D0466136

DEAD ENDS

DEAD ENDS

Sandra Balzo

Severn House Large Print
London & New York

This first large print edition published 2015
in Great Britain and the USA by
SEVERN HOUSE PUBLISHERS LTD of
19 Cedar Road, Sutton, Surrey, England, SM2 5DA.
First world regular print edition published 2012 by
Severn House Publishers Ltd., London and New York.

British Library Cataloguing in Publication Data

Balzo, Sandra. author.
    Dead ends. – (Main Street series)
    1. Griggs, AnnaLise (Fictitious character)–Fiction.
    2. North Carolina–Social conditions–Fiction.
    3. Detective and mystery stories. 4. Large type books.
    I. Title II. Series
    813.6-dc23

ISBN-13: 9780727872807

Severn House Publishers support the Forest Stewardship Council™
[FSC™], the leading international forest certification organisation. All
our titles that are printed on FSC certified paper carry the FSC logo.

MIX
Paper from
responsible sources
FSC   FSC® C013056
www.fsc.org

Typeset by Palimpsest Book Production Ltd.,
Falkirk, Stirlingshire, Scotland.
Printed and bound in Great Britain by
T J International, Padstow, Cornwall.

For Michael and Lisa, who have shown they really <u>will</u> 'love me forever.' And I, them.

One

'But that's what Daisy told me to do,' Joshua Eames insisted, blue eyes wide and innocent as he used his work boot to sweep away a brown long-legged spider that was angling toward them.

While AnnaLise Griggs was prone to believe the young man – and grateful for his intervention with the creepy-crawler – his boss apparently wasn't buying it.

'If you're going to kill the thing, Josh, kill it.' Fred Eames, Josh's father and proprietor of Eames High Country Builders, stomped hard on the still-wriggling spider to make his point.

Eames was tall and muscular like his son, but with a belly more like a keg than a six-pack. Just a quarter-barrel for now under the blue plaid shirt, but AnnaLise was betting he'd be up to a half-barrel girth by the time he hit fifty if he kept putting away hunks of breakfast coffee cake like the one he delicately set down on the cross-piece of a sawhorse. 'Why do you think I give you written orders?'

Mr Eames picked up the orders in question, a yellow-tissue carbon of Eames company letterhead stapled over a drawing and, below that, a memorandum. 'I told you before, son. You don't change nothing – for Mrs Daisy Lorraine Griggs or nobody – without talking to me first.'

The memo at the bottom of the stack was

courtesy of AnnaLise. The twenty-eight-year-old journalist might not know *how* to do what she wanted done, but that didn't stop her from outlining the end game – basically running electricity to her mother's ancient two-car garage and installing new twin garage doors and openers.

A simple thing, not perhaps worthy of the three double-spaced, spell-checked pages, except that the finished job had to satisfy the detailed, exacting specifications of not only her mother – the Daisy in question – but also Daisy's neighbor and co-garage owner, Mrs Peebly.

A police reporter in Wisconsin, AnnaLise had taken a leave of absence from her job until the end of the month – that month being September and today already the twelfth – for 'personal business' in her hometown of Sutherton, North Carolina.

But whether in the upper Midwest or the mountains of North Carolina, AnnaLise's exposure to the legal system in general – and one Wisconsin district attorney in particular – had taught her to lay out her expectations in clear, unambiguous terms. Especially important in this case, since AnnaLise might well be leaving the state before the job was completed.

In fact, if Daisy's lab work came back OK and the appointment with the neurologist . . .

AnnaLise registered that Josh was speaking to his father. 'Daisy said didn't I think one big door instead of two—'

'Did ya tell her I don't pay you to think?' Eames interrupted. ''Cuz if I did, boy, you'd sure owe me a refund.'

2

The 'boy' – though Josh had to be twenty by now – flushed.

Not that the elder seemed to notice. 'Were you "thinking" last week, when you put up that DETOUR sign 'stead of the DEAD END one and nearly sent half a dozen cars off the side of Big Sweet?'

Big Sweet was Sutherton Mountain's highest ski run, forming a vertical gash in the trees that covered the southern face of the mountain.

But Big Sweet aside, AnnaLise didn't like Eames bullying his son – especially if Daisy's increasing mental confusion may have been the indirect cause. 'Now, Mr Eames,' she interrupted, consciously weaving a bit of her native south back into her tone, 'I don't think there's any cause to blame Josh for this little misunderstanding.'

'Little misunderstanding?' Eames repeated, removing his cap. 'Tell that to your mama's friend, whose deck we were working on at the time. Ida Mae Babb nearly had a brand-new junk-yard for her view, 'stead of the ski slope.'

Nestled in the Blue Ridge Mountains, Sutherton was closer in both distance and general attitude – not to be confused with *altitude*, though this was true as well – to the mountains of Tennessee and Virginia than it was to North Carolina's own beaches and golf resorts.

'You see that?' Eames pointed at the irregular chunks of mortar and cinder block littering the sidewalk in front of the shared garage. 'If I hadn't checked on this, that whole garage would've come tumbling down.'

'Now that's not exactly true,' Josh said, as the

3

double-beep of a text message came from AnnaLise's phone somewhere in the nether regions of her purse. 'There's a big old steel beam running right across the tops of those doors, so I was thinking—'

'I told you, I don't pay—'

'Enough!' AnnaLise, having dug out her cell, checked it and unceremoniously dumped the thing back into her bag. 'I have an appointment in Boone. You two figure this out. Civilly.'

She eyed Eames, then Josh.

Josh nodded, but Eames looked like he was going to protest.

Time to be straight with the man. 'Can I have a word with you alone, Mr Eames?'

The boss hesitated. He looked like he'd prefer to keelhaul his son, but then he tipped his head toward Josh. 'Go get the big flashlight out of my truck so we can see up in that garage. Damndest thing to build somethin' even forty years back without putting in electricity. It'll cost an arm and a leg to add, especially with that Scotty doin' it, though I don't see there's a choice.'

Josh safely out of sight, Eames turned to AnnaLise. 'Now don't you be telling me to go easy on that boy. He's been in and out of trouble since his mama ran off ten years ago. And mostly "in."'

Who could blame the kid? Josh had been barely ten when his mother took off with another man, leaving Fred and Josh without so much as a goodbye. AnnaLise's father had died when she was five, but even back then she knew he'd have stayed with them if he could.

4

'Didn't you tell me when you put Josh on this job that he's a good worker?'

Now it was Eames turn to flush. 'Why, I sure did. And it's the truth. The boy just needs focus and I'm focusing him.'

Well, God knows we all needed someone to do that sometimes, if not quite with the alacrity of the man in front of her. 'I'm certain you are, Mr Eames, and I'm sure Josh appreciates it. Now I need to pick up my mother and get her to a doctor's appointment. Umm, you may have heard—'

But Eames was already holding up his hands like two heavily calloused stop signs. 'Not another word, AnnaLise. Josh and me, we'll figure things out so's it'll work real good. You just tell your ma not to worry about a thing.'

AnnaLise's 'ma,' Daisy, even now just fifty years old, was having . . . well, 'spells' might be what Eames would call them, though accidentally draining Mrs Bradenham – the mayor's mother, of all people – of an extra pint or two at Sutherton's annual blood drive less than two weeks before might be pushing the definition's envelope.

'I'm sure Daisy will be fine,' AnnaLise said, trying to reassure Eames about something that scared the hell out of her. 'Her confusion when Mrs B was donating blood and all . . . well, it's probably just a vitamin deficiency or something.'

'Or dehydration,' Eames offered. 'Remember, the air can be mighty dry up here in the mountains. You tell Daisy to drink water, lots and lots of it. Fix her right up.'

5

'I'll do just that,' AnnaLise said, now uncon-sciously slipping into the rhythm of speech she'd largely abandoned since leaving western North Carolina to enroll at the University of Wisconsin. 'And if you would, just ask Josh to run any suggestions Daisy might have past both you and me? And Mrs Peebly's . . . thoughts, as well?'

Eames broke a grin at the thought of the retired elementary school principal, bent over her walker but never, ever broken. 'Now that I'm not sure I can promise. I'm no match for Mrs Peebly, so I can't hold out much hope for poor Josh.'

'I'm not sure anyone is a match for Mrs Peebly.' AnnaLise was reminded of the time she'd acci-dentally dinged the passenger door of one of the series of black Cadillacs their neighbor had owned over the decades. Sixteen-year-old AnnaLise had lived in fear of discovery for exactly forty-three minutes before blurting out a confession.

At ninety, Mrs Peebly still managed to inspire that kind of fear. And respect.

AnnaLise extended her hand to the man in front of her. 'I appreciate your taking this job on at such short notice, Mr Eames.'

'Happy to do anything I can, AnnaLise. For you *or* for Daisy.'

As they shook on it, AnnaLise was reminded how often, in the High Country, calloused hands were matched to the still- unhardened heart of a true and utter gentleman.

A characteristic as refreshing, she thought, involuntarily glancing down to her purse with the cellphone buried inside, as the clean mountain air itself.

Two

Leaving Fred Eames, AnnaLise Griggs hurried up the sidewalk toward Sutherton's Main Street, which rimmed the southern shore of Lake Sutherton. To the north across the lake – you guessed it – Sutherton Mountain could be seen.

Admittedly not the most imaginative collective, but what was lost in grandiosity was gained in clarity. You always knew where you stood in Sutherton – literally *and* figuratively.

AnnaLise passed the door to the over-and-under apartment where she'd grown up and her mother still lived. The building also housed the corner storefront that had been Griggs Market, a small grocery store and deli Daisy had owned and operated until a few months back. The space was now leased to a coffeehouse-cum-nightclub called Torch, and it took all of AnnaLise's resolve to resist the aroma of freshly-brewed caffeine wafting out from that new incarnation as she rounded the corner.

Tucker Ulysses Stanton, the club's young owner, had decided to open mornings to serve espressos, lattes and cappuccinos and then reopen at night with a full bar and live entertainment. The latter sometimes included Tucker on the bongos punctuating his recital of various haikus, all of which seemed suspiciously to echo 'There was an old man from Nantucket.'

If Torch could be described as a coffeehouse day or night, though, it was the beatnik, poetry, cool-cat kind, like in the classic TV show *The Many Loves of Dobie Gillis*, with Tucker as an African American Maynard G. Krebs.

Barely able to raise the stubbly goatee required for the image, Tucker had needed his physician father to apply for a license to serve alcohol, Tucker himself being too young to drink.

Practically overnight, though, the place had become a success. And, for Daisy, it was a home away from home, tucked under and in front of her long-time abode.

Or *another* home away from home.

As AnnaLise rounded the corner onto Main Street proper, the true heart-and-soul of Sutherton, the town, as well as Griggs, the family, came into view: Mama Philomena's restaurant. Phyllis Balisteri, aka 'Mama Philomena,' was Daisy's oldest and dearest friend. Between the two women, they'd managed not only to raise AnnaLise after Timothy Griggs died, leaving the widowed Daisy with a five-year-old, but to keep both Griggs Market and the restaurant afloat.

Not that it hadn't been without its challenges.

Going by the restaurant's name, red-and-white-striped awning and big plate-glass window, you'd expect Mama Philomena's to offer family-style Italian meals. And you'd be . . . well, more dead wrong than disappointed. True disappointment would come only if you tried any of the Italian delicacies that Phyllis had tried to replicate from her mother Philomena's original menu.

Mama, as Phyllis and her mother before her were inevitably called, had been tipped to the town's opinion of her early efforts immediately, of course. Sutherton natives were not known to mince words, especially when the tourist industry – the town's bane or its boon, depending on who you were talking to and at what time of year – could be affected.

Because no matter how much they enjoyed complaining about the influx of out-of-towners, including students attending the University of the Mountain, the locals knew that the reason Sutherton continued to thrive was that its cool mountains, picturesque lakes, and beautiful trout streams drew people trying to escape the heat of the deep South all summer long, foliage-gawkers in the fall, and skiers through the winter.

For better or worse, Sutherton had an eleven-month tourist season and Mama Philomena's on Main Street – listed in every tour book and travel website – could not be allowed to founder on the rocks of inedible meals.

Facing mounting pressure, Mama had turned to what she, herself, had survived on while her own mother provided authentic Italian cuisine to the rest of the town: convenience foods and the easy recipes found on the backs of the boxes, cans and bottles in which those brand-name favorites were packaged.

And so Mama Philomena's had survived, as had its standing as the hub of life on Main Street. The restaurant served as Sutherton's tribal camp-fire, where stories were swapped and information shared. Sort of a brick-and-mortar Wikipedia, right down to the occasional questionable source.

Mama's Monday LUNCH SPECIALS, hand-written on a bright pink sheet of paper, were already up on the door, strategically placed between a flyer advertising next month's annual Woolly Worm Festival in nearby Banner Elk and a second circular, this time for Beary Scary Halloween on neighboring Grandfather Mountain.

AnnaLise read the menu: Corn Flakes Crunchy Baked Chicken, Bennett's Chili Sauce Brisket and Beans and, for dessert, AnnaLise's own favorite: Grape Nut Pudding.

'What's the occasion?' AnnaLise asked, pushing open the door to find her own mother on the other side of it.

Daisy had a roll of tape in her hand, presumably having just posted the specials. Now she plunked both fists, tape in one of them, on her hips. 'AnnaLise Griggs, you can't tell me you've forgotten the Woolly Worm Festival. You haven't been away that long.'

Ten years, if you were counting. And, of course, her mother would be.

'Please,' AnnaLise said, 'one does not forget the whole county coming out to watch Woolly Caterpillars race up strings and then using the color pattern of the winner's bristles to predict the coming winter's weather.'

'Hey there, AnnieLeez.' The voice came presumably from the kitchen and undeniably from Phyllis 'Mama' Balisteri. 'Don't you go making fun of our Woolly Worms. They pump a whole lot of dollars into the county's coffins.'

AnnaLise bit her tongue to avoid correcting

that to 'coffers.' She'd long ago sublimated Mama's butchering of her own given name.

'Not to mention Mama's cash register,' Daisy said, setting down the tape roll. 'It's only a month away. Maybe you won't miss it this year, AnnaLise.'

There was a wistful tone to Daisy's voice, tinged with a hint of fear. Both mother and daughter knew that if AnnaLise stayed beyond the end of September it would be because of Daisy's spells. And AnnaLise didn't think either of them really wanted that, Woolly Worms or not.

She changed the subject. 'By "occasion," I was referring to the menu. Brisket? Grape-Nut pudding? Sounds like Mama's pulling out all the stops.'

'I think it's a reaction to the doctor,' Daisy said, pushing blonde curly hair away from her sun-darkened face. 'Sort of a last hurrah.'

AnnaLise felt like she'd been punched in the stomach. Was Mama, who admittedly knew Daisy best – better even than AnnaLise herself – so worried that she'd, in effect, prepared the 'condemned' woman her final meal of favorites?

'Grape-Nut should have a hyphen,' was all AnnaLise could think to say.

Afraid to make eye contact with her mother, she plucked a Wheat Chex out of a small bowl of snack mix set in the middle of a nearby booth.

A palm lightly but crisply slapped her hand. 'Complimentary Chex Mix is for the paying customers. Don't you go digging in there or the Health Department will shut me down.'

AnnaLise whirled to face her 'other' mother, who was often mistaken for her biological one

11

– much to Daisy's dismay. But it was true that AnnaLise's dark hair and eyes echoed more Phyllis Balisteri's coloring than her own mother's blue-eyed blondeness.

'Besides,' Mama continued, laying paper-napkin-wrapped sets of silverware next to matching placemats already on the table, 'you eat too much junk and you'll get fat.'

Well, there was a new sentiment from Mama, who was known to slather doughnuts with butter before frying them up. 'When I arrived just a week ago this past Saturday, you told me I was too skinny and made me drink whole milk,' AnnaLise pointed out. 'And eat cake.'

'You asked for that hunk of cake, AnnieLeez Griggs.'

Mama was right, but then AnnaLise had needed to gird herself for her return to Sutherton in response to Mama's panicky call about Daisy's blood-drive gaffe. Bacardi Rum Cake was as close to a cocktail as AnnaLise could justify at ten a.m. in the morning.

AnnaLise opened her mouth to say so, but Mama apparently wasn't done. 'And don't you dare be telling me any different, you hear now?' With that, the restaurant owner whisked the snack mix off the table and disappeared into the kitchen, looking for all the world like she was going to break into tears.

'My God,' AnnaLise whispered to Daisy, while keeping a lookout over her shoulder, lest Mama reappear. 'Is she truly so worried about your appointment with the neurologist?'

Specters of what her mother's best friend might

12

know – or suspect – were dancing in the younger woman's head.

'*My* appointment?' Daisy had moved on to cleaning the glass display case that held the restaurant's cash register on top and ancient candy and bric-a-brac below. 'Don't be silly. Phyllis is just upset about what the doctor said after her annual physical yesterday.'

Mama returned with a fresh bowl of the snack mix and slapped it on the table, sending Chex flying. 'Fat my southern-fried ass, Jackson Stanton!'

Dr Jackson Stanton was Tucker's father. The Stantons had been summer visitors until Theresa – Jackson's wife and Tucker's mother – died. The summer after her death, the widower came with Tucker anyway, and they just never left.

'He didn't say you were fat, Phyllis,' Daisy said. 'He said your cholesterol was up and you should cut *out* fat.'

'And how am I supposed to do that?' Mama asked. 'I have a restaurant to run.' She swept the errant cereal off the table and plopped it in her mouth.

Before AnnaLise could delve further, if she indeed dared, the electronic chime on the door signaled the arrival of a new customer; one that AnnaLise was very happy to see. 'I'll get this,' she said, grabbing a menu from the front counter's stack and turning to the man who had entered, newspaper tucked under an arm.

James Duende was about six-one, with shaggy dark hair and eyes the color of melted Hershey's milk chocolate.

But that wasn't what interested AnnaLise. She was still untying slip-knots from her last romantic entanglement.

'This booth is ready, James,' she said, sweeping a hand toward the one Mama had just set.

'Thanks, AnnaLise,' he replied, taking the offered menu as he slipped past her to slide onto the bench facing the front window. Duende was a recent addition to Sutherton – a writer, and a closed-mouthed one at that.

'So good to see you back,' she said pleasantly. 'I heard you were away on assignment for a few days. I hope it went well.'

'Last week?' he asked, unfolding his copy of the *High Country Times*. 'It went fine.' He took a red Flair from the inside of his jacket and laid it on top of the paper before looking up at her. 'Though not as good as yours, I understand.'

Uh-oh. AnnaLise took the bench across from him and leaned forward. 'I take it you've heard that Dickens Hart hired me to do his memoirs?'

'Dickens Hart?' Duende repeated, leveling those chocolate eyes on her. 'You mean your father?'

AnnaLise squirmed. 'At the time I took the job, I didn't know that was the case.'

And still refused to acknowledge him as such. The man was a womanizer and an egomaniac, the former witnessed by AnnaLise's very existence, and the latter by the boxes of journals he'd kept 'for posterity' and which now filled AnnaLise's childhood bedroom as future research material for *Dickens Hart: The Poor Man's Hugh Heffner*.

Probably *not* the final title, admittedly, but it was the way AnnaLise thought of the project. Still, the money was beyond anything she could earn as a reporter and an outright godsend, given her current suspended state of employment.

AnnaLise glanced over at Daisy, who was arguing with Mama. Business as usual between the two mothers. The last thing AnnaLise needed was an illegitimate father in the mix. But then, we get less of what we want and more of what we deserve.

'Listen,' she said to Duende. 'We both know you're a legendary biographer – the male Ramona Ravens.'

That chocolate in his eyes hardened. 'I'm a legitimate, highly credentialed author.'

Presumably Ramona Ravens, the queen of unauthorized biographies, thought the same about herself. The likes of Frank Sinatra, Nancy Reagan and the British Royal Family might beg to differ.

Nonetheless, AnnaLise held up her hands in apology. 'I'm sorry. I know the sensationalized, unauthorized bio isn't your thing.' Unless it paid well enough. 'But you know that I had nothing to do with Dickens choosing me to write his autobiography over you. In fact, I tried to price myself out of the market. Unfortunately, I didn't realize he'd gone,' a sheepish grin toward Duende, 'upscale.'

That elicited an answering smile from Duende. 'A reporter who didn't do her research.'

'I didn't know who you were then, or that you were here for the job. Believe me, if I could back out of it I would, but . . .'

15

She involuntarily glanced toward where her mother was exchanging the glass cleaner she'd been using for her purse, presumably toward leaving for the doctor's appointment.

Duende put his hand on AnnaLise's as she checked her watch. 'How is your mom doing?'

AnnaLise shrugged. 'Fine. For now. I mean, until the next time she's not.' The reporter colored up. 'Sorry. Not my best syntax. Maybe you *should* be writing the Dickens Hart story.'

Duende didn't let go of her hand. 'Did you have to take an unpaid leave from the paper?'

She felt her cheeks go warmer. 'Yes, but—'

'AnnaLise? Are you ready?' Daisy stood by the cash register. 'We need to make a stop on the way, remember?'

'Of course.' AnnaLise smiled and slid her fingers out from under Duende's. 'I have to go. But thanks for understanding. Or . . . uh, at least not being mad.'

Geez, what was it about sitting across from this man that made her incapable of stringing together a proper sentence? AnnaLise Griggs who, as Mama was fond of saying, not only corrected everyone's grammar, but would copy-edit their thoughts if she could access them.

Granted, the man was a multi-published author, with more than a couple of *New York Times* Bestsell—

'AnnaLise?' Daisy sounded impatient and for good reason. The woman had to be nervous about what her doctor might say.

'I'm sorry, Daisy,' AnnaLise said, sliding to the end of the bench.

As she did, Duende caught her hand again. 'If you need anything, please just ask.'

AnnaLise hesitated.

'I mean with the biography,' Duende said, his olive skin getting a little duskier. 'I've written a ton of them and you're pretty much a . . .'

'Virgin?' AnnaLise asked, thinking it felt good to flirt again, so long as it could be done safely.

'Well, I was going to say "rookie," but—'

The electronic chime rang out again.

'Thank God we found that inn,' an adult female voice said. 'At least *it* has a little charm.'

With a smile of thanks to Duende, AnnaLise turned to follow Daisy and stopped.

At the door stood Benjamin Rosewood, district attorney of Urban County, Wisconsin and, until about a month ago, AnnaLise's lover.

And with him, his wife and daughter.

Three

Tanja Hobson Rosewood. Suzanne Rosewood.
AnnaLise knew them from their photos. The
framed ones on Ben's desk. And on his walls.
Or candids with Ben in the papers.

Tanja, daughter of self-made billionaire Lenny
Hobson. Tall, slim and well-kept, her hair was,
eerily, the color of rosewood and so thick and
shiny it could have been a lacquered, curvy plank
of same. She and Ben met while they were class-
mates at Northwestern University north of
Chicago. Married in the fall of 1992.

From the social columns, AnnaLise knew
Tanja loved white roses. From Ben, she
knew Tanja hated seat belts because they wrinkled her clothes, and oral sex because . . . well,
just because.

As for Suzanne, or 'Suze' as she was known,
any information on the teenager came nearly
entirely from Ben. Determined, a Rosewood trait,
when he agreed with her. Spoiled, a Hobson
trait, when he didn't. She had her father's blue
eyes and mother's patrician nose.

'AnnaLise Griggs?' The voice was Ben's.

Hide in plain sight, he'd always told her. If you
think someone might have seen us together, walk
right up to them and say hello.

'Hello?' she replied, striving for a 'do I know
you?' tone because seeing him here, now, was

18

so totally out of context. And so totally beyond comprehension.

'Why, District Attorney Rosewood,' she continued. 'I'm sorry, I just didn't recognize you. It's such a surprise to see someone from home – my new home – down here.' AnnaLise tossed an apologetic look toward her mother.

'Please, call me Ben. No need to be formal so far from the office. After all, you're part of the reason we're here.' Rosewood shook hands with AnnaLise before turning to Daisy. 'I'm Ben Rosewood. You're . . .?'

'Oh, I'm sorry,' AnnaLise said again, trying to grasp the idea that Ben was here – with his wife and daughter – because of her somehow. 'This is my mother, Daisy Griggs.'

'A pleasure,' Ben said with his best politician smile. Sun-streaked hair, blue eyes, a firm hand-shake and a record as a Gulf War hero completed the picture. 'And this is my wife, Tanja, and my daughter, Suzanne.'

'Good to meet you,' AnnaLise said, turning her attention to the two women. At about five-nine, Tanja Rosewood was a better physical match for Ben than five-foot AnnaLise. Even without stilettos, Tanja's head would rest on the D.A.'s shoulder when they danced, whereas AnnaLise's—

'Are you visiting U-Mo?' AnnaLise heard Daisy ask.

U-Mo, the nearby University of the Mountain, where one needed either brains or money to get in. While AnnaLise had the brains, she would have needed a full-ride to go there and, truth be told, she'd wanted to go away to school. Living at home while attending school, at the time, wasn't what she'd envisioned.

But then again, neither was this.

'I'm already a student,' said Suzanne brightly, all the while scanning the diners over AnnaLise's shoulder.

AnnaLise glanced around, seeing only James Duende watching their little group.

'As of Tuesday last week,' her mother said dryly, as AnnaLise turned back. 'Thanks so much for the recommendation on the school, by the way.'

She didn't look thankful. In fact, brows raised to form inverted 'V's over both eyes, Tanja seemed speculative, almost accusing.

AnnaLise willed herself not to think it had anything to do with her and Ben – or what used to be her and Ben – but coming face-to-face with Tanja for the first time, it was all she could do to not break down and confess, throwing herself on the betrayed woman's mercy.

Tanja continued: 'One visit here last spring and Suzanne was entranced. She wouldn't hear of going anywhere else for some reason.'

AnnaLise, who had no memory of 'recommending' U-Mo or any other school, was saved from saying something that might have contradicted whatever Ben had told his wife and daughter.

Saved, that is, by the district attorney himself. 'When Suze indicated she wanted a real college campus experience in a picturesque place, I asked Katie to come up with suggestions. She included the university here, said you'd spoken glowingly about the area.'

Katie was a paralegal in the D.A.'s office. And, apparently his beard. Or their beard, in this case. Much more likely for a lowly reporter to be talking to an equally lowly paralegal than to the big man himself.

'Quite honestly?' Tanja threw AnnaLise a tight smile. 'When Suzanne made her decision, I was as surprised as you seem to be.'

Perhaps, though AnnaLise doubted it.

'*She* wanted me to go out east.' But now the girl was craning her neck to look out the window behind her.

'There are schools with absolutely lovely campuses in the northeast corridor,' Tanja said, turning away from AnnaLise. 'And with, I might add, five-star hotels nearby.'

'Sutherton is picturesque, dear, and you enjoy staying at country inns.' Ben seemed embarrassed by his wife's attitude.

'I said I "enjoyed" the White Gull Inn in Door County, Wisconsin's vacationland.' She idly set her hand on the glass next to the cash register, but quickly snatched it back, rubbing the tips of her fingers together. 'We were dating at the time. Must you hold me to it twenty years later?'

While Daisy's eyes had narrowed at the suggestion her newly polished counter wasn't as clean as it might be, AnnaLise was contemplating the lovely bed and breakfast in Fish Creek, Wisconsin. The White Gull Inn apparently had not been quite the serendipitous discovery Ben had claimed when he took her there.

Nor, presumably, was the University of the Mountain.

'I'm sorry to run,' AnnaLise said, lying through her teeth, 'but I need to drive my mother to an appointment.'

Daisy glanced at the clock behind the counter. 'It's not for an hour, AnnaLise, if you want to stay and chat.'

'I thought you had an errand to do en route,' said the prodigal daughter.

'Yes, but we're already cutting it too close.' Daisy was looking at AnnaLise curiously. 'We'll just stop on the way back.'

'And,' AnnaLise continued, 'we should let these good people eat in peace. Besides, who knows what the traffic will be like in Boone.'

'Traffic?' This from daughter Suzanne. 'The town's not exactly New York City.'

'Suze.' A warning look from Ben, much like the one he'd directed at his wife. Poor guy, having to keep all the women in his life in line. 'New York City isn't built in the mountains, either. There are only so many roads people can use for travel.'

'And we'd best get on one.' AnnaLise moved past them to the door. 'Before we're late.'

'What time is it, anyway?' Tanja slipped open the flap of her handbag and pulled out her cellphone. 'I have an appointment at three thirty for an afternoon treatment at the Sutherton Spa.' The wife looked up. 'How long will it take me to get there?'

'Sutherton Spa?' AnnaLise said uncertainly, looking at Daisy. 'I don't think I know—'

'Yes, you do,' said her mother. 'It's where Tail Too used to be, in the Hotel Lux.'

22

'Really?' AnnaLise asked. The Hotel Lux was the 300-room, ten-story facility at the top of Sutherton Mountain. Popular with skiers, it was considered an eyesore by the rest of the community. In fact, its construction had resulted in a law prohibiting the building of multi-story structures on ridge lines.

But it wasn't the spa's location in the Hotel Lux that had surprised AnnaLise; rather that it meant the last vestige of the old White Tail Club was finally gone. White Tail – a sixties knock-off of the Playboy Club, but with 'Fawns' instead of 'Bunnies' – had been located on the fifty-acre island which dominated the northern part of Lake Sutherton. For ski seasons, owner Dickens Hart had maintained a smaller, satellite club in the Lux, though it, too, had been closed for years. 'Hart opened a spa?'

'Ask your mother,' Mama said, throwing a look at Daisy. 'By all accounts, she knows Dickens Hart better than any of us.'

Daisy, who'd dared to keep the truth about AnnaLise's male parentage secret, even from her best friend, squirmed, just as Mama had intended. She'd eventually let Daisy off the proverbial hook, AnnaLise knew, but in the meantime Phyllis Balisteri had no compunction about throwing in the occasional barb.

As for AnnaLise, she preferred to let sleeping biological fathers lie. And mothers, likewise.

'Not really,' Daisy explained. 'Dickens turned the space over to his ex-wife about a year ago when he decided to turn the club on the island into condos and shops.'

'His ex-wife? You mean Joy?' Joy Tamarack had been Hart's third wife, and though the marriage between the then twenty-five-year-old blonde physical trainer and the aging playboy had lasted but a year, Joy had managed to leverage 'ex-wife' into a full-time paid position with*out* benefits. 'But just last week Joy was pressing Hart to give her space for a spa in Hart's Landing now that she's staying here permanently.' Hart's Landing being what Dickens Hart modestly had named his new mixed-use development on the island.

'That will be a second location for the summer season,' Daisy said. 'But in the winter, when the skiers—'

'While this is endlessly fascinating,' Tanja Rosewood broke in, 'could someone please answer my question?'

Daisy, Mama and AnnaLise – all three of them stared at her, none of them seeming to quite remember what that question had been.

AnnaLise hit the answer button first. 'Tail Too, or whatever it is now, is all the way up the mountain.' She looked at Daisy for consultation. 'What would you say? A half hour, maybe?'

Daisy laughed. 'Only because you drive like a snail.' She turned to Ben's wife. 'Instead of following Main Street around the lake to Sutherton Mountain's lower entrance, take the highway north to the upper entrance. That way you can use the Sutherton Bridge and bypass some of the curvier mountain roads. It shouldn't take you more than fifteen minutes from here. Twenty, if you want some cushion.'

'Then ten for you, Mom,' Suzanne said, still seemingly preoccupied with who else she might see either in the restaurant or outside it. 'And if *I* was driving the Porsche, I bet I could—'

'Over my dead body,' Tanja Rosewood said, cutting her off.

She stepped close to AnnaLise as if confiding – so close that AnnaLise got a whiff of her menthol cough drop. 'I'm not a good "sharer," you see.'

AnnaLise felt her eyes go wide. Fingers already on the doorknob, she twisted it now, backing as she went. 'Yes, well, enjoy your lunch and, Suzanne, I hope you have a great year at U-Mo.'

'Oh, I will.' Porsche apparently forgotten, the girl had caught sight of what – or who – she'd been looking for. 'Be right back.'

Her mother followed her gaze, a sour look pinching her face. 'Suzanne, I will *not* have you chasing after that boy. He has no—'

But Suzanne was already pushing past AnnaLise and cleared the doorway before the electric chime had a chance to bong.

'We should probably take my car,' Daisy said as they rounded the corner.

'Your car?' AnnaLise said, stopping by her mother's Chrysler, parked on the street for the duration of the garage's renovation, as was AnnaLise's Mitsubishi Spyder convertible. 'I thought you wanted me to drive.'

'I do, but I thought you might prefer my car on Sutherton Mountain. I know how you hate the steep ups and downs.'

'I hate all the mountain roads,' AnnaLise said, unlocking the Spyder's passenger side door for her mother. 'But I'd prefer a car I know.' Besides, compared with the pert little Mitsubishi, her mother's car drove like a boat wallowing on the waves.

AnnaLise swung open her door. 'Why are we driving up there anyway? The neurologist is in Boone and that's the opposite direction.'

Daisy slid into the passenger seat and half-turned to regard her daughter as she got in on the other side. 'I promised Ida Mae Babb we'd come by and she'll still expect it, even though now it will be after my appointment, instead of before it.'

Ahh, the 'errand.' 'Sorry,' AnnaLise said, thinking it was true in more ways than one. Not only had she held up her mother, but now, instead of driving on the mountain safely at midday, it might be late afternoon or even early evening before they'd be knocking on Ida Mae's door two-thirds of the way up Sutherton Mountain.

'Well, you sure didn't seem in any hurry,' Daisy said, 'while you were chatting up James Duende. Then your friend from way up north comes in with his family and you're practically shoving me out the door. It struck me as a touch rude – not to me, but to them.'

'Well, I felt guilty for keeping us at Mama's and didn't want you to miss your doctor's appointment on account of me.' AnnaLise started her car and pulled away from the curb, turning left onto Main Street. Just past Mama Philomena's she saw Suzanne Rosewood next to a parked yellow sports car, talking to the driver of a pimped out – for outdoor business, not indoor pleasure – black pick-up truck. The yellow car was a Porsche. AnnaLise knew that because Ben had bought it for his wife last Christmas. 'Isn't that Joshua Eames—'

'Please, AnnaLise,' Daisy continued, unimpeded, 'give me credit for knowing my own daughter.'

'Knowing . . .?' AnnaLise slowed at the intersection of Main Street and the state highway and glanced anxiously over at her mother. Had Daisy sensed something between her and Ben? 'You're saying I *wanted* to make you miss your—'

'Oh, no. I'm saying you looked guilty, all right. I just didn't think your reaction was because of keeping me waiting.'

AnnaLise floored it, turning left onto the highway and narrowly missing getting T-boned by a white truck. The bushy-bearded man driving the vehicle didn't lean on the horn, or even throw her the finger.

'Daisy, people are just so damn *nice* here. It's not natural.'

'We just recognize which side our bread is buttered on,' Daisy said. 'That was Lester Moose in that truck. He might be on the elliptical trainer at Peak Fitness tonight, talking about the idiot who pulled out in front of him, but he'd never be rude to a tourist outright.'

AnnaLise hadn't gotten past the image of a big mountain man like Lester Moose on an elliptical trainer. 'I'm not a tourist,' she muttered.

'No?'

27

Daisy was hazing her and AnnaLise knew it. She also knew that continuing the discussion about guilt wouldn't lead to anything but her connection to the Rosewood clan. Then again, Daisy's appointment with the neurologist was probably not her mother's first choice of topic, either. That left: 'So why are we stopping by Ida Mae's?'

'She suggested we come by to take a look at the new deck Fred Eames put on, seeing as he's doing work for us. If you ask me, Ida Mae's just looking for a little company. Gets lonely up there now with her husband gone.'

'You don't have any real worries about Fred working on the garage, do you?'

'Not so long as he confines himself to Monday through Friday on our project. Weekends, I hear, he drinks.' Daisy twisted to look behind them. 'AnnaLise, the speed limit is forty-five on this stretch and you're doing barely thirty. You'd best step on it or people might not wait until they hit the gym to work out their frustration with you.'

AnnaLise glanced in her rear-view mirror to see at least a dozen vehicles stacked up behind the Spyder. Then she glanced at the cliff that had been cleaved to form the highway. 'The sign says Caution: falling rock.'

'That sign has been there since you were a little girl. You just never paid it any mind.'

'Well, I'm older and wiser now.'

'Older and scared-er,' Daisy said, and AnnaLise could feel the weight of her gaze. 'And scared isn't a good way to live, no matter your age.'

'I'm not scared,' AnnaLise said, startled. She'd

been working very hard at convincing herself that Ben's wife did not know about the affair. That it truly was the Porsche Tanja was talking about sharing, *not* her husband. But if she could look that murderous just about a car, how would she feel about—

'You *are* feeling scared,' Daisy said, 'and you are feeling guilty. I just don't know why. I'm hoping it's not over me.'

There was just a hint of a sniffle at the end.

'You?' AnnaLise asked, ashamed that in addition to Daisy worrying about her own very real problems, the older woman was troubled about her daughter's hypothetical ones as well.

But what to do? Confess to her mother she'd had a year-long adulterous affair with a man who was now sitting in Mama's restaurant with his betrayed wife and daughter?

Granted, AnnaLise had come to her senses and ended it, but that didn't excuse it. Didn't excuse her, either, from the stupidity that made the journalist – of all people – believe that she and Ben were different. That only she understood him and that he and he alone 'got' her. That she must be pretty and smart and funny, because this man – this intelligent, powerful, older man – said so.

And, biggest lie of all, that if nobody found out about their affair, no one would be hurt.

AnnaLise, Daisy would say if she knew, *a married man?*

And, worse, a married man, who – as cool as Ben Rosewood had played it – now didn't seem to be able to simply let go, witnessed by the text messages and emails she'd been systematically deleting without reading after the first two or three from him.

AnnaLise had finally sent one last text message, composed painstakingly on her computer first, so she'd be sure to get it right. A clear and concise argument written in parallel structure and using the 'Rule of Three' Ben followed in making his closing arguments to juries.

AnnaLise could hear the district attorney now, explaining why 'three' was the magic number: 'Think about it. Julius Caesar's *Veni, vidi, vici* – I came, I saw, I conquered. Lincoln's *We can not dedicate – we can not consecrate – we can not hallow – this ground.* Even FDR's very own advice to speakers: *Be sincere, be brief, be seated.* We remember them, we repeat them, we live by them, all because of the Rule of Three.'

Even the man's explanation of the rule was in triplicate. So, in answer to Ben's 'Why can't we be together?' AnnaLise had replied: 'Three reasons – you have a wife, you have a daughter, and I have a mother who needs me. Do not text me, do not email me, do not call me.'

If only she'd thought to break the 'Rule of Three' to add a fourth: 'And don't *ever* show up on my doorstep.'

Four

The appointment with the neurologist was a huge relief or a colossal waste of time, depending on which of the two Griggs you believed.

The doctor had been two hours late, meaning they'd finally gotten in to see him at 4 p.m. When he'd entered the exam room, where they'd been waiting another twenty minutes, he'd asked Daisy a few questions and suggested memory exercises she could do at home before saying she should call his medical assistant – who'd already left for the day, naturally – to schedule a CT scan and MRI 'just to be safe.'

'Talk about the bum's rush,' AnnaLise said as they drove back toward Sutherton.

'The man had an emergency,' Daisy said, looking like the cat who swallowed the canary. Or worse, the Cheshire Cat who swallowed the canary. She seemed so smug, in fact, that AnnaLise wanted to scream.

'Besides,' Daisy continued, '*I* had no trouble with his little tests. On the other hand, when *you* tried to "play" along . . .'

'Nobody uses analog clocks anymore,' AnnaLise muttered. 'How the hell should I know where the big and little hands are supposed to be?'

'But you do know how to count, right?' The suppressed grin in Daisy's tone was palpable.

'I'm a word person, so sue me,' AnnaLise

exploded. 'Besides, who counts backwards from 100? By sevens, no less.'

'And the date? I suppose—'

'Last Monday was Labor Day,' AnnaLise snapped, 'and a short week is always confusing. Besides, when I'm working—'

'I'm sorry, dear. I didn't realize Wisconsin was over the international dateline,' her mother said mildly. 'Or perhaps you time travel at the newspaper?'

Daisy was having way too much fun with this. And why shouldn't she? The woman had just been given a reprieve. Besides, for the most part, Daisy herself was unaware of the memory blips that AnnaLise all too clearly noticed. The lost keys or forgotten clothes in the washer didn't bother AnnaLise. Who *didn't* do those things occasionally? No, it was more the two incidents, both witnessed by other people, in which Daisy Griggs, the mid-life woman, slipped back into Lorraine Kuchenbacher, the teenage girl.

It had given AnnaLise the creeps, so she'd told the doctor about them. And what had he replied?

'Interesting,' Daisy's daughter repeated, starting the car. 'He said your memory glitches were "interesting." And where does he get off keeping us waiting all afternoon? What could he have been doing for two hours? Performing—'

'Brain surgery?' Daisy finished for her. 'Could be, I suppose. Or maybe neurologists leave that to the neurosurgeons. Whichever, dear, it does no good to sputter. Besides, you went next door to the office supply store. I was the one cooling my heels in the waiting room.'

'I invited you to come with me,' AnnaLise said stubbornly. 'And I'm not sputtering.'

'Yes, you are. And for the record, even reading old magazines is preferable to following you around while you shop for printer ink and red Flair pens. Besides, I wanted to call Ida Mae and let her know we were going to be late.'

'What did she say?' AnnaLise looked at the clock – the *digital* clock – on her dashboard. 'It's past five thirty, maybe we shouldn't—'

'Honestly, you are such a worrywart, AnnaLise. Besides, we could have cut a good ten minutes off our trip if you'd taken the Blue Ridge Parkway. *And* we'd have gotten off before the section that spooks you.'

The Blue Ridge Parkway runs nearly 470 miles through the mountains from Shenandoah National Park in Virginia south to Great Smoky Mountains National Park in North Carolina. A breathtakingly beautiful drive with scenic vistas that drew people from all over the world, the local stretch of Parkway provided a handy shortcut between the town of Boone to the south and upper entrance of Sutherton Mountain, at least when the route wasn't packed with rubber-necking tourists.

But it wasn't the gawkers that, in Daisy's words, 'spooked' AnnaLise. Her problem started at the Parkway's Milemarker 303.4: the Linn Cove Viaduct. The viaduct skirted Grandfather Mountain, essentially Sutherton Mountain's big brother to the west, so as not to destroy that mountain's delicate ecosystem. Seeing it from a distance, you would swear the snaking concrete span and the vehicles crossing it were suspended in thin air. And they were. Above forty-one hundred feet of nothingness.

AnnaLise didn't like nothingness. In fact, she even hated the viaduct which performed the same function on their own mountain. Not nearly as long or impressive – a simple 'c' curve tucked against the mountain, as opposed to the Linn Cove Viaduct's long, sweeping 's' – the Sutherton version had been dubbed simply a 'bridge' rather than the more pretentious 'viaduct.' Semantics aside, Sutherton Bridge still danced a precarious semicircle around a gorge deep enough to give AnnaLise conniptions.

'Well, not to worry,' Daisy said. 'It won't be dark for another couple of hours, so you don't even need to concern yourself about getting down the mountain before nightfall. Besides, the people who stay at Hotel Lux drive up and down it without a problem and some of them are two or three times your age.'

'That's because they have cataracts as thick as quarters and cars the size of cabin cruisers. They just point downhill and let 'er rip so they won't miss the early-bird specials at Mama's.'

'"They," and the rest of our visitors, keep this town solvent,' Daisy scolded. 'I won't have you bad-mouthing them.'

Sure, AnnaLise thought, until they ignore the no-parking sign in front of your garage and block you in. Again.

But she didn't say it. Instead, she told Daisy: 'I just meant that Ida Mae might have given up on us and is having dinner.'

'Sure you did.' The dollop of sarcasm was

34

unmistakable. 'Here, take Main Street, but don't forget to bear left toward the mountain.'

AnnaLise turned onto Main Street and then bore left, as ordered. The opposite direction would have taken them home. Instead, though, she was reluctantly circling Lake Sutherton clockwise on Main Street, a route which would eventually take them up Sutherton Mountain.

The western side of the lake was dominated by large homes with names like Miller House, Preston Place, Watkins Nest and Cranswick Cottage. Then came the north boat launch, the post office and Lucky's Bait Shop. A handy arrangement since during the summer months, mail was delivered to the lake homes by boat.

Tourists paid fifteen dollars a head for the fun of riding along to cheer on the college-age runners who hopped off the boat on one side of the property, raced to the flagged boxes to deliver and collect the mail and then, with luck, hopped back on the vessel – which never stopped or slowed – before it was out of leaping range.

Lake Sutherton was cinched at the waist like a figure of eight and just below the belt was Bradenham, Mayor Bobby Bradenham's home-stead. Just north of Bradenham was the turn-off for what had been White Tail Island, now converted into 'Hart's Landing.'

A half-mile north of Hart's Landing was where Main Street began to climb the mountain. This so-called 'low entrance' took visitors past the strategically placed Sutherton Real Estate office, which handled properties on both the lake and mountain. AnnaLise's friend Kathleen Smoakes headed the rental division.

'How far along are the Eames on Ida Mae's deck?' she asked her mother as the little Mitsubishi passed the first tee of the eighteen-hole golf course and then six clay tennis courts, already covered in fallen, wind-blown leaves.

'Done, I hope. That rickety thing was practically falling off the place. As tight as the woman is with money, I finally convinced her that she'd best fix it before someone landed on the expert slope without wearing any skis.' Ida Mae's place was one of the many stilt-supported chalets on the fringe of the ski hill.

'I hear you.' AnnaLise nodded at a rustic wooden lodge diagonally across the road from the tennis courts. Located at the base of the ski hill where all the runs came together, the place would be jammed with parka-sheathed skiers in a couple of months. Now, though, the lodge was nearly deserted, the metal benches for the chair lift detached and lined up on the grass, half of them looking newly painted. 'Speaking of skiing, it looks like they're getting a jump on the season.'

'The lodge has to be ready for the first snowfall, whenever that should come,' Daisy said. 'Besides, they've taken to doing ski-lift rides on fall weekends. I hear it's beautiful, what with the changing leaves and all. We should do it this weekend before you leave.'

Again, that push-pull in Daisy's voice. Wanting her daughter to stay, but hoping she wouldn't need to.

'Sounds good,' AnnaLise said, though the very thought of it shot acid into her stomach. Someone born and bred in the High Country should not be afraid of heights, but there it was.

AnnaLise stepped on the brake to make the tight left turn onto Ridge Road, which would take them up the mountain without needing to cross the Sutherton Bridge. As with most things in life, though, there was a price: the narrow switchback roads. They were especially a problem for AnnaLise's Spyder, which had an amazingly wide front axle and long wheelbase for a car so small, meaning that while it held the road very well, the convertible had the exaggerated turning radius of a tractor-trailer.

'You're going to have to give it some gas, you know,' Daisy said, looking back at a shiny black panel truck emblazoned with the words 'Scotty the Electrician' coming up fast behind them. 'The road climbs about five hundred feet in elevation during this section.'

Said 'section,' in AnnaLise's estimation, being maybe the equivalent of only eight city blocks. The grade was so steep she was afraid her poor Mitsubishi's twin tailpipes were scraping.

But AnnaLise stepped on the gas and the little car leapt forward, just in time for another hairpin turn. She slammed on her brakes and was rewarded with a screech of tires behind her and the sound of a horn.

Negotiating the bend, they continued to climb, the panel truck on their tail. 'Back off,' AnnaLise said into the rear-view mirror.

'He's likely just trying to get to a job,' Daisy

said mildly. 'You could jack up your speed to ten miles an hour.'

'I'm going fifteen.' She rolled down her window. 'Jackass!'

'AnnaLise Griggs, I will not have you talking that way. And the last thing you want to do is alienate the only electrician in town before that garage is wired. Though,' she squinted into her side mirror, 'I don't think that's Scotty himself.'

'Back off, Jack,' AnnaLise muttered, putting the window back up. 'Or whatever your name is.'

'If the tailgating bothers you so much,' her mother said in a reasonable tone, 'take the road up here on the left.'

AnnaLise slowed to make the turn, the other vehicle nearly clipping her as he roared past.

'Asshole,' Daisy called after him.

'Daisy Griggs, and you're scolding me for my—' She interrupted herself. 'Did that sign say Dead end?'

'It did, but you've lived up here long enough to realize that some ends are deader than others. We can get through, you just have to know how.'

AnnaLise glanced at her mother as they passed one lone round house that probably backed up to the ski hill, but from this side resembled one of those Sweet Tart lollipops that looks like a space ship on a stick. Except wooden and rustic, of course. 'Are you sure this connects? Preferably to where we want to go?' Which, increasingly for the younger woman, was down.

'At least where *I* want to go,' Daisy said. 'Here, slow up so you can make this right.'

'Onto what?' AnnaLise asked, following orders. The little convertible's tires crunched. 'Oh, goody. A gravel road, and this high on the mountain.'

'More like a trail. We used to take this all the time when I was a girl. Just keep the car centered and we'll be fine.'

The tailgating SUV was looking better and better by comparison. AnnaLise ducked instinctively when a low-hanging branch came into view, despite having left the car's canvas top up against the autumn chill in the air. Which brought to mind another problem.

'With the convertible roof closed the sightlines in this car are obstructed enough, without having to trail-blaze our way through,' AnnaLise griped. She'd slunk down so the top of her head was about level with the apex of the steering wheel. 'Not to mention that the Spyder rides so low, we're going to get hung up. This car isn't made for off-roading.' Nor was AnnaLise.

'Honestly,' Daisy said, 'stop being such an old lady. We won't get stuck – the turn-off is right up here.'

Her *mother* was calling her an old lady.

AnnaLise tried to buck up, carefully keeping the car centered and moving forward. Finally, a break in the trees. Hallelujah – an end was in sight. 'I turn here?' she asked, edging over toward the enticingly level clearing.

'No!' Daisy practically shouted.

AnnaLise jerked the little car back onto the road. 'My God, Daisy, why— Holy shit! Was that a gunshot?'

'More than likely.' Daisy was calmer now. 'There's a new range at the base of the mountain.'

It had sounded a lot closer than that to AnnaLise. She flexed her hands on the steering wheel, trying to loosen up. 'Firing range?'

'The county put it in. Mostly for law enforcement, though your police chief friend Chuck let me squeeze off a few rounds when it opened.'

Reassuring to know her friends were taking such good care of her mother, even to deadly force practice. What would they expose her to next, mixed martial arts? Cage fighting?

'Here!' her mother said, pointing. '*That* break in the trees.'

AnnaLise sat up a bit so she could see that there was indeed solid ground where Daisy wanted her to turn. She nosed the Spyder between two stands of sugar maples, already turning a vibrant red-orange. 'This will get us back on the road?'

'Yes'm,' Daisy said, self-satisfied. 'That wasn't so bad, was it? Now goose the gas over this little embankment and we'll be on the road just south of the bridge.'

'The *bridge*?' AnnaLise slammed on her brakes, but the car, having surged forward on Daisy's directions, went up and over the rise, landing crossways to block the road. 'Why would you make me—'

As AnnaLise spoke, she was stepping on the gas but getting nothing. The Mitsubishi had died.

Hands shaking, AnnaLise turned the key in the ignition, willing it to catch. Nothing. More

40

turning, the same: not a sputter, not a grinding, not even a pathetic *tick, tick*.

The road they now blocked led onto the curving bridge, the north end of the 'c' in view across the gorge. Sutherton Bridge was never a welcome sight to AnnaLise, but even she preferred the bridge's low concrete wall and rail to the stretch of road they were now stuck on – as high above the ground as the bridge itself, but with only a gravel shoulder.

'Relax, AnnaLise, there's no one coming.' Despite the reassuring words, Daisy was craning her neck, trying to watch for cars that might be speeding down the mountain via the curved bridge. 'If you panic, it'll just—'

'Park. The car has to be in park.' AnnaLise stepped on the brake and moved the gear shift from D to P, then turned the key again. Now the engine caught.

'Thank God,' she said, shifting the car back into drive. 'Last time I let you talk me into taking a clearly marked dead—'

A black truck came barreling toward them.

AnnaLise Griggs let go of the wheel and screamed.

Five

AnnaLise didn't remember closing her eyes, but later she would remember opening them. And seeing nothing.

'Daisy?' she called out. 'Are you all right?'

'I think so,' came her mother's voice, very nearby. 'You?'

'I . . .' AnnaLise blinked and her eyes still didn't clear. 'I can't see anything. Is it . . . is it night-time?' She tried to stifle the panic that was bubbling up. 'Have we been here for—'

'It's just a quarter to six. Or thereabouts. Are you delirious?'

'But, but . . . Mommy,' the word sprang from AnnaLise's lips only in times of crisis or illness, 'I can't see. I think . . . I think I might be blind.'

AnnaLise could barely make out the wail of a siren in the distance, but would it matter? Was hearing going to substitute for eyesight? Would she ever see another sunset? The man she would marry? The face of her newborn—

'Oh, for God's sake, AnnaLise, do we really need the scene from *Dark Victory* right now? Your frickin' convertible top collapsed on us. I can't see a thing either.'

'Hello?'

AnnaLise recognized the voice.

'Joshua Eames?' she called.

'Yes – is that AnnaLise Griggs?' His voice was

42

close to her left ear now, just on the other side of what AnnaLise realized actually *was* the Spyder's canvas top.

'It is. Are *you* OK, Josh?'

'I am, but I've lived close by here on the mountain my entire life and I have to say it's not a good idea to stop in the middle of a blind turn like you did, AnnaLise. Especially crosswise.'

'I'm so sorry,' AnnaLise said, trying to figure out where the glass from the driver's-side window had gone when the roof collapsed. 'Thank God you weren't hurt.'

A *snap/whirr* next to her signaled Daisy's seat belt being undone.

'No, ma'am,' Josh's voice said. 'Though I'm afraid *you're* in a bit of a fix. I can't see if you've got yourself a passenger, but I sure wouldn't get out of that side of the car.'

Both women froze.

'Joshua Eames,' Daisy said carefully, the south in her voice more pronounced under stress, 'are you telling me that this car is hanging out over the edge?'

'No, ma'am.' The sound of him moving around the back of the car to look. 'Just seems like the two wheels on your side are perilously close.'

'Perilously close' – under normal circumstances, AnnaLise, a big fan of descriptive language, would delight in the expression. Now, though: 'Josh, can you call nine-one-one, please?' Pretty goddamned please.

'Already did.'

'That's good, Josh. Thank you.' AnnaLise was trying to sound calm and measured, despite

43

feeling neither. 'We can't see how we're situated here, but can you tell if it's safe for us to slip out my door?'

Assuming she could find the handle. They couldn't very well shimmy through the window opening because the frame of the fallen convertible top was blocking the way.

'I'm not moving an inch,' Daisy's voice said, 'and don't you either, AnnaLise Griggs. You climb out of there and I tip over the mountain like the fat kid on the end of a teeter-totter.'

'I'm sure we're not that bad off,' AnnaLise said. 'Besides, listen. Help is already on its way.'

The siren she'd heard earlier was getting closer, presumably Fire and Rescue from town, though with the road zigzagging up the mountain, the sound waxed and waned as it approached.

'Are we on the bridge, Josh, or the road leading to it?'

It didn't feel to AnnaLise as if the car was tilted like the wheels on her mother's side had climbed the railing, so she was betting the latter. She didn't know which was worse: the 'teeter-totter' her mother was envisioning over the bridge's low wall, or their car clinging to the edge of the road without even a railing between them and a sheer drop.

'Joshua?'

The only answer was the distant wailing of the siren.

Six

'Have you given any thought to maybe getting out?' Chief of Police Chuck Greystone asked, a chuckle burbling just below the tone of his voice.

AnnaLise, who had a blanket over her shoulders, tried not to let her trembling hands slosh coffee out of the Styrofoam cup she held. 'Unless I'm having an out-of-body experience, I believe I *am* out. Daisy, too, thankfully.'

AnnaLise gestured toward the ambulance where her mother stood talking with Coy Pitchford, one of the town's uniformed officers. As Chuck turned to look, Daisy put her hands over her eyes, opening her mouth in a mock scream of terror. Coy bent over, laughing uncontrollably.

'Very funny,' AnnaLise muttered.

'It is, a little,' Chuck said, green eyes contrasting with the tanned planes of his face. Chuck was fifty-percent Cherokee, fifty-percent Irish, and a hundred percent gay. 'Since you're both safe.'

'Thanks, I think.' AnnaLise and Chuck had dated through high school, though the relationship had never gone much beyond the close friendship they still shared. Upon returning to Sutherton the prior week, she'd finally discovered why. 'So when you said, had I thought about—'

'Getting out? I meant "of town," Dodge, whatever.' He cracked a grin, reminding her again why she'd loved him. And still did, in fact.

45

'That's a fine thing to say. I thought you were glad to see me.'

'I am,' Chuck said. 'You're just sort of . . . High Country high-maintenance.' He nodded toward the Mitsubishi, now being hoisted by a tow truck's hook like the sole trout on a fisherman's stringer. The vehicle hadn't been quite as close to the edge as she'd imagined, though her imagination – at least when it came to heights – was the stuff recurring nightmares were made of.

As the pathetic-looking Spyder dangled by the bumper, the front right hubcap fell off and rolled. One of the wrecker's crew trotted after, retrieving the cap before it could go over the edge.

'Nice of him, but I'm not sure it's worth salvaging,' AnnaLise said, trying not to look at the gravel shoulder where her car's passenger-side tires had been moments ago. If they'd had a little more rain, if the soil was a bit softer, if the slope had been a mite steeper, the bridge a yard nearer . . .

'The hubcap or the whole car?'

'The whole . . .?' AnnaLise glanced guiltily at the little vehicle like it could hear her, 'The entire thing looks totaled, I'm afraid. And it's fifteen years old so—'

'Shit!' the man who'd caught the hubcap had stopped his momentum at the side of the road. But he was looking down. 'We got another one.'

'Please, don't bother,' AnnaLise started. 'Whatever fell off doesn't—' She stopped when the mechanic turned and she could see the expression on his face and the name patch on his coveralls.

46

'Earl?' Chuck, tensing in the lowering light, left her side and went to join the other man.

Then the chief turned as well. 'We're going to need some help. There's a car down there.'

Seven

'Well, I'm very glad you had the officer bring you up here, rather than trying to drive back down the mountain after everything you've been through,' Ida Mae Babb said.

They were sitting on Ida Mae's new deck, sipping wine. AnnaLise was in a chair backed so close to the sliding glass door into the house that the heating from the interior was keeping her warm.

On the other hand, both Ida Mae and Daisy had afghans tucked around them and sat out as far as they could, the better to see the crazy quilt of leaves on Grandfather Mountain as the sun sank below its peak.

'Next time you're going to be so late, though,' their hostess continued, 'I'd appreciate a call. I was expecting you closer to noontime.'

AnnaLise glanced toward Daisy. Hadn't her mother said she'd called Ida Mae from the neurologist's waiting room to tell her friend they'd be late?

But Daisy didn't protest her friend's gentle scolding. 'We do appreciate your hospitality, Ida Mae. Especially given we didn't have a vehicle to drive down the mountain ourselves, and the chief and his officers already had enough on their hands without worrying about ferrying us all the way home.'

'You were lucky you weren't killed,' Ida Mae said. 'But the other car, the one in the gorge. Do they think it flew right off the bridge itself?'

AnnaLise took a sip of red wine. 'Chuck says there are indications it went off the road on the approach to the bridge, but on the opposite end from where we came to rest.'

'So likely before the railing.' Ida Mae, a porcelain-skinned woman of about sixty-five, shook her head. 'I don't think a day goes by that some yahoo doesn't stand far too close to that edge for my comfort. Pedestrians aren't allowed on the bridge, so they pull over there to look out.'

'It *is* a view you can't get anywhere else on the mountain,' Daisy admitted. 'Breathtaking, really.'

AnnaLise shivered. A mother's 'breathtaking' was her daughter's 'heart-stopping.'

'Do you know what I'm thinking?' Ida Mae asked. 'I'm thinking that other car might have pulled over to look and the earth gave way. I'm sure it's not the first car to slide into that gorge, never to be seen again.'

'No way of telling, yet, when this one happened,' Daisy said. 'In fact, if Earl from the Sutherton Auto hadn't nearly gone over the side trying to show off for AnnaLise, I'm not sure anyone would have known it happened at all.'

'Show off for AnnaLise?' Daisy's daughter repeated. 'He just stopped my hubcap from going over. Probably an environmentalist.'

'Apparently you didn't see the looks he was sneaking at you.'

Ida Mae frowned. 'Are you talking about Earl

49

Lawling? Now, he's much too old for AnnaLise. Bobby Bradenham is a better fit, or that writer who's staying at the inn . . . Dandy?'

'Duende,' AnnaLise supplied. 'And the last thing I need is a new man in my life.'

Daisy pounced. 'A "new" man?'

Oh, dear. Having Ben and his family in town was bad enough, without AnnaLise making verbal slips like this. 'I do date, you know. Just not anyone in particular.'

'Uh-huh,' Daisy said slowly.

'But back to this other accident,' AnnaLise said to change the subject. 'When we left, the police were processing the scene where the car went off.'

'I can't imagine there's any chance someone survived a fall like that,' Ida Mae said.

AnnaLise had stayed well back from the cliff and hadn't seen the remains of the car. Still, 'It's a long way down.'

'Amen,' Daisy said. 'Coy Pitchford tried to point out the wreck to me, but all I could see was a glint of yellow. I honestly don't know how Earl Lawling knew that was a car down there.'

'Yellow?' AnnaLise felt the bottom drop out of her stomach.

Daisy cocked her head. 'Yellowish, at least. But I just got a glimpse.'

And so, AnnaLise assumed, it would be no use to ask her mother if the car had been a Porsche.

Eight

'. . . Totaled her car and could have killed poor Josh,' Daisy was saying.

AnnaLise was still grappling with the possibility that the 'yellowish' car her mother had seen far below them was Tanja Rosewood's Porsche – the one AnnaLise had seen daughter Suzanne standing next to as the girl spoke to Josh.

'Poor Josh?' she repeated weakly, wanting to appear she had some grasp of the conversation.

The Porsche parked on Main Street had to be Tanja's – the high-end import wasn't exactly ubiquitous in Sutherton. And Tanja had planned to drive up the mountain this afternoon. In fact, Daisy had given her directions to the bridge near where the car – the yellow car, if AnnaLise's mother was to be believed – had gone over. Had Suzanne been with her? Or Ben?

AnnaLise gave an involuntary shiver. She wanted to ask how sure Daisy was that the car was yellow, but didn't trust herself to bring the Rosewoods into the conversation in a casual enough way that didn't give away her past relationship with Ben. Besides, Daisy already seemed to sense something – guilt, she'd said, and her mother had hit the nail on the head with that one.

'Yes, poor Josh,' Daisy was saying. 'Eames Trail is just south of that bridge. I imagine he was anxious to be home and done with his day,

51

and there you are stalled in the middle of the road like that.'

'Eames Trail?' AnnaLise repeated. 'There's a road named after the family?'

'More like a long driveway,' Ida Mae said. 'When the new nine-one-one system was put in, all the roads and trails, big or small, had to be named. Most folks just called them after themselves or their animals. Like Ruff Road, down the way. Get it, AnnaLise? R-u-f-f.'

'Got it.' AnnaLise managed a weak smile. 'Cute.'

Daisy eyed her daughter. 'Are you all right?'

AnnaLise pulled herself together. 'Fine, considering everything. And I'm glad the same is true for you and Josh, though I don't understand why he left before the police got there.'

'Simple,' Ida Mae stated.

Daisy frowned at the unkindness. 'I really don't think he's simple, Ida Mae. I know he spent a lot of time by himself as a boy, but—'

'Of course he's not simple,' Ida Mae said. 'Why would you think that? I meant his reason for leaving the scene was simple.'

'And what would that be?' This could be a very long evening.

Ida Mae shrugged. 'Joshua Eames has had his run-ins with the law, him hanging out in the woods, drinking and the like. His mother was as wild as they come, so he comes by it honestly, I suppose.'

'It didn't help that the boy was big for his age so people expected more of him,' Daisy offered. 'Or that Joshua was awful at the very things his father loved, like hunting and fishing. Not that Fred had much time for either, what with a wife who loved money and a business that wasn't—'

'My point,' Ida Mae said, glaring at her for the interruption, 'is that I wouldn't be at all astonished if Joshua Eames is driving without a license.'

'Nor I,' Daisy said, nodding. 'That's why I didn't mention his being there to the chief.'

'But that's silly,' AnnaLise said, though truth be told, she hadn't either. 'Josh, himself, called nine-one-one, and he's probably going to need the police report for his insurance—'

'Why? Besides, AnnaLise, we owe him. If it weren't for him, we might still be sitting in that car – or worse,' Daisy said stubbornly. 'As far as I'm concerned, an unidentified vehicle came at us, but sailed right on past while you were busy bouncing us off that rock wall. End of story.'

Fine. Let Daisy have it her way. 'Nice deck, Ida Mae.'

'And how would you know that, either? You've only set foot on the first five boards of it.'

'Leave the girl alone,' Ida Mae said, getting up. 'AnnaLise, can I get you another glass of wine?'

AnnaLise looked at her glass, which was surprisingly low. 'That would be very nice, but shouldn't we be going?'

'Going?' Ida Mae asked. 'But how?'

AnnaLise felt herself color up. 'Well, I thought maybe you could give us a ride.'

'Heavens, I don't drive down at night. Besides,

didn't you say the road was blocked, what with the police vehicles and all?'

'Well, yes, but we'd hate to presume on your hospit—'

'Nonsense. It's my pleasure to put you up and God knows there's all sorts of space. Four bedrooms, remember?'

'I'd forgotten, honestly,' Daisy said. 'How many people can you sleep?'

'Eight, officially, but I'm certain the skiers manage to fit in a few more on the floor and what-not.'

'Are you renting the place out in the winter, Ida Mae?' AnnaLise asked. 'I'm not sure why, but I thought you stayed on the mountain year-round.'

'I most certainly did, when Robbie was alive. He loved the snow, and I did, too, as long as it behaved itself. I'd tell God, "You keep it on the grass and let the streets stay clean, and we'll get along just fine, thank you very much."'

AnnaLise laughed, eliciting a chuckle from their hostess. 'My husband thought that was funny, too. Said, "Ida Mae, you don't honestly bother God with that, do you?" and I would shrug and tell him, "Well, now, Robbie. He *knows* how I feel."'

Ida Mae was still smiling at the memory. Robbie Babb was Ida Mae's late husband. Not to be confused with their son Robbie Jr, Bobby Bradenham or any of the myriad Robbies and Bobbies who seemed to dot the area, possibly because of the large Scottish population that had settled there centuries before.

54

In fact, if AnnaLise forgot a man's name, she'd trot out Robbie or Bobby – maybe mumble it, so they couldn't tell which one she was saying – and stand a good chance of being right.

Or, at the very worst, getting a polite 'No, ma'am, that's my brother.' Or father, uncle, cousin or neighbor.

'Ida Mae has a grandbaby now,' Daisy was saying. 'Though you certainly wouldn't know it by looking at her.'

'Robbie Jr and his wife have been trying and trying,' the new grandmother said, pulling a smartphone out of her pocket. 'This will likely be their one and only but she's a keeper all right.'

'Congratulations,' AnnaLise said, her mind only partially on the conversation. She was still thinking about the yellow speck Daisy had seen in the rocky wilderness at the base of the mountain. 'Where are Robbie Jr and,' she couldn't remember his wife's name, 'his family living now?'

'Down in Charlotte.' Ida Mae rose and gave the phone to her. 'Isn't she a darling?'

A bald butterball with dimples that didn't stop, the baby was undeniably cute, though the only way you could gauge gender was by the tiny pink bow velcroed to the downy fuzz on the top of her head.

'Adorable,' AnnaLise said, trying to hand the phone back to the proud grandmother.

'Oh, there are lots more,' Ida Mae said, returning to her chair. 'Just use the touch screen.'

Oh, goody. AnnaLise loved babies, but in her estimation a picture was worth the proverbial thousand words, the emphasis on the singular article 'a.'

Still, being left to her own thoughts as she scrolled through wasn't so bad. Thank God, with new technology, people didn't make you peer over their shoulders while they showed you shot after shot in a computer slide show anymore.

Ida Mae did, though, keep up a running commentary on her new granddaughter, whose name AnnaLise missed and whose current age she couldn't guess from the pictures.

No matter, the reporter was consumed with other thoughts, the phone in her hand reminding her of her own, on top of her handbag in the other room. Should she try to call Ben? If now, a couple of hours after the accident, she remembered that Tanja Rosewood's car was yellow, would it seem so odd that she called to make sure the family was safe?

The truly odd thing might be that she, AnnaLise Griggs, had Ben Rosewood's personal cellphone number. Especially if their acquaintance was as casual as they'd pretended in front of his wife and daughter.

Speaking of the family, wasn't the Porsche a two-seater? If so, Ben or Suzanne could have been with Tanja, but not both of them. The same was true, of course, on the drive from Wisconsin. So how had all three gotten here? Perhaps they'd rented a truck or a van – something that Ben would have driven – to transport Suzanne's clothes and things to school. With a one-way rental, Ben could turn in the truck here and drive back to Wisconsin in the Porsche with—

'Wouldn't it, AnnaLise?'

Daughter looked at mother. 'Pardon?'

'Ida Mae offered to drive us home tomorrow morning after breakfast.' Daisy raised her eyebrows at AnnaLise.

'Oh, I'm sorry. I was just enjoying the photos,' she said. 'That's very nice of you – above and beyond the call of duty, really.'

'Nonsense,' Ida Mae said. 'We're practically family. Did you know I used to babysit for your mother?'

'No,' AnnaLise said, looking back and forth between the women. At sixty-five, Ida Mae was fifteen years older than Daisy, so it made sense. 'I had no idea your family was here that long ago.'

The oldest of the three women laughed. 'That long ago – you make it sound like ancient history.'

'Not ancient, certainly,' AnnaLise said, 'but has anybody done a history of Sutherton? Or documented who settled here and when?' She'd had an idea prompted by the memory games the neurologist had suggested for Daisy, and this seemed an opportune time to trot it out.

'Not that I know of,' Ida Mae said. 'There was that lady in Foscoe, who wrote up something and sold it at her jam and honey stand on the highway, but I think that was just her own family.'

Daisy was regarding her daughter. 'Whatever are you thinking, AnnaLise? That you'd do it?'

In truth, AnnaLise was trying to think about anything other than the Rosewoods. 'Heavens, no. I haven't even started combing through

57

Dickens Hart's journals toward doing his memoirs yet. No, I was thinking more of a blog on the town website, maybe, where people could share their memories and family stories.'

'Sounds like fun,' Ida Mae said. 'But does the town even have a website?'

'Joy Tamarack and Sheree Pepper have been talking about doing one for visitors,' Daisy contributed, though her face had turned guarded at AnnaLise's mention of 'memories.'

Sheree Pepper was the owner of the Sutherton Inn and one of AnnaLise's oldest friends. Though AnnaLise hadn't run this brainstorm past Sheree or Joy, who she was also close to, she was certain they would buy in. Especially if it were to help Daisy.

'Well, I think it's a fabulous idea,' Ida Mae said, getting to her feet. 'But I'm starving. Shall I get dinner started?'

'Sounds wonderful,' AnnaLise said, getting up to hand Ida Mae her phone.

As their hostess took it, the thing gave off the tweet-tweet signaling a text message.

'Sorry,' Ida Mae said. 'Barbara Jean – she's the one who lives on Ruff Road – was having stomach pains earlier and her daughter insisted she call down for the paramedics.'

Slipping on reading glasses, Ida Mae surveyed the message and typed in one of her own, before slipping the phone back into her pocket. 'All's well, thank the Lord. Though it took the fire department over an hour to get there, can you believe that?'

Daisy glanced at AnnaLise. 'Given the two

accidents where we were, the town's emergency services were probably severely taxed.'

Or they couldn't find 'Ruff Road,' AnnaLise thought. 'Did they take your neighbor in for observation?'

'No, but they did confiscate her North Carolina Hot Sauce. Honestly, you'd think the woman would learn.' Ida Mae waved her guests into the house.

'Truly, Ida Mae,' AnnaLise said, 'thank you so much for both the hospitality and for driving us home tomorrow.'

'Not a problem at all,' Ida Mae said. 'I have to see Kathleen at Sutherton Realty anyway and work out the rental arrangements for the ski season.'

Ida Mae and Daisy continued through the living room into the kitchen, while AnnaLise went to retrieve her handbag and the cell on top of it from the couch. The room was dark now that the sun was fully down, and she could see a red light on the phone, signaling a new text message.

She picked it up with trepidation, but found only a Tweet from the newspaper where she worked in Wisconsin, a tease of the next day's special section on fall lawn care. Glancing toward the kitchen door where the other two women were talking she punched in Ben's number.

It was impulsive – the text equivalent of drunk-dialing – but in this case the act was driven more by anxiety than the wine AnnaLise'd had. The affair might be over, but she'd loved the man and not knowing if he was OK was intolerable. If all was well and he was with his wife and daughter, AnnaLise could claim that she was simply being hospitable, making sure they didn't need anything during their—

Daisy popped back in. 'Ida Mae wants to know if rib-eyes on the grill and baked potatoes are all right.'

AnnaLise reflexively pushed 'end' on the phone. 'More than all right.' And it was true. After a week of meals eaten largely at Mama's, something prepared simply with*out* condensed soup, canned tuna or elbow macaroni sounded great.

'Can I help?' AnnaLise followed Daisy into the kitchen, glad now that her mother had interrupted the ill-advised call before Ben could answer. She looked around, starting to relax a bit from the wine. 'Wow, this is beautiful.'

'I thank you,' Ida Mae said, going to mute the small television that blared *The Mountain News* in the corner. 'This was my remodeling project last year.'

'Eames Construction?' Daisy asked.

'Josh did the woodworking,' Ida Mae said, pointing to the hickory kitchen cabinets. 'That boy has a real talent. Every corner, every angle, is perfectly square. No mean feat in old houses built on the sides of mountains.'

'Good to know,' Daisy said. 'Aren't you glad you hired Eames for the garage, AnnaLise?'

But her daughter wasn't listening. She was watching the silent TV image of a barely recognizable yellow Porsche being tow-lined onto the ramp of a flatbed truck.

Nine

'It's my fault, you know,' Daisy was saying to Phyllis Balisteri the next morning.

'Yours? Why?'

AnnaLise's surrogate mother held up the coffee pot to offer her a refill, but the younger woman shook her head. Seated with Daisy in Mama's private booth, she'd barely been able to keep the first cup of java down.

'I told that woman to take the bridge,' Daisy said, turning to face AnnaLise across the table. 'You were right about it, you know. The thing's a death trap.'

'Daisy Lorraine Kuchenbacher Griggs,' Mama said, 'you're making yourself all too important in this drama. The woman – from what, Minny-sota?'

AnnaLise forced herself to offer, 'No, Wisconsin.'

'Same difference. She didn't know the mountain and went barreling back down too fast and ran off the road, pure and simple, with plenty of examples beforehand. That's her fault, not yours.'

Mama did have a way of separating the wheat from the chaff. Whether you wanted it separated or not.

'Well, then they should put up a railing along that stretch, Phyllis. AnnaLise and I nearly went over at the identical spot on the opposite end of the bridge, didn't we?'

61

'So what would you have the town do, Daisy? Fence off the entire mountain? And then there's the lake, all them college kids and tourists wandering in and drowning? Maybe we should build a stockade around that, too.'

Phyllis put the carafe back on the heating element of the coffee brewer and came back, moving a copy of *Best Recipes from the Backs of Boxes, Bottles, Cans and Jars, 1979*, before sliding in next to AnnaLise across from Daisy. 'Round here, we don't figure it's our job to protect people from their own stupidity.' She twisted her head toward AnnaLise. 'No offense.'

'None taken.'

Ever since Ida Mae Babb had dropped them off at Mama's restaurant earlier that morning, the accident had seemed to be the main topic of conversation. The media coverage hadn't identified the woman whose body was found in the car, confirmed as a Porsche with Wisconsin plates, but everyone seemed to know. In Sutherton, both news and conjecture traveled at warp speed.

'Had to be the mother of that girl who's dating Joshua Eames.' Mrs Peebly, Daisy's next-door neighbor and garage co-owner, was seated at the booth across from them, her aluminum-frame walker blocking the aisle.

Weird, AnnaLise thought. The people of Sutherton seem to know more about the Rosewood family than she did. 'So Josh and Suzanne *are* a couple?' she asked, thinking back to when she saw the two talking outside Mama's. 'Since when?'

'I think it might be stretching it a bit to say

they're dating,' Daisy said. 'Though I did see that girl with Joshua last year during U-Mo's open-house week.' She looked at Mama. 'We helped with refreshments, remember?'

'I do.' Phyllis bobbed her head. 'Though I can't say I've seen the girl between then and now.'

Mrs Peebly snickered. 'Don't mean they haven't been seeing each other. There's this thing they call the Internet now, you know, and Skope.'

'The mouthwash?' Mama seemed puzzled, and that didn't happen often.

'I think she means Skype,' AnnaLise forced herself to participate. 'It's—'

'Hell's bells, I know what Skype is,' Mama said. 'You think I was born yesterday, AnnieLeez?'

More like a half-century of yesterdays, though Mama and Daisy seemed less set in their ways at fifty than AnnaLise was at the age of twenty-eight.

'Love at first sight, those two,' Mrs Peebly was saying. 'Nice girl, even if her father and mother, bless her soul, come on uppity. Sheree Pepper says the woman was nothing but trouble.'

'Well, it does take one to know one,' Mama said, moving aside the walker to get past. 'Sheree Pepper sure doesn't have a halo on that blonde head of hers.'

'Not *that* kind of trouble,' Mrs Peebly said, with a glint in her eye. The shrunken ninety-year-old loved a good dirty story that she could then declare 'disgraceful' even as she was laughing about it. 'Sheree gave them number seven and eight, the best rooms in the inn, and the woman still found fault.'

'Two rooms?' Mama asked as she slipped onto the bench next to her. 'She and her hubby don't sleep together?'

AnnaLise felt her cheeks flame, having been wondering the same thing.

'Now, hush,' Daisy scolded. 'That second room was probably for their daughter—'

The electric chime on the door rang out and Suzanne Rosewood, herself, entered, eyes red. She was with Joshua Eames, Josh's arm wrapped around her protectively.

Mama stood up to seat them, but AnnaLise slid out after her.

'I'll take them,' she said, gesturing for Mama to sit back down.

Not sure if she was trying to assuage her conscience or simply protect the two from 'inquiring minds,' AnnaLise pulled two menus out of the stack and greeted Josh, then turned to his companion. 'I am so sorry about the accident, Suz—'

The young woman's face twisted. 'I bet you are.' She snatched the menus from AnnaLise's hand and pushed past her to a table at the back. Josh trailed after her, throwing AnnaLise a puzzled look.

Well, that pretty much settled that. Tanja must have known about the affair and either told her daughter, or Suzanne had sensed it. AnnaLise closed her eyes, drawing in her breath slowly and releasing it the same way, before she opened them.

Daisy and Mama were staring at her from opposite sides of the booth. Phyllis said, 'Now what in the world was that all about?'

Daisy just sat, her lips tightened into two narrow – and probably disapproving – lines.

'I'm not sure,' AnnaLise mumbled miserably. 'Maybe, umm, maybe she blames me for them coming up here at all.'

'I don't think it's Sutherton she has the problem with,' Mama said, looking toward the back of the restaurant. 'She seems to be getting along just fine with parts of it.'

AnnaLise followed her glance to the table where Josh and Suzanne were locked in a kiss. A long kiss. 'I guess this explains why Suzanne was so adamant about coming here.'

'Your pocketbook is vibrating,' Mama said, passing the bag from the bench next to her.

AnnaLise pulled out her cellphone, which showed a text from Chuck, who she'd been trying to get hold of all morning. It read: Here, if you want to come by.

'I have to run,' she said. 'I'll catch you later.'

'Do you need my car?' Daisy called after her.

'Not for this, but thanks,' AnnaLise said, hesitating at the door and coming back to give her mom a kiss on the cheek. 'I'm sorry I almost killed you.'

Daisy flushed with pleasure. She and AnnaLise weren't given to shows of affection.

'Now don't you be saying that,' Mama said, waving the younger woman off. 'Your mother already likes to make herself the center of attention.'

Which, of course, was where Mama thought her own rightful place was. AnnaLise gave her a cheek-kiss as well. 'Well, she certainly has a right, what with her side of the car practically hanging over the cliff last night.'

'It was?' Mrs Peebly asked, eyes rounding. 'What . . .?'

AnnaLise let herself out the door as Daisy recounted the story, accompanied, no doubt, by the Greek chorus pantomime of Mama's eyes rolling.

AnnaLise was sitting in one of the two guest chairs in front of Chuck's desk.

The last time she had been here, the other seat was taken by their friend Mayor Bobby Bradenham and the two of them – AnnaLise and the mayor – had engaged in a shouting match.

Now Bobby, who'd had a rough past week, had taken off for a few days. AnnaLise missed him. Not only had she and Bobby been friends since kindergarten and first grade respectively, but he was the only one she'd confided in about Ben.

Granted, the revelation had been inadvertent and accompanied by an epic and uncharacteristic torrent of tears – hers, not his – but it felt good, nonetheless, to tell someone.

Not that she planned to tell anyone else, especially Chuck, given the circumstances.

'Your car is totaled?' he asked, lacing his hands behind his head and leaning back in the chair to stretch. Chuck's green eyes always looked a little dreamy – Mama insisted on calling them 'bedroom' eyes – but now the chief looked downright tired, the result of a long night which, according to Chuck, had culminated in the positive identification of Tanja Rosewood as the driver of the Porsche.

'And how. The mechanic who answered the phone at the garage said, "Well, ma'am, we can fix it, but this is the one time the whole will not be greater than the sum of its parts. In fact, I'm not sure we can even *find* all the parts."'

'That would have been Earl.' The chief took a swig of his Diet Coke. 'The man does have a silver tongue to go along with his eagle eyes.'

'He's the one who spotted the car yesterday.' Her own Diet Coke, untouched, was sitting on the desk.

'Yup. And good thing. There were no signs at the spot the car went off the road and it wasn't the first.'

'There's more than one car down there?' AnnaLise was feeling very lucky all of a sudden.

'At least two, though the other one's slipped deeper into the gorge, so we'll need some time and equipment to recover it. Could be just a stolen car someone was trying to get rid of, or maybe the poor folks *did* go over like Mrs Rosewood. If Earl Lawling hadn't spotted the yellow of that car before the leaves and eventual snow covered it and the spring thaw sent water into that gorge, God knows when we'd have found it.'

'I assume Mrs Rosewood died on impact?' From the horror AnnaLise had experienced just being close to the edge, she couldn't even fathom what it would feel like to be hurtling over it.

'It's a long way down and, despite the law, Mrs Rosewood wasn't wearing a seat belt.'

'They wrinkled her clothes,' AnnaLise said reflexively.

Too late, she saw Chuck's sleepy eyes sharpen, like they'd just hopped out of bed and strapped on six-shooters. 'And just how would you know that?'

AnnaLise felt her face get warm. 'I'm sorry, I thought you knew. Ben is the district attorney for the county I work in.'

'"Ben" being Mr Rosewood?'

There she went, digging herself in deeper. The less said the better. 'Yes.'

'Well, Mr Rosewood certainly made it clear he's a D.A. there in Wisconsin, but he didn't mention you two were acquaintances. You know the family quite well then?'

Maybe Chuck should have been a district attorney, though interrogational skills certainly came in handy in police work, too, as witnessed by . . . well, right now.

'The family? No,' AnnaLise said, following her own mental advice to keep it short, stupid. 'We were introduced just yesterday at Mama's.'

'Which is when Mrs Rosewood volunteered the information that she hated seat belts?'

What was Chuck doing? Auditioning for a position with the prosecution? 'No,' AnnaLise screwed up her face, like she was thinking. Which she was, fast and furious. 'I'm not sure how . . . Oh, I know, it must have been my friend, Katie, who mentioned it. She works in the D.A.'s office and, well,' a smile, 'you know how girls talk.'

Katie, AnnaLise's own mother and every

woman who supported the equal rights amendment would shoot her. *Should* shoot her.

'Huh,' was all Chuck said.

'Anyway, that's pretty much all I know.' AnnaLise shrugged. 'Besides the fact that Suzanne Rosewood just started at U-Mo and . . . oh, you do know that Tanja had a spa appointment up at what used to be Tail Too, right?'

'The Sutherton Spa? Yes.'

A rise by any other name. 'Fine, Sutherton Spa. Did she keep that appointment?'

'She did, though she arrived a few minutes late for her three thirty, according to Joy.'

'Joy?' AnnaLise sensed an opportunity to turn the conversation from what she might know about the Rosewoods to something more mundane. 'I heard just yesterday she owns the place, but is she actually working up there now?'

Chuck seemed to accept the deflection. 'Honestly, Lise, it's tough to know just what Joy is doing. Or intends to do. I never knew her when she was married to your daddy, but—' He eyed her.

'Don't mess with me, Chuck,' she warned. 'I know where all your skeletons are buried, too.'

'My only skeleton was being gay and that one was stuck in the closet, not buried.'

'Not anymore,' AnnaLise said, happy that her friend was content, but a little sad for herself. Why did the best-looking, nicest guys have to be gay? Though it did make her feel a mite better about the wheel-spinning in their relationship. At the time, she'd thought it was her and her desire to leave Sutherton, see the world, all that rot.

Now, she realized, the wavering was on both sides.

'But you're right about Joy being full of ideas,' AnnaLise went on. 'I would think, though, that it's a graveyard up there before ski season.'

'Hence her interest in a second location in Hart's Landing.'

It made sense, AnnaLise guessed. Life in their part of the High Country revolved around the lake in summer and the mountain in the winter. Joy could allocate staff seasonally between the two, depending on demand.

But back to directing the subject at hand. 'So, Joy saw Mrs Rosewood when she arrived at the spa?'

'Unfortunately.'

AnnaLise cocked her head. 'Why unfortunately? At least you know Tanja was driving down the mountain – instead of up – when the accident happened. Though I suppose that's most often the case. People gaining speed and taking the curves too fast.'

'True. Though very occasionally you'll come across your over-achiever who tempts disaster on the way up as well.'

'Meaning me, I suppose.'

'If the lead foot fits, Lise.'

AnnaLise didn't bother going into the role her mother's shortcut played in the fiasco. God knows AnnaLise's panic had an equally important part.

'. . . liability for Joy and the spa,' Chuck was saying.

'I'm sorry?'

The chief shook his head. 'You know, if you're

70

going to come all the way to my office to pump me for information, the least you can do is pay attention.'

Chuck knew her too well, AnnaLise thought ruefully. 'It was only a short walk. You were saying?'

He leaned forward. 'I was *saying* that while Mrs Rosewood may have been speeding, that's likely the secondary cause of the accident. Preliminary reports show her blood-alcohol levels were over the legal limit.'

Ben had mentioned his wife's love of the grape over pillow talk one night. A riff on the prototypical cheating husband's 'she doesn't understand me,' no doubt. Still, it could well be true – not that AnnaLise had any intention of sharing this tidbit with Chuck after the seat belt comment sparked such interest.

The police chief could – and certainly would – interrogate Ben on the subject of his wife's drinking.

'But what does that have to do with Joy and the spa?' AnnaLise asked.

Another overhead stretch from Chuck. 'Seems that when Mrs Rosewood arrived late for her appointment, Joy offered her a glass of wine while she waited for the next opening.'

'That's not unusual in a spa or upscale salon,' AnnaLise said. 'Besides, a single glass shouldn't have made her drunk. Presumably, Tanja had eaten lunch at Mama's before she left for her appointment.'

Chuck shrugged. 'People were coming and going and the bottles were opened and left in the

71

waiting area, so we can't be sure how much Mrs Rosewood ultimately drank there. We do know, though, that an open bottle of wine was recovered from her car.'

'Doesn't mean it came from the spa,' AnnaLise protested. 'And even if Tanja Rosewood did pilfer a bottle when she was up there, it certainly wouldn't be Joy's fault. It's not the spa's responsibility to protect people from their own . . .'

AnnaLise realized she had been about to echo Mama's earlier statement about fencing off the mountain and the lake to protect people from their own stupidity.

'You might believe that,' Chuck said, going to pick up his phone. 'But I've got an inkling from what your friend "Ben" said, that he's not in total agreement.'

Ten

AnnaLise tried Joy Tamarack's cellphone on the walk back home, but the call went immediately to voicemail, a sure sign that the cell tower coverage was spotty wherever Joy was – not unusual in the mountains.

Turning off Main onto 2nd street, AnnaLise unlocked the door to her childhood home. Half of the two-story concrete block building's first floor was allotted to the retail space now rented to Tucker Stanton for Torch, so the front door of the unconventional living space opened directly into the kitchen. A tiny parlor completed the lower level, with a staircase leading up to the second. The upper level had twice the square footage of the lower, since it ran above not only the kitchen and parlor, but also all of Torch.

'Daisy?' AnnaLise called, not expecting an answer. When her mother wasn't down the block, helping Mama with the restaurant, she was at Torch, doing ditto for Tucker. In fact, Tucker had become the son Daisy never had and AnnaLise was grateful to have his back-up when she wasn't around.

Getting no response, AnnaLise dug the phone book out of the bottom of a desk drawer to look up the Sutherton Spa at the Hotel Lux. Finding no listing, she searched the pages for Tail Too's old number.

Bingo.

Suspicious, AnnaLise checked the date on the phone book. As she suspected, the thing dated back to the last time she'd been home, five years ago.

The sound of keys in the door and her mother entered. 'What are you doing?'

'Looking for a phone number for the Sutherton Spa.' AnnaLise showed her the date on the book. 'Where's the new one?'

'Heavens, who uses phone books anymore? If I need a number, I just go online. Wherever did you find that old directory?'

'In the desk drawer under the mailing supplies.'

'Well, that explains why I didn't see it,' she said, taking the book and dumping it in the wastebasket under the sink. 'I never go in that drawer.'

'You don't send things?'

'Of course I do, but not snail-mail. I even pay my bills online.' Daisy pulled a small roll out of the drawer in question. 'You know what these are?'

'Stamps?' AnnaLise tried, anticipating one of her mother's trick questions.

'Not just stamps,' Daisy said, 'but "Forever" stamps. The U.S. Post Office doesn't issue the first-class ones with denominations anymore. You know why that's good?'

'Because these stamps can be used forever?'

'Correct! Which is how long a single roll lasts these days.' Daisy tossed the stamps back into the drawer.

AnnaLise wanted to cry for the poor feckless stamps, as well as their unloved brethren:

74

stationery and envelopes. And don't even get her started on cursive writing.

'The post office is going bankrupt because of you,' she pointed out.

'Hey, evolve or go the way of the dinosaurs.'

'I'm not sure dinosaurs died out because they didn't evolve,' AnnaLise said, defending her kind. 'Scientists think maybe a meteor or—'

'Meteor, shmeteor,' Daisy said, punching something into AnnaLise's computer. 'You know what I mean, AnnaLise, so why do you insist on correcting me?'

'I . . .' She paused to reflect. 'Well, I'm not sure, honestly. It's just what I do.'

'It's the reporter in you, I suppose,' Daisy said, in the same tone one might blame a black sheep on the other side of the family. 'Here.' She stepped aside.

'Sutherland Spa at the Hotel Lux,' AnnaLise read on the screen. 'Nice website.'

'Joy Tamarack put it up,' Daisy said. 'That's why Sheree Pepper talked her into helping with the Sutherton visitor site.'

'I imagine Joy didn't take much convincing,' AnnaLise said, writing down the phone number. 'Both of them are businesswomen and have a stake in Sutherton's future.'

'And they embrace it, something you might try sometimes.'

'Embracing Sutherton's future?' AnnaLise asked with trepidation. No matter how long she needed to stay in Sutherton for Daisy, she clung to the belief that she'd be back at her job in Wisconsin, sooner rather than later.

75

'No, not *Sutherton*'s future, just *the* future. You know, modern times. Honestly, sometimes I think *you're* the mother.'

AnnaLise wouldn't say it, but sometimes she felt the same, and had since she was five and Timothy Griggs had died.

'OK,' said AnnaLise, taking the sticky note she'd written the phone number on. 'I'm going to call to see if Joy is at the spa. If she is, can I use your car?'

'Sure,' the real mother said, starting up the stairs. 'I'm just amazed you want to drive up there so soon after our accident.' She made the turn at the landing where Timothy Griggs' gun cabinet still stood, and disappeared.

'Wanting and having are two different things,' her daughter called after her.

As it happened, no drive up the mountain was necessary, because Joy had 'gone home,' according to the young man who answered the Spa phone.

With Joy still not answering her cellphone, AnnaLise was left with one option: tracking her friend down at home. The only problem was that for the time being, Joy was living at the Sutherton Inn – the very same place the man AnnaLise planned to warn her against was also staying.

District Attorney Ben Rosewood did not believe in accidents. If something happened – a person killed or hurt – then someone must be responsible and made to pay. It was the way the man ran his office. And his life. Only now his wife was the decedent and AnnaLise feared it would be Joy who paid.

76

Pulling on a light jacket against the fall weather, AnnaLise called up to Daisy that she was leaving and stepped outside.

The inn was only a few blocks down Main Street and on a beautiful day, with the leaves changing, it should have been a nice walk.

But instead, AnnaLise was thinking about a stormy morning in Wisconsin this past spring, when a sixteen-year-old girl's car slid on wet pavement and jumped a curb, killing her best friend who she was going to offer a lift.

To Ben, it was a crime – vehicular homicide, to be exact. To AnnaLise, it was a heartbreaking accident that had already taken one young life and now threatened to ruin another's. The issue wasn't the only thing the two disagreed on, but it was one of many reasons that had led to AnnaLise re-examining their relationship.

Climbing the steps to the front porch of the Sutherton Inn, AnnaLise said a little prayer of gratitude for Sheree Pepper, who'd saved the graceful structure from the wrecking ball and converted it into a money-making venture that made the most of the building's charm. The California bungalow was built on the east shore of Lake Sutherton in 1916 by a wealthy cotton broker so he and his family could escape the heat of Charlotte's summer. Other wealthy moguls followed, but though 'McMansions' like Bradenham and Preston Place still lined the west shore of the lake, most of the truly original palatial homes that graced the east had been long-since razed.

Not that this sad fact stopped tour-boat operators from taking unsuspecting visitors out for 'historical' cruises of the elegant lakeside estates only to be subjected to two hours of, 'See that stump? That's the spot where the legendary (fill in the blank)'s home stood . . .'

AnnaLise tapped on the stained-glass panel of the inn's door, and then tried the knob, which turned. Stepping into the lobby, she gave a shout: 'Anybody home?'

Check-out at the inn was 11 a.m. and check-in not until 4 p.m., so Sheree often took advantage of the five hours in between to run errands.

AnnaLise checked her watch: noon.

'Hello?' James Duende's dark-haired head appeared around the stair banister.

'Just me,' AnnaLise said, setting her handbag down on the hall table next to a rust-colored potted mum plant. 'Sorry to bother you, especially if you're working, but I was looking for Joy.'

'I haven't seen her *or* Sheree, for that matter, but I've been tied to my computer screen all morning.' Duende came down the steps. He was wearing jeans and a blue dress shirt, the sleeves of which he rolled down to his wrists as he descended. 'In fact, I was just going to break for lunch. Care to join me?'

'Thanks,' AnnaLise said, thinking how he looked every inch the writer, holed away in room thirteen of a country inn. 'But I had a late breakfast.'

'At Mama Philomena's, presumably,' Duende said, buttoning the cuffs of the shirt as he covered the last few steps. 'You and I should move in there.'

78

The smile he gave her would have been enticing, if room thirteen – the room directly above Sutherton Inn's dining room – wasn't the one Sheree reserved for eligible males she was interested in herself.

'What can I say?' she'd said, when AnnaLise had noticed the trend. 'Thirteen's my lucky number. Besides, with the exception of breakfast, there's no one to disturb below.' A wink. 'These antique beds do squeak a bit.'

How 'lucky' Sheree had gotten with James, AnnaLise didn't know. And didn't necessarily want to know.

'I was practically brought up at Mama's,' AnnaLise said now to James. 'And I'm sure it's convenient for you, since there are no other restaurants within walking distance, except for Sal's Tap on the beach across the way.'

'Which is where I'm headed, I think,' Duende said, continuing to where she was standing in the front hall. 'Sure I can't treat you to a greasy burger with matching fried onions and jalapeños?'

'As enticing as that sounds, I'll have to take a rain check.' Stepping back so he could get to the door, AnnaLise bumped into the bow-front foyer table. The mum tipped, spilling dirt, and as she tried to prevent further damage, AnnaLise managed to sweep her handbag to the floor.

Duende bent down to retrieve the purse and set it on the table before he said, 'Can I hold you to that?'

AnnaLise, at barely five foot, had to look up over twelve inches to meet his brown eyes, which at this close distance she could see were flecked with gold.

'To what?' she asked as the door behind Duende opened.

The eyes sparkled, but he didn't step back. 'The greasy lunch.'

'Sounds delightful,' Sheree's voice said, though AnnaLise couldn't even see the statuesque blonde beyond Duende's solid frame. 'Was that an invitation?'

'Well, *there* you are,' AnnaLise said, sweeping the spilled soil from the plant into her hand and stuffing it into her jeans pocket, before popping out from behind Duende. 'I was looking for you.'

'Oh, I bet you were.' There was a predatory look on Sheree's face as she glanced between them. AnnaLise would have taken it personally, if it hadn't been Sheree's modus operandi whenever a prospective male target was in the room.

An M.O. since AnnaLise and she were in the ninth grade and Chuck Greystone was the male in the triangle. Chuck had chosen AnnaLise back then, probably because super-sexed Sheree had scared the shit out of him.

'If you two want to go to lunch, it's fine.' AnnaLise was signaling surrender before the battle – even if only in Sheree's mind – could begin. 'I was actually looking for Joy.'

'She's probably up at the spa,' Sheree said. 'I know she left before I did.'

'I didn't hear her come back,' Duende said. 'Though I like to put instrumental music on when I write, so I may have missed her.'

'I'll go up and knock on her door. If she's not there, I can always leave her a note to call me,' AnnaLise said.

'Good plan,' Sheree said, then turned to Duende. 'And we're going to lunch?'

'Sure, but I've got a hankering for Sal's,' Duende said. 'Take it or leave it.'

'I'll take it.' Sheree linked her arm with his to usher him out the door.

'You sure you won't come, AnnaLise?' Duende asked, turning at the threshold.

'I am, but thank you.'

As the door closed behind them, AnnaLise mounted the steps toward the business at hand: finding Joy.

Passing by twelve, eleven and ten, AnnaLise tapped on the door of room nine. No answer, but by this time she'd expected that. Digging out a pad from her purse she scribbled: *Joy, call me – it's important. AnnaLise* and her number. Then she slid the paper under the door and started back down the hall.

As AnnaLise reached the top of the stairs, she heard the front door open and voices in the foyer. Sheree hadn't locked the door, but given that guests who were staying more than one night would need to come and go that wasn't unusual. The only other guests that AnnaLise knew of besides James Duende and Joy Tamarack, though, were the Rosewoods.

She froze, not sure why.

'I'd just appreciate it if you'd stay here with me.' Ben's voice, though not the way AnnaLise was used to hearing it. He sounded vulnerable.

'Instead of going back to the dorm or going out with this Josh.'

'Joshua,' Suzanne corrected, sounding like a snotty eight-year-old. 'And why should I stay? You'll just be on the phone. Or your computer.'

'You're a fine one to . . .' her father started, then seemed to catch himself. 'You're right. I'll have to make a lot of calls, notifying . . .' He let that trail off, too.

'I'm sorry, Dad.' The sound of a hug, if a hug can make a sound. 'How about I come back in time for dinner?'

'That would be good, Suze. I should be done with my calls by then and we can talk.'

Even without seeing him, AnnaLise could imagine Ben's expression. Warm. Endearing, even. Worked wonders with juries. Hell, it had worked wonders on her, too.

'Do you need a ride?' he continued.

'Joshua's picking me—' She stopped. Then, 'I . . . I almost started to make up a story about Joshua picking me up by the lake in his father's car, because I knew Mom would hate my being seen in his truck.'

'You forgot your mother is dead,' her father said. 'That's not unusual, Suze. And it's certainly not anything to be ashamed of. It's going to take . . .'

An embarrassed laugh. 'Time, I know. Listen,' a sniff, 'I better go or Joshua will be worried.'

The sound of the inn's front door opening and then closing.

Decision time, AnnaLise thought, stepping down onto the first step and hesitating. Should she take the opportunity of Suzanne's absence to talk to Ben and offer her condolences? Still intimate or not, the two had known each other for five years now and AnnaLise wished him only well. If she could undo the whole thing . . .

Too late, she heard the door creak open again and a voice say, 'Need my jacket,' followed by the pounding of teenaged feet on the steps.

Eleven

AnnaLise retreated a step, but Suzanne Rosewood just brushed by, continuing on to a room beyond Joy's and returning seconds later with the forgotten jacket. Suzanne pounded back down the stairs, ignoring AnnaLise and apparently Ben as well, as she exited the inn, slamming the door behind her.

Slowly, AnnaLise descended the steps one-by-one, only to see the district attorney standing in the arch from the foyer, her open handbag in his hand. 'Ahh, I thought this was yours, AnnaLise. It's really not a good idea to leave valuables in the front hall, where anybody outside could see them through a window.'

AnnaLise took her handbag from Ben, not bothering to remind him that this was Sutherton, North Carolina, not Urban County, Wisconsin, and that she had a better idea of what was 'a good idea' around here than he did. 'I'm sorry about Tanja, Ben. Do you want to sit and talk?'

The D.A. nodded and they moved into the parlor, where the bright yellow walls and white-washed woodwork were in direct contrast to the mood in the air. AnnaLise took a cherry-red over-stuffed chair while Ben chose the floral couch perpendicular to it.

The sheer force of the district attorney's personality usually made him look taller and broader

84

than his five-eleven and 175 pounds. Now, though, he settled onto the couch elbows on knees, forehead in hands, his trademark longish, sandy-brown hair making him look more like a little boy who'd lost the family puppy.

This was the Benjamin Rosewood that AnnaLise had fallen in love with. The private one, and it was all she could do to stay in her chair and not go to him.

But stay she did. 'Suze . . . I'm sorry that she saw me. I'm afraid she thinks I was meeting you here.'

Ben ratcheted up his head; his blue eyes seemed confused. 'You mean an assignation? Why would she believe that?'

AnnaLise wanted to slap herself. The man had lost his wife and obviously was having trouble with his daughter and yet, to AnnaLise, this – like everything else in life – was all about her. 'I just . . . I just assumed Suze knew about us.'

'I don't believe so. Why would you think that?'

AnnaLise was surprised he could be so obtuse. 'When I saw Suzanne this morning and told her how sorry I was about her mother, she said something like "I bet you are." Not to mention just now, when she ignored me and slammed the door on the way out.'

'She's a teenager.' Ben shrugged. 'Sometimes you just have to forgive them for their youth.'

This from the same man who charged some-body else's teenager with vehicular manslaughter.

'So you didn't tell Tanja about the affair?'

'No.' Ben stood. 'Why? Did she find out?'

Before AnnaLise could answer – not that she

had an answer – he started to pace. 'Are you telling me that my wife died thinking I'd been unfaithful to her?'

AnnaLise glanced toward the parlor door. 'Ben, you *were* unfaithful to her. We,' she pointed back and forth between the two of them, 'cheated on Tanja.'

'But you and I were over,' Ben said. 'There was no reason for her to know now.'

'I didn't tell her,' AnnaLise protested. 'I thought maybe you did, when she made that pointed remark in the restaurant yesterday morning about not liking to share. I assumed Tanja meant you.'

'Ohh.' Ben sat back down on the couch. 'She did, actually. But it was more of a warning-off than an accusation.'

'Like . . .' AnnaLise was looking for a more diplomatic way of putting it, but settled on, '. . . marking her territory?'

'Exactly.' Ben projected that pleased-teacher look. 'You should be flattered – Tanja only does it to women she views as real competition.'

'Flattered,' didn't quite describe it, but AnnaLise *was* relieved. She also noticed the use of present tense. 'I'm really sorry about the crash. I think that' – she looked down at her hands, which she seemed to be wringing – 'that, despite everything you've said, you loved Tanja.'

'I did. Still do. And always will.' The rule of threes.

AnnaLise cleared her throat. 'I was surprised to see you up here yesterday.'

A rueful grin from Ben. 'Well, then I got what I planned, I guess.'

'I don't understand.'

'What I said about putting the university on Suze's list was true. Because of the glowing way you'd spoken about the area. Though Katie, of course, wasn't the conduit of those sentiments.'

Conduit. Another reason the journalist had fallen for the lawyer: his large – and apropos – active vocabulary.

'Really?' AnnaLise leaned forward. 'I hadn't been home for five years. And, besides, I'd run, not walked, from Sutherton in the first place. What could I have said that was so "glowing"?'

'It wasn't your words, per se.' Ben extended his hand toward her. 'It was that *you* glowed. Anytime you talked about this area.'

They both looked at the hand stretched out between them. Then, simultaneously, they stepped away from the abyss – she retreating into her chair, and he retracting his hand.

AnnaLise said, 'You didn't mention Suzanne had applied or been accepted.'

Another grin, this one more sheepish than rueful. 'I thought I'd surprise you.'

'Well, that certainly is accurate.'

'I know. And I'm sorry about it, but you handled the situation deftly.'

Deftly. 'You trained me well.'

Ben laughed. 'This is sounding like the airport scene from *Casablanca*.' This time he did reach over, chucking her chin.

'You know, the "here's looking" line wasn't scripted,' AnnaLise said. 'Bogart—'

'Yes, Movie-maven,' said Ben, rolling his eyes.

'Bogart ad-libbed it based on something he'd said to Bergman while he was teaching her poker between takes. You told me.'

AnnaLise just smiled. Feature films remained the one thing she knew more about than he did.

Ben sighed. 'I miss you, AnnaLise. Miss just talking to you. I know we're over, and that's for the best, especially given . . .' The enormity of what had happened seemed to wash over him and he closed his eyes. When they reopened, tears brimmed in them. 'I . . .' Ben cleared his throat. 'I have to pay a lot of attention to Suzanne now, try to repair our relationship. I've been an absentee father, and not even a very good one of those.'

'I know,' AnnaLise said, and she did. Not only how little Ben had been there for his daughter, but how it felt not to have a dad. 'If there's anything I can do – or my mother, or Mama or any of our friends, assuming Suzanne plans to stay in school at U-Mo.'

'She wants to, given the young . . . beau.'

Beau. Lovely. 'Joshua Eames. From what I've seen, he's grown into a pretty good guy. Got into some trouble when he was younger, but his mom had abandoned him, and the father—'

'Birds of a feather,' Ben said musingly. 'No wonder he and Suze are drawn to each other. His mother left him and I wasn't around for her. And now with Tanja gone, they'll have even more in common.'

It was true, though AnnaLise hadn't thought along those lines.

Yet another aspect at which Benjamin Rosewood

excelled: empathy, knowing instinctively how other people felt.

But whether that 'empathy' translated into 'sympathy,' she wasn't as sure.

Twelve

The parameters of the district attorney's tolerance were about to be tested.

Ben had followed AnnaLise to the foyer and as she prepared to leave, the front door of the inn opened.

'Joy!' AnnaLise said. 'I've been looking for you.'

Joy Tamarack was wiry, with spiky, nearly white blonde hair. A tiny bundle of restless energy and contradictions, she weighed maybe a hundred pounds – all of it muscle – and, despite being a physical trainer, smoked like the proverbial chimney.

Less than a year after marrying Dickens Hart, she'd found her groom – direct quote – 'helping himself to a little tail.' In other words, one of the White Tail Club's 'fawns.' Joy may have been young herself, but she was also a shrewd business woman even then. She'd promptly divorced Hart, coming away with a very nice settlement. So nice, in fact, that the speculation was that Hart's 'little tail' had been very little.

As in under-aged.

Yet another reason AnnaLise was unwilling to recognize her own parentage on the paternal side.

As for Joy, while she'd maintained business interests in Sutherton thanks to her divorce settlement, she'd moved away to manage an Indiana fitness club. Each year, though, the fitness trainer would return for a girls' weekend, where she and a dozen of her sorority sisters – another direct quote – engaged in 'drinking, smoking and aural, that's a-u-r-a-l, sex. Meaning we listen to each other lie about it.'

At the most recent 'Frat Pack,' as the group called the reunion, Joy had announced she planned to return to Sutherton full-time.

AnnaLise wondered whether her friend might want to reconsider that, should District Attorney Rosewood stay true to his stripes.

The least AnnaLise could do was to get the two off on the right foot and make it very clear to Ben that Joy was a friend of hers. And clear to Joy that Ben should be taken seriously.

'Joy Tamarack,' AnnaLise said, 'this is Ben Rosewood, the district attorney of Urban County, where I live now. Ben, Joy is a very good, long-time friend of mine.'

Ben shook Joy's hand. 'You're the owner of the spa that served my wife alcohol before sending her careering down the mountainside.'

So much for hoping things would go well.

Though AnnaLise couldn't help mentally applauding his use of the word 'career,' as in the verb meaning rushing onward while lurching or swaying, as opposed to the more common 'careening,' which meant just swaying or swerving while moving.

But, perhaps, a distinction without a difference, especially under the circumstances.

Mouth open, Joy looked at AnnaLise and then back to her accuser, and promptly broke into tears.

91

'What in the world is *wrong* with you?' AnnaLise said to Ben as Joy dashed away and up the stairs.

'What's wrong with *me*?' he asked. 'Maybe you should ask your "very good, long-time friend" that.'

'Your wife is dead not even a day and you're already considering litigation?' AnnaLise said. 'I ask, again, what is *wrong* with you?'

'Absolutely nothing,' Ben said, running a hand through his hair. 'My wife is dead and someone has to pay.'

'*She* paid,' AnnaLise said, almost unconsciously falling into debate mode with him. 'I mean, Tanja did. She had some wine, took our mountain roads too fast and died as a result, sadly. Case closed.'

Early in their relationship the debating had been a game they played – almost their version of pillow talk. Back then, the district attorney seemed gratified and even proud that the feisty little reporter had the guts to stand up to him. He had even said AnnaLise would have made a good lawyer. Now, apparently, he was not so entranced.

'A case is not "closed,"' Ben said through his teeth, 'until I say it is.'

Wonderful. AnnaLise had wanted to help, but probably had only managed to make things worse for Joy.

Try another tack – reason disguised as empathy.

'I'm sorry,' AnnaLise said, holding up both hands, palms out in apology. 'You're under enough strain without my adding to it. I only thought that given . . .' She let her sentence drift off.

'Given?' Ben said, also standing down.

AnnaLise looked around and lowered her voice. 'Given what you told me about Tanja's drinking . . .'

'What about it?' The walls were back up.

'Well, I'm just not sure that Joy's spa could be held responsible for what Tanja drank before she got there.'

'Who says she had anything earlier that morning?' Ben demanded.

AnnaLise shrugged. 'I smelled it on her breath in Mama's restaurant, when Tanja made the remark about not being a good sharer. Or I should say I smelled a menthol cough drop. As I don't have to tell you, cough drops – and mouthwash and *peanut butter*, of all things – are all ploys alcoholics use to disguise the booze on their breath.'

Now AnnaLise forced a smile. 'The cough drops have the added plus of keeping the germ-aphobics a fair distance away.'

'Tanja had a cold.'

'She didn't cough or sniffle the entire time we spoke.'

'Then apparently the cough drop did its job.'

'Deny it all you want,' AnnaLise said, tiring of the game. 'But you told me Tanja was an alco-holic and I'll testify to it if I have to.'

'Hearsay. And besides, the fact she was an alcoholic doesn't prove that she was, indeed, drinking that morning.'

If AnnaLise was a television lawyer, she'd have followed up with 'Ahah! So you admit your wife

93

was an alcoholic.' But this wasn't court and she wasn't a lawyer, though apparently she played one in the foyer.

So instead, she said: 'But presumably the serum blood alcohol test will indicate approximately how much Tanja had to drink, and if it's more than she could have gotten at the spa . . .' AnnaLise performed the shrug of the foregone conclusion.

Ben, however, wasn't done yet. 'Fine. Let's say my wife was an alcoholic and she'd been drinking – was even drunk – when she arrived for her appointment.'

When Ben made his point in court, he had a perfectly crafted way of showing it. No shit-eating grin, of course: he was too good. No, the D.A.'s lift of his eyebrows was a non-verbal 'so there,' serving to cue the jury that the next few questions would be significant and that they should take note.

Now his brows rose. 'All that means, AnnaLise, is that Sutherton Spa as an entity and Joy Tamarack as a person are even more liable. they served alcohol to someone they knew – or should *have* known – was already intoxicated and, despite that, let her leave to drive down an unfamiliar mountain.'

'But,' AnnaLise looked puzzled, 'maybe they didn't know.'

Ben's turn to shrug. 'The standard is whether a reasonable person should have known, and you yourself just testif— Sorry, you just *said* that you did.'

'True.' AnnaLise seemed to give it some

94

thought, then gave Ben a little smile. 'But you *have* told me that I'm smarter than most people.'

He met her smile and raised one himself, seeming to relax after scoring the win. 'I told you that you are one of the smartest women I've ever met. And I meant it.'

'You know, I never quite believed you about that, but now,' she moved toward the inn's front door, 'I think you may be right.'

He opened it for her, smiling down. 'So, what changed your mind?'

'I realized that if Tanja had been drinking and *I* noticed, certainly her husband would have.' AnnaLise ducked under Ben's braced arm and stepped out.

When she turned back, Ben's eyes had narrowed. 'Your point?'

'My point,' she said, 'is that if you then let Tanja get behind the wheel, *you* would be legally responsible. Especially,' a lift of her own eyebrows, 'if she was driving a car you gave her as a gift, but – knowing you – kept in your name. In fact, Ben, you're very lucky your wife didn't kill anyone else.'

Not being the man, or the lawyer, Benjamin Rosewood was, AnnaLise allowed herself a shit-eating grin as she started back down to the sidewalk.

Thirteen

'Do you honestly think that little debate will keep the man from suing me?' Joy Tamarack asked.

AnnaLise got up from her mother's kitchen table to pour them each another margarita from the blender pitcher. Given the subject of the last hour or two, perhaps not the best idea, but at least no one would be driving anywhere.

'More so than your crying act. Damn!' The last of the frozen margaritas had plotched out, overflowing Joy's glass and hitting the table. AnnaLise eyed her empty glass as well as the now equally empty pitcher and went to get a spoon out of the drawer. 'What good did you think tears were going to do? The man is a hardbitten lawyer.'

'And an asshole to boot, from what you've told me. Cheating on his wife.'

'Like I said, I have to take half the blame in that category.' AnnaLise had settled down at the table and was carefully ladling half of the slush from Joy's glass into hers.

AnnaLise drew the line at slurping any drink off the table, but just barely. Today – including just having told Joy about the affair with Ben – had taken its toll and the margaritas were going down mighty easy.

Joy pulled her glass away. 'Believe me, I'm not absolving you. You'll recall a certain incident with a "fawn" in my marital bed.'

AnnaLise was reminded of *The Godfather*. 'Better than a horse's head.'

'Yeah, my luck,' Joy said dryly. 'I had the horse's ass, instead.'

'Wait a second,' AnnaLise said, admittedly a little tipsy, 'that's my father you're talking about.'

'Yeah, well, "stupid is who stupid does," to paraphrase another of your favorite movies. Your mother and me, sleeping with the same guy. Doesn't that strike you as a little creepy?'

'It strikes me as a *lot* creepy, though happily it wasn't simultaneously. Hey,' AnnaLise looked up from her drink, sensing a margarita mustache on her upper lip, 'does that make you my stepmother?'

'*Si, Señor*,' Joy said, leaning across the table to wipe the tequila-mix residue off her friend's face. 'And my step-motherly advice to you is to give yourself a break. Fact is, you're young and you made a mistake with Rosewood.'

'I honestly believed that as long as we were careful, as long as no one found out, it would be OK,' AnnaLise said, now tending toward miserable again. 'Nobody would get hurt.'

'But you ended it. And didn't you just tell me that Rosewood's wife never *did* know?'

'The basic premise was flawed, Joy. The mistake – the thing I should have been worried about – was the affair itself, not getting caught.'

'You were in love.'

'I thought.'

'You're not the first one to have made that mistake.' Joy leaned forward. 'Don't get me wrong. Like I said before, I'm not saying it's no blood, no foul. But . . . well, have you stopped to think that maybe this has something to do with your father?'

'So, what – I inherited the "philander" gene?' AnnaLise put her hand on her heart dramatically. 'My God, you're right – I was doomed from the start.'

'Not your biological father, dunce. Your functional father: Timothy Griggs.'

'My "functional father" died when I was five. I barely knew him.'

'But that's what I mean. Geez, AnnaLise, can you possibly be this dense? You're a journalist – you probably even read occasionally. Ink on actual paper and everything.'

AnnaLise let the insult to the printed word pass. 'All right, so you're trying to say I have a father fixation?'

'You've told me that after your dad died, your two "moms" – Daisy and Phyllis – teamed up to take care of you, while they were also running the market and the restaurant.'

'Joy, if you're saying I suffered from the arrangement, you're wrong. I never questioned that I was loved.'

'Loved, yes, but—'

AnnaLise interrupted. 'And, before you go any further, yes, I was praised. *And* got positive reinforcement *and* was made to feel good about myself. Almost to the point of nausea, in fact. When I got an "A" on a test or report, Mama would post the paper right next to the menu board.'

'I'm sure they did everything they could, but,'

Joy started to reach across the table toward her, but was stopped by the sticky drink spill, 'honey, they couldn't be your father.'

'I don't believe it.' AnnaLise kept hold of her margarita glass. 'You, of all people, think women can't do everything men can?'

Joy's eyes narrowed. 'I do not. I just think they – we – do it . . . differently.'

'Right.' While AnnaLise's tone was skeptical, she feared there was more than a kernel of truth to what Joy was saying. Maybe not so much in that AnnaLise had suffered from a lack of a father figure growing up, but more . . . well, mothers, no matter the number, *had* to love you, right? At least in her experience, Daisy and Mama had doted on everything the little AnnaLise had done or said.

But that wasn't *earning* it. Having someone you admired, hell, the whole county admired, say you were smart, or funny or—

'. . . so intoxicated by the feeling,' Joy was saying, 'that nothing else seems to matter.'

This time, AnnaLise didn't interrupt. The feeling she'd had at the height of the affair – thinking about Ben, being with Ben – had been very much like being high without realizing you were drunk. Right down to waking up the next morning ashamed of yourself.

'. . . and no matter how stirred up we get, eventually we're left with exactly what we started with.' Joy nodded significantly at the overflow of their frozen margarita, melted and running on the table between them. 'Three people. Like the ingredients of a margarita. And whatever you do, your love and his spouse will always be its main ones – tequila and lime juice.'

Against her will, AnnaLise was impressed. 'Go on.'

'You, my friend – all you ever can be is the triple sec. The splash of flavor. My metaphor is, forgive me, brilliant, right down to the triple in triple sec. The third wheel.'

Joy's expression suddenly changed, and she pointed at the rivulet of green liquid just starting to trickle off the edge of the table and onto the thighs of AnnaLise's jeans. 'Leaving you home alone, with nothing to show for it but a sticky crotch.'

Joy Tamarack managed to stand up in one, graceful motion. 'Now *that's* a metaphor.'

Fourteen

Joy Tamarack was both crude and . . .

No, 'crude' pretty much captured it.

Nonetheless, before her friend left, AnnaLise had broached the subject of including a blog on the new Sutherton visitor website. Joy had liked the idea and suggested they get together, sans margaritas, at the spa at nine a.m. the following day.

The more the journalist thought about it, the more she thought the blog was a good idea. The doctors – first Tucker's father, Dr Jackson Stanton, and now her mother's neurologist – had suggested writing and word games like crossword puzzles and the like to keep Daisy's mind engaged, especially now that she was no longer running the store.

Now, on Wednesday morning, one foot in the leg of her jeans – a clean pair, thank you very much – as AnnaLise dressed toward driving up the mountain to the spa, something occurred to her: her mother's cognitive 'shifts' had started after she had closed the shop and rented the space to Tucker. Though Daisy continued to help Mama – writing up the menu boards as she had for as long as AnnaLise could remember, and hostessing, and handling the cash register – Daisy no longer had the day-to-day responsibility of running a business on her shoulders. Or on her mind.

Good, in some ways, but could it be part of

the reason she'd slowed down so noticeably?

AnnaLise wasn't sure, but an added benefit of the blog was that, perhaps once up and running, Daisy should be able to take over responsibility for its coordination. People like Mama and Ida Mae would have plenty of stories to tell and their contributions would keep the job from becoming too burdensome in the search-for-Sutherton-anecdotes sense. Not only would it be good for all of them, but it was a great way of preserving the area's history and lore.

Who knows, maybe there was even a book in it. AnnaLise zipped up her jeans, wishing she hadn't had that extra half-margarita yesterday. The things had a ton of calories in them, as fastening her top button confirmed.

Grabbing her cellphone and handbag, AnnaLise descended the stairs from her room and left via the front door, locking it behind her. Daisy had already been up and gone when AnnaLise awakened late – and groggy – at quarter past eight. Yet another reason to regret the margaritas. She wasn't going to make her 9 a.m. meeting with Joy.

Happily, Daisy hadn't gone farther than Mama's, so AnnaLise had the use of her mother's car, still parked conveniently down the street while the garage work was being done. She started the Chrysler and pulled away from the curb.

As AnnaLise passed the garage, she saw Joshua Eames patching the concrete wall between its doors. Apparently, Mr Eames had won the one-door-or-two issue, resulting in the status quo of a pair.

'Morning, Josh,' AnnaLise said, coming to a

stop and turning off the engine after having driven all of twenty feet. At this rate, she wouldn't make the spa before first snowfall.

'Morning,' Josh echoed, wiping his palms on a rag before shaking hands with her through the driver's-side open window. His blue eyes were sad. 'I'd like to apologize for my friend's behavior yesterday at Mama's. Suze was upset.'

'She has reason to be,' AnnaLise said.

'Yes, ma'am, but not at you, and I told her that. Suze said to tell you she was sorry when I saw you.'

Suzanne hadn't looked 'apologetic' when she and AnnaLise had practically run into each other at the top of the stairs at the inn, but given the affair AnnaLise'd had with the girl's father, she had no right to criticize Suzanne's behavior. Or, for that matter, her protective clan instincts.

'That's a very nice gesture, Josh, but truly neither Suzanne nor you has anything to apologize for. How is she holding up?'

He gave a little head-tilt. 'Hard to tell, I have to say. I don't know a lot of people from the Midwest, so maybe they handle this manner of thing differently. She just seems . . . mad? Says her mother killed herself.'

AnnaLise's heart stopped. 'Killed herself? Like in . . . suicide?'

'That's what I thought at first, when Suze said it, but no. Turns out her mama,' Josh looked around to see if anyone was passing by and therefore could overhear, 'she liked to drink.'

'Oh.' AnnaLise didn't have anything else appropriate to contribute.

103

'According to Suze, her mother was always telling her not to drink alcohol and not to drive too fast, but she didn't take her own advice.'

'I guess a lot of us don't practice what we preach.'

'That's just what I told Suze.' Josh's blue eyes turned sadder. 'I also said she was lucky to have had her mama for as long as she did, but that just made Suze, like, more . . . bitter?'

Poor Josh. AnnaLise feared he'd be no match for Suzanne's biting intellect and, if half of what Ben said about his daughter was true, legendary temper tantrums.

AnnaLise touched his arm. 'Suze is very lucky to have you.'

'Thank you, ma'am, but I'm not sure she's feeling that way right about now.'

'Some people find it less painful to be angry rather than sad. She'll get past it.' AnnaLise checked her watch. Five more minutes late. 'Well, I'd best go. I'm due at Hotel Lux in ten minutes.'

'Don't think you're going to make it, less'n you fly.'

'I crawl, more like it. Which reminds me,' AnnaLise couldn't believe she'd forgotten, 'I'd like to pay for any damage to your dad's truck from yesterday afternoon. That way you won't have to report it to your insurance company, especially since my mother already told the police officers at the scene that we hit the rock wall, not another vehicle.'

'That's good, because that's exactly what you did. Don't you remember?'

'No, actually, I don't.' Great, now the town would be talking about AnnaLise's memory quirks as well as Daisy's. 'I think I must have closed my eyes.'

A grin twisted the corners of Josh's mouth, despite what seemed his best effort to control it. 'That's not a real good thing to do when one's behind the wheel.'

'I may have been behind the wheel, but I wasn't driving,' AnnaLise said. 'My car stalled in the middle of the road.'

'Well, that might be so, but when I came up on you, that little car of yours jumped right across the road, bounced into the rock wall and back again to the edge.'

'Huh,' AnnaLise said, thinking. 'Now that you mention it, I remember putting the car into park and finally getting it started. I must have hit the accelerator in panic.'

'Sure looked that way to me, ma'am.'

AnnaLise kicked herself for thinking at the time that Josh had fled the scene, when he'd simply been a Good Samaritan, stopping to help and call 911.

'Well, I'm very glad I didn't damage your father's truck. How do you like working for him?' She was already going to be late, so might as well add another couple of minutes assuaging her guilty conscience.

'My dad can be difficult, I won't lie, but I do like the work.'

'From what I've heard, you're also very good at it.'

She was rewarded with a pleased smile and

AnnaLise had a hunch she'd have seen a blush if Josh wasn't so tanned from his outdoor job. 'I thank you, though Suze and me've been talking about my maybe going back to school.'

'College?' AnnaLise asked, wondering if this was Josh's idea or Suzanne's. Either way, the journalist thought it would be a good thing. Fred Eames might love his son, but he couldn't be doing much for the young man's self-esteem.

Josh tilted his head. 'Well, I really do like the work and it pays the bills, but it sure would be nice to have a little something left for my back pocket.'

AnnaLise loved the syntax and rhythm of High Country English. 'And you think that won't happen if you stay in your dad's business?'

'*Hasn't* happened, even for him. Besides, eventually, the mountains will be built out, at least as far as the county will let them be. Then the only work will be renovations like this one and, no offense, that's not where the big money is.'

'I hear you,' AnnaLise said, impressed by the amount of thought Josh had given the subject. 'And believe me, I'd be the first one to advise you to get your degree. Have you considered where?'

'I can't afford U-Mo, where Suze is, but I was thinking maybe Lees-McRae right down the road in Banner Elk. That way it wouldn't be too much of a financial burden and Suze and I would still be close by each other. Maybe even get an apartment together.'

Wow, AnnaLise thought as she gave Josh a wave before turning the key again in the

106

ignition. A one-eighty turnaround for the troubled kid who'd barely made it through high school. Maybe Joshua Eames and Suzanne Rosewood would turn out to be good for each other after all.

Fifteen

Not wanting to follow Daisy's example of Monday afternoon, AnnaLise called the spa to warn Joy she was running late, only to find that her friend had a training client for the next hour anyway.

Given the extra time, AnnaLise decided to take the state highway to the upper entrance of the mountain. The highway route would take her past the garage where her poor Spyder had been towed, so she could claim any property from the little car before it went to the parking lot in the sky.

AnnaLise turned off at a sign trumpeting *Sutherton Auto Sales, Service and Scrap.* Talk about your cradle-to-grave operation, she thought, following the bend of the gravel drive past the main sales building to the service garage.

She parked the Chrysler in the shadow of the building. Earl Lawling was inside one of the bays busy with a tire, but it wasn't him AnnaLise had come to see.

The scrap yard was wisely hidden behind a slight rise and it was on that hill – the limbo between repair and salvage – that she found her Spyder. Poor thing looked like it had been scalped and left for dead, canvas pate on the ground next to it.

As AnnaLise observed a moment of silence,

Lawling emerged from the repair bay. 'Come to say your goodbyes?'

'And pick up anything I might have left inside,' she looked at the fully-detached roof, 'if it's still there.'

'If I were you, miss, I'd just be counting my blessings I got out, unlike the poor lady in that one.'

He pointed and AnnaLise turned to see the Rosewood's Porsche, three tires blown and one wheel completely missing.

'By the by,' Lawling continued. 'I have a nice selection of new and used cars if you're in the market.'

If she was in the market? AnnaLise couldn't drive her mother's car forever and, besides, she'd certainly need something to drive back to Wisconsin the end of the month. Still, it seemed too early to replace the Mitsubishi when the car hadn't even been given a proper burial.

'I haven't decided whether I'll buy a car here or wait until I get back to Wisconsin.'

'I think you'll find the prices here more to your liking and I'll make you the same deal I offered the Porsche's owner.'

Ben was already looking to replace his wife's car? 'What deal is that?'

'Once we come up with a fair price, I'll subtract the salvage value of your old vehicle.'

AnnaLise glanced over at the remains of the Mitsubishi.

'I admit it's not as much of an incentive for you,' Lawling continued hastily, 'as it would be for Mr Rosewood. Your whole car wasn't worth what I'm likely to get for the Porsche's parts.'

'Well, that's not surprising, is it? I mean, considering my car is totaled and therefore worthless.'

'No, ma'am. I don't mean your Mitsubishi as it stands now. I'm talking about as it stood at the dealer's lot in Wisconsin, brand-spanking new.'

Well, that seemed a little cruel.

'Though it's true that comparison will have to wait a bit,' Lawling continued, 'seeing as the police are sending a wrecker over to the Porsche.'

'They are?' AnnaLise asked, but she was thinking, *Now what's Ben up to?*

'Well, I don't like to brag, but it appears I discovered something they missed. I probably shouldn't say more than that.'

Eagle-eyed Earl had spotted something. The question was, what? AnnaLise glanced toward the repair bay. The wheel the man had been working on when she'd arrived was balanced on a couple of sawhorses. 'Do you think one of the tires was to blame?'

She was remembering a case they'd studied in one of her marketing classes: millions of tires recalled and millions more in dollars awarded in damages for 'deaths and catastrophic injuries' caused by faulty tires.

Ben would have a field day with this one, if it were true. But better he take on a conglomerate with teams of lawyers on retainer rather than Joy.

But the loquacious Earl seemed to have buttoned his lip. 'I surely would hesitate to speculate on the matter, ma'am.'

'Wise of you, I must say. Especially if a lawsuit

should arise from all this,' AnnaLise said, unintentionally falling into his pattern of speech. By the time she got back to Wisconsin, she'd have a full-fledged High Country accent and would be walking out of restaurants without paying, like she was used to doing at Mama's.

'We do live in a highly litigious society,' Lawling was saying. 'Well, here now. Just like I said.'

He was looking toward a cloud of dust being kicked up by two vehicles on the gravel driveway. The first was a Sutherton squad car and behind it, a police wrecker. When the first got close enough, AnnaLise saw Chuck in the passenger seat.

The chief of police out for a product-liability case? Seemed like overkill, though Ben was certainly willing and able to throw his weight around, even as an out-of-state D.A.

Lawling pulled a grubby white envelope out of his pocket and went to meet them.

Curious, but not wanting to be shooed away at the outset, AnnaLise went about her business. She retrieved the contents of the sprung glove compartment in her Spyder, along with a parking pass from the dashboard, all the while keeping an eye on Chuck and Earl who were now in the repair bay. Leaving the cassette tapes in the hope that her next vehicle would have a CD player, she moved on to the trunk, where she found a stuffed Bucky Badger wearing a University of Wisconsin sweatshirt.

'Say goodbye to our Spyder,' AnnaLise said, turning the stuffed mascot to face the car.

Bucky didn't answer. Badgers aren't much for sentiment.

Dropping everything in the trunk of her mom's car and closing it, AnnaLise hurried over to where Chuck now stood alone by the sawhorses. 'So, what's going on?'

'Who's asking?'

AnnaLise looked around. 'Who's asking? Me, of course.'

'But are you asking for your friend?'

Friend. Careful now, girl. 'You mean Joy?'

'I mean Ben Rosewood.'

'No, I'm not asking for Ben, though I'd hardly call him a friend.' Which was true, so far as it went. The district attorney had been much more than that. 'I'm on Joy's side, assuming that's what this is all about. Though if a tire company is involved, I don't have a side.'

Chuck shook his head. 'Whatever are you talking about?'

'Joy,' she reminded him. 'You said Ben Rosewood was suggesting the accident was her fault?'

'Oh, right.' Chuck seemed to honestly have forgotten. 'Looks like the glass of wine Mrs Rosewood had up at the spa is no longer a major issue.'

'Because she was already drunk?'

'Apparently.' If Earl Lawling's lips were buttoned, Chuck's were zipped up tight.

'But what about the tires?'

'The tire?'

'Tire, singular?' This was like Twenty Questions. Animal, vegetable or mineral.

112

Chuck looked skyward. 'I don't know why I play these games with you.'

'Me, neither. You might as well just tell me. You know Earl's not going to be able to keep his mouth shut for long.'

Since AnnaLise had known Lawling all of two days, it was a guess, but apparently a good one. 'Point taken.'

'So, give.'

'While Tanja Rosewood's blood-alcohol level was likely a contributing factor, it may not have been the initial cause of the accident.'

'But something in the tire was? What's the manufacturer?'

'Hard to tell. Remington, Hornady, maybe? Likely not UltraMax.'

'Hornady? UltraMax?' Sounded more like condoms than tires. There was probably a 'Where the rubber meets the road' joke in there somewhere, but AnnaLise had no intention of trotting it out just now. 'I'm sorry, Chuck, but I don't understand. Are those tire manufacturers?'

'Tire? No.'

'Barely a minute ago you said one of them was at fault. I was asking what type of tire.'

'That's a little like blaming the victim, Lise.' He pointed toward the sawhorses. 'Tires don't kill people, at least in this case. But bullets do.'

Sixteen

Gentle scents of jasmine and lavender wafted through the doorway of the Sutherton Spa, carried on the piano strains of Katie Kuhn, George Winston, and David Lanz.

All very peaceful and Zen-like.

In direct contrast to the woman who ran the place.

'Wait. Someone shot out her tire?' Joy Tamarack demanded.

She and AnnaLise were sitting in Joy's office. AnnaLise had arrived in the parking lot of Hotel Lux a little before ten.

The outside of the big hotel looked much as it had the last time she'd seen it: tall, white and ugly. In AnnaLise's opinion, a building built on a mountaintop should reflect its surroundings. This one just . . . reflected. No matter what time of day or where you were, the thing glowed like an opalescent sore thumb. Made it real easy to find.

Walking through the door and past the concierge desk to the lobby, AnnaLise had to admit the inside of the Lux was a lot more appealing than the outside, though just as modern. Three restaurants, one a coffee shop and the others open for lunch and dinner with night-time entertainment. A beauty salon and barber shop. Two upscale clothing stores – one for men, the other for women – and a ski shop that carried everything you might need for more money than you ever imagined. And, of course, Joy's spa and fitness facility.

Hotel Lux was, in a word, lux. Once there, the only time you'd have to go outside would be to ski.

Yet another High Country activity, like shooting, that AnnaLise had never taken up, though this one she regretted. Living in Wisconsin or the mountains of North Carolina, it was practically a sin not to take advantage of the winter sports that drew others there.

The journalist resolved to put it on her bucket list. Though at age twenty-eight, the bucket was more pink plastic sand-pail.

But it was autumn, not winter, that AnnaLise loved most in the High Country. The bright red sugar maples punctuating the greens – soon to be yellows and oranges – of the oaks, chestnuts and—

'And again I ask,' Joy snarled, pulling AnnaLise's attention away from the vista outside the office window, 'someone shot out Tanja Rosewood's tire?'

Joy had been finishing up a fitness training session with a sixty-something female 'half-back' – someone who retired to Florida to escape northern winters only to come halfway back when the heat got oppressive in June – when AnnaLise arrived.

Since the older woman's biceps put hers to shame, AnnaLise willingly retreated to Joy's office to wait. Her friend joined her a few minutes later, sinking comfortably into the desk chair and reaching for a pack of Marlboros.

Once Joy was settled, AnnaLise had filled her in on recent developments, though apparently not as completely as said friend would like.

AnnaLise sighed in response to the repeated question. 'All I know is that Chuck told me Earl at the garage found a rifle slug in a front tire.' And that Remington, Hornady and UltraMax were ammunition, not tire, manufacturers.

'Well,' Joy sent a smoke ring into the air, 'unless the bears have armed themselves, I think that means somebody shot out her tire.'

'Fine,' AnnaLise said, holding up her hands, 'I'll stipulate that a human being fired the gun. Most likely a hunting accident.'

'Except it's bow season,' Joy pointed out. 'Besides, the town outlawed hunters of *any* kind on Sutherton Mountain years ago, supposedly because they tended to cut down unsuspecting visitors right along with the deer.'

There was that. And the theory that the thinning of the tourist herd wasn't necessarily accidental. 'Be that as it may, poachers know no season.' AnnaLise was sipping a Honeydew Melon, Pineapple and Lemongrass Juice Smoothie, a nice counter to the toxic fumes floating across the desk from the physical trainer's cigarette.

'More so in the woods around the lake than here on the mountain, I would think.' Joy tapped the ash from her cancer-stick onto a piece of aluminum foil molded into a makeshift ashtray. 'Especially with the police range nearby. Chuck and his troops hear gunfire that's not theirs, they might come looking.'

The gun range. 'Daisy and I heard what sounded like a shot from there as we drove up the mountain on Monday.'

'What time?'

'Five thirty, quarter to six?'

'Then it didn't come from the range. It's only open nine to one on weekdays. Is it possible you heard the shot that took out the woman's tire?'

'I suppose so.' AnnaLise was trying to recall the circumstances. 'It was as we were off-roading on Daisy's shortcut. Given the way things echo up there, I suppose it could have come from above us.'

'Are we talking about the dead end that leads to the bridge?'

'Not much of a dead end, by my definition,' AnnaLise sniffed.

'Don't be such a grump,' Joy said. 'We're getting somewhere here.'

By way of a dead-end road. 'If you're right, Tanja Rosewood's car went off the road just moments before Daisy and I nearly got killed ourselves.'

'What?' Joy's smoke was out and, though AnnaLise would have liked to believe her friend was more concerned about the answer to her question than getting the next one lighted, soon there was evidence to the contrary.

'You'd have no way of knowing,' AnnaLise said, 'but my car stalled crossways on the approach to the bridge Monday. We nearly went over the cliff and the car was totaled.'

117

'Damn. Who hit you?' Creature comforts taken care of, Joy actually looked concerned.

'Well, no one, as it turned out. I don't remember much, but according to Daisy and Joshua Eames, when his truck came up behind me just after I got the Spyder started, I must have panicked and hit the gas, sending us into the rock wall.'

'I thought you almost went over into the gorge.' Joy sounded disappointed. 'The wall is on the mountain side of the road.'

'We must have bounced back across, because when the car came to rest, it was right on the edge. Luckily, Josh warned us, or Daisy would have climbed out of her side of the car, right into the gorge.' AnnaLise gave a shiver. With Tanja Rosewood's plunge off the road, their own near miss seemed even scarier. And AnnaLise and Daisy, even luckier.

Joy seemed to mull that over. 'And this happened within minutes of the Rosewood woman's car going over.'

'If it was a shot I heard, *and* the one that blew out her tire.'

'Did it sound like a deer rifle or . . .' AnnaLise could feel Joy reading the expressions on her old friend's face. 'I don't even know why I ask, as much as you like guns. I wasn't even born here and I'm probably a better shot than you are.'

'Don't pat yourself on the back,' AnnaLise said. 'There are toddlers in Sutherton who could say the same. My father just never got around to teaching—'

Joy opened her mouth to say something, but AnnaLise held up two hands to stop her. 'I know,

I know. Yet another sad result of growing up fatherless.'

'Actually, that's not what I was going to say, smartie. I was going to ask what happened after your accident – how you got out of the car and when the Rosewood car was discovered. There could only have been an hour or maybe two of daylight left at that point.'

'Like I said, Josh arrived and warned us to stay put, then called nine-one-one. They were there within minutes, thankfully. It was Earl Lawling, the guy who came with the wrecker to tow my poor Spyder away, who spotted the Porsche. Good thing, too, because Chuck says that, with leaves falling, followed by the snow and summer floods, it might never have been found.'

'Earl?' Joy repeated. 'Didn't you also say he's the one who discovered the slug in the tire?'

'So what?' AnnaLise asked. 'You think he was up there with his tow truck taking pot shots at cars, only to point out the Porsche so he could ultimately indict himself by discovering that a bullet blew out the tire and then reporting it to the police?'

'First of all,' Joy said, ignoring what *some* might call sarcasm or, at least, facetiousness, 'it's damn lucky there was a slug for him to find. With a high-powered rifle, which is what you'd need to take out a tire even if your Mrs Rosewood was taking it slow like I advised her to, you'd be more likely to have a through-and-through. The thing must have hit the rim, which means it'll be so badly damaged they won't be able to tell anything but the caliber. Maybe.'

119

AnnaLise squinted at her friend. 'And you know this how?'

'I read.' Joy puffed out another smoke ring and leaned forward earnestly in her chair. 'But back to this Earl – maybe he's one of those freaks who gets off on being important. You remember that movie about the firefighter who torched buildings so he could be a hero?'

AnnaLise didn't answer.

'What? I finally stumped the movie expert?'

'*Backdraft*, starring Kurt Russell and Billy Baldwin,' AnnaLise said, 'but you've got the motive wrong.'

Joy waited. 'Well?' she said finally.

AnnaLise looked up, startled. 'What?'

'What was the motive?'

'You know what?' AnnaLise met Joy's gaze. 'I honestly have no idea.'

Seventeen

AnnaLise steered her mother's Chrysler away from Hotel Lux and down the mountain toward the Sutherton Bridge. Although she was trying to keep her mind on the drive, purposely choosing the route that Tanja Rosewood had used to descend, AnnaLise kept returning to one thing.

Joshua Eames.

If the sound Daisy and she had heard was the gunshot that took out the Porsche's tire, Tanja went over the cliff only a few minutes before AnnaLise had accidentally hit her Spyder's accelerator.

From that moment onward, she'd been blocking the road. No other vehicles had come or gone – *could* have come or gone – with the exception of Josh's truck. Had he seen or heard what had happened to Tanja? Or, much worse, had he been responsible for it?

If so, why? As Joy had asked about the movie *Backdraft* – what was the motive? Tanja certainly—

AnnaLise stepped hard on the brake, slowing the Chrysler to the point of crawling as she rounded a blind curve. In front of her lay the bridge and, just before the concrete span started, the place where the Porsche had apparently sailed off the road. The spot was nothing more than a patch of dirt and gravel – more worn down from use than intentionally created, though it wasn't big enough to get a car of any size fully out of the road.

Not that it stopped people, as evidenced by the minivan now being parked with its butt sticking out. Before the wheels had stopped moving, occupants of the vehicle spilled out with cameras.

'Stand over there, Sarah,' a man said, pointing to the edge.

Just the thought of being that close to the edge made AnnaLise white-knuckled and she used her death grip to steer past the group and onto the bridge. At least driving down, she was on the mountain side of the road, not hanging out over nothing. Or, more precisely, the gorge that had swallowed Tanja's car.

By the time AnnaLise and the Chrysler reached the end of the bridge – and to the place where the Spyder had met its own end – her right foot was shaking so badly she was afraid to touch it to the gas pedal. Happily, the downgrade made that unnecessary, and the brake was considerably more forgiving. And reassuring.

Coasting down now and relaxing some, she tried to think. No matter how much a trouble-maker Joshua Eames had been when he was younger, he seemed to have his act together now. Worked for his dad, had a respectable girlfriend, even planned to go to college.

While Tanja may not have been thrilled about her daughter's relationship with someone she would no doubt consider 'a townie,' she'd allowed Suze to come to school here and was an intelligent enough woman to know that a relationship in the freshman year of college would likely die

122

a natural death, even without parental interference.

So what would Josh have had to fear from Suzanne's mother? It didn't make sense.

Now on the lower half of the mountain, AnnaLise caught up with an SUV pulling a trailer laden with boxes. Most likely more summer folk, moving back to their homes in other parts of the south for the winter.

Gradually the mountain and the lake would start to feel deserted, leaving the locals to enjoy their town as the weather turned crisper. Before you knew it, the signs would be up, warning people not to drive on the mountain without snow tires, chains or four-wheel drive vehicles. In fact, AnnaLise should talk to Daisy about outfitting the Chrysler for the winter. It was the least AnnaLise should do, given she was driving her mother's—

Damn.

She'd gone up to talk to Joy about the Sutherton website and had completely forgotten to raise the subject. Maybe she deserved the look her friend had given her when she'd spaced out while they were talking about the movie.

The SUV turned out onto the highway at the high entrance, but AnnaLise continued on the smaller streets to Main Street, not wanting to pass the garage where her Spyder sat looking not unlike the arachnid that Fred Eames had stomped into the sidewalk in front of the Griggs' own garage.

Passing Mama's, which looked like it was hopping for lunch, AnnaLise turned right onto Second Street, pulling up to the curb in front of their apartment door. The black pick-up was parked on the other side of the garage. Now was as good a time as any to talk to Joshua Eames for the second time that day.

'Josh?' she called.

Mr Eames stuck his head out of the garage, holding a power drill. 'Not here. Will I do?'

'Of course,' AnnaLise said. 'Hope that drill is battery-operated or you're going to need a long extension cord.'

'It is. Though by tomorrow night, you'll have electricity in here, even if it's not run everywhere Daisy needs it yet.'

'Scotty is coming?' AnnaLise practically clapped her hands.

Scotty the electrician was notoriously tough to pin down. In fact, if Josh wanted to make 'back-pocket' money, maybe he should consider an apprenticeship with the company instead of college.

Assuming he wasn't a cold-blooded killer.

'Says they'll be here tomorrow in the a.m.,' Mr Eames said, 'though that's what Scotty told me nearly a week ago. And they've been holding me up nearly a month on a job down Church Street. We've gotten as far as we can on both without the wiring run.'

'That's certainly not fair to you.'

'No, ma'am, it's not. Especially given people don't take kindly to paying for jobs that aren't finished. But don't you worry – I'm taking steps to make sure it doesn't happen again. In the meantime, I'm tidying up so Scotty's slugs won't have another excuse not to put in an honest day's work.'

'Is Josh coming back?' AnnaLise asked.

'I'm not sure,' Mr Eames said, settling the drill into its case and carefully snapping it closed. He seemed embarrassed. 'Josh, he . . . uh, he had to go see the chief.'

AnnaLise felt her own blood go cold. 'Chuck asked him to come in?'

'No, no,' shaking his head, 'Josh just said he'd been thinking about something and he'd feel better if he went to the police and got it off his chest.'

'He didn't tell you what it was that was bothering him?' By now AnnaLise was following Eames as he went back and forth to his truck, emptying the garage of framing materials and tools.

Eames stopped. 'Josh is twenty now and doesn't exactly think I need to know everything that goes on in his head.' Eames turned away from the bed of his truck to face AnnaLise. 'Probably your mama has had a similar experience with you.'

'I . . . yes, I suppose she has, now that you say it.'

'Oh, I'd pretty much bet on it.' He swung what looked like a heavy toolbox into the truck effortlessly. 'The books and TV doctors talk about growing pains and kids wanting to be independent and such, but they never really get to the heart of the matter from the parent's side.'

'Empty-nest syndrome.'

Eames snorted. 'That's their label, like it's just a matter of gaining a spare room. Josh still lives with me on the mountain, so it's not *him* being there I miss. I miss *my* being there – in his head,

I mean. Or at least feeling like I had a right to be.'

Now Eames shook his own head. 'Ah, don't mind me, AnnaLise. Josh wasn't an easy child, growing up – wouldn't talk to me about most things, so what do I know?'

AnnaLise touched the man on the shoulder. 'More than I do about it, that's for certain. Anything I can help you finish up here?'

'Not a bitty thing.' He swung up the gate of the pick-up. 'I'll be on Scotty to make sure he gets here and runs that wiring so we can finish up.'

AnnaLise followed Eames into the garage. 'Are the openers here yet?'

'At my shop. Even in Sutherton, I'm afraid they might take a walk if I left 'em here with the doors not hung yet.' He knocked on the fresh two-by-fours framing the opening on Daisy's side of the garage. 'Josh did a nice job of getting this all plumb and laying the tracks, so once Scotty is done tomorrow, he and I should be able to hang the openers and the doors on Friday and your mama and Mrs Peebly will have their garage back by the weekend.'

'That's wonderful. Thank you so much.' AnnaLise couldn't believe it had been so quick. She impulsively hugged the man.

Looking surprised, Eames said, 'You're most welcome, AnnaLise, but I do have to tell you that installing electric garage doors, even in a structure as old as this one, isn't a major undertaking.'

'You have no idea, Mr Eames,' AnnaLise said,

moving back onto the sidewalk. 'You honestly have no idea.'

Feeling good about the garage doors, which had been fourteen years and countless arguments toward modernizing them, AnnaLise made herself lunch at home.

The pickings in the refrigerator were sparse, as usual, since both generations of Griggs took most of their meals at Mama's. AnnaLise settled for peanut butter on toast and a glass of orange juice. Pretty much the perfect meal, in her estimation, and one that had been a staple for her in Wisconsin.

It was good to be alone, she thought, settling down at the kitchen table with her plate and glass. It hadn't happened much since she'd returned to Sutherton, now eleven days ago.

Picking up her orange juice, she smiled at the glass. It was a Welch's jelly jar, part of the manufacturer's 'Winnie the Pooh collection,' this one featuring Winnie and Eeyore. When her mother had started collecting them for her, AnnaLise had been nearly seventeen years old. Too old for Disney glasses, not that it had stopped Daisy.

And now AnnaLise took nostalgic solace.

She took a sip of orange juice as she gave some thought to what Mr Eames had said. The truth was AnnaLise had been eager to move away from her admittedly loving, but also meddlesome, dual-barreled mothers.

Obviously she'd never told them about Ben back in Wisconsin, but she'd also told them very little of even her day-to-day life there, embracing her independence and, truth be told, resenting their occasional phone calls. Not because she didn't love Daisy and Mama, but because the calls felt like interrogations rather than what they likely were: attempts to have a continuing role in AnnaLise's adult life. To feel as much a part of her as she still was – and always would be – of them.

Hell, what would it have cost AnnaLise to telephone and ask Daisy for an opinion? Or Mama, a calorie-laden recipe? Beyond the pounds, of course.

AnnaLise's 'freshman fifteen' in college had been a weight loss, not gain, when she'd gone away to school. In fact – she pinched an inch at her waist just to check – she'd best be careful not to gain it back in the time she'd be here.

Going to the dishwasher, AnnaLise moved aside a Revere Ware copper-bottomed kettle that pre-dated her about twenty years, slid in her plate and glass and gave some thought to how she would spend the afternoon.

Then, closing the dishwasher, she picked up her jacket.

AnnaLise arrived at the Sutherton police station about 2 p.m., just in time to see a red Toyota Camry pull out of the parking lot with Suzanne Rosewood in the driver's seat and Josh sitting next to her.

The two seemed to be in a heated conversation, so much so that AnnaLise didn't think either of the occupants of the Toyota saw her skip out of the way as they blasted out of the parking lot. Watching the car disappear alarmingly quickly, given the twenty-five-miles-per-hour speed limit, AnnaLise noticed Wisconsin plates. Suzanne's car, mostly likely still in Dad's name. Given the way the girl drove, he'd be wise to get this one out of his name, too, assuming that was possible given Suzanne was only eighteen.

Entering the police station, AnnaLise waved at the officer staffing the front desk. 'Afternoon, Charity.'

Charity Pitchford and her husband Coy were both on the force. Like AnnaLise, Coy was born in Sutherton and had gone away to school. When he came back last year, it was with Charity, a Charlotte native who was also studying criminal justice. The two had married earlier in the year and, according to Chuck, were a welcome addition to the department.

'Afternoon, AnnaLise. You looking for the chief?'

'I am, if he has a minute.'

'I'm sure he does for you, though that door of his should be a revolving one today.'

'A lot of visitors?' AnnaLise asked, coming through the swinging half door Charity held open for her.

'I'm told it's busy for this time of year, though I don't have the historical reference to judge.'

'How do you like Sutherton?'

'Just fine.'

'But this will be your first winter, right?'

'It will, though I think I'd be happier about it if y'all didn't ask that question with the outright glee of the cat that swallowed the canary and had me in mind for its next meal.'

AnnaLise laughed. 'You'll be OK as long as you have a four-wheel drive vehicle.'

'The other piece of advice I've been getting. In fact, Coy is out looking at one as we speak, which is why I'm covering the desk for him. What about you? Will you be staying for the winter?'

'God, I hope not,' AnnaLise said.

'You'll be OK as long as you have a four-wheel drive vehicle,' Charity mimicked.

AnnaLise laughed. 'Afraid I don't have a vehicle at all right now. My car was totaled.'

'So I heard. I was on the desk, here, but Coy said Monday late afternoon into evening was about as crazy a few hours as he's ever experienced. One call sends our guys plus fire and rescue out there, only to stumble on something altogether unexpected.'

'Tanja Rosewood's car already in the gorge. And ours, very nearly so.'

'That gorge has definitely proved to be the gift that keeps right on giving.' Charity ran a hand through strawberry blonde hair. 'The recovery of the Porsche was no picnic, but that second vehicle down there? And God knows what we'll find beneath that. It's like we have our very own archeological . . .' She squinted at AnnaLise, searching for the word.

'Dig?' AnnaLise guessed.

'Exactly,' Charity said, head bobbing in approval. 'A mode of transportation for every decade. By the time we reach the bottom, we'll be down to chariots and mastodons. Sure glad Daisy and you aren't the ones we're scraping up down there right now.'

'Amen,' said AnnaLise, as Charity glanced back toward the desk.

'The chief is off his phone, so you can go on back if you like. Just rap on the door before you go in.'

AnnaLise thanked her and followed the instructions, only to get a testy 'What?' in response to her knock.

She stuck her head in. 'Am I disturbing you?'

'Yup,' he said, gesturing for her to take a seat. 'But why on earth should you be any different around here? Besides,' he continued without giving her a chance to answer his rhetorical question, 'I have a bone to pick with you.'

'With me?'

Another tap on the door and Charity stuck her head in. 'Sorry to disturb you, Chief, but Mr Rosewood is on my line.'

'Would you tell him I'll call him back? Thanks, Charity.' When the door closed he turned back to AnnaLise. 'I have all the sympathy in the world for your friend Ben Rosewood, but the man is becoming a pain in the ass.'

'He's not my friend,' AnnaLise insisted, though she probably was protesting too much, 'but he has over the years in Wisconsin expanded and perfected the squeaky wheel. Why? What's going on?'

'With him? Nothing I should be complaining about, I suppose. The man just lost his wife, after all.' Chuck ran his hand through his hair.

131

'Is he pressing for information?'

Chuck shrugged. 'He's presumably used to being treated like an integral part of the law enforcement effort back home.'

'Direct quote?'

Chuck sighed. 'Within a word or two.'

'I thought I recognized it from a campaign speech of his I had to cover.'

'Even before this happened, he was calling. Wanted to use the shooting range at odd hours, though I said that wasn't possible. Needless to say, he wasn't happy.'

'I can't imagine there's much information to share with him anyway,' AnnaLise said. 'He knows about the tire being shot out?'

'He does. Even made some helpful suggestions on how we might pursue the investigation.'

AnnaLise could imagine. 'You just got your hands on the slug this morning, so there can't possibly be anything back from ballistics yet, right?' AnnaLise was fishing.

'Right.' While Chuck wasn't quite swallowing the bait, he hadn't spit it out, either.

'I suppose it just could have been an accident.'

'There's essentially a rock wall, road and cliff there. Not someplace where you'd be out hunting or target-shooting, even if it were legal on the mountain. As for whether the shooter could know the car would go over? Probably not, but they could be assured of a bad crash. And with Mrs Rosewood impaired by alcohol . . .' Chuck spread out his hands.

'With all this contact between you and Ben, has he told you his wife had a drinking problem?'

132

To her surprise, Chuck nodded. 'He did, though he asked me to keep it quiet and given that while it was a contributing factor, it wasn't the cause, I'm going to do my best.'

'Doesn't her blood alcohol have to be in the report?' AnnaLise asked.

'It does,' Chuck said, pushing back from the desk. 'What I don't have to include is that she had a chronic drinking problem, especially since there's nothing on the record – no DWIs –'

'It's OWI, in Wisconsin – operating while intoxicated.'

'– so we just know what Mr Rosewood has told us. Which reminds me: I told you I had a bone to pick with you.'

AnnaLise didn't like the sound of that. Had Ben told Chuck about the affair? Or had Chuck found out for himself, though AnnaLise didn't see . . .'

'. . . slipped your mind?' the chief was saying.

'Pardon?'

Chuck looked skyward. 'I asked why you or your mother didn't mention Joshua Eames.'

'Josh?'

'Yes, Josh. According to him, he came around the corner and there you were. He was lucky to be able to stop.'

'I know,' AnnaLise said. 'And I'm sorry I didn't mention it, but I was a little shook up that night, as you'll recall. Though given he didn't hit us anyway—'

'Whether you two collided or not, it would have been helpful to know there was someone else on that road.'

133

'Did Josh see anything?'

'See? No. But he heard a shot and it's very possible . . . what?'

AnnaLise was waving her hand like a kid in school. 'Daisy and I heard that shot, too. While we were cutting through the dead end road between Ridge Road and the bridge.'

'Lise, that trail is closed for a reason. It's a hazard to vehicles on the road, your popping out of nowhere like that.'

'Daisy's the one who insisted,' AnnaLise said, having no problem with hanging her mother out to dry.

'You tell Daisy I'll run her in if I find her up there, just like my dad, when *he* was on the force. Besides the danger you pose to other drivers, if you'd have taken a right at the lookout instead of the second clearing, you'd have landed smack on top of the folks we're *currently* trying to peel off the bottom of the gorge. Made my job considerably more difficult.'

'Sorry,' AnnaLise said, suppressing a smile. Chuck was so cute when he was grumpy. 'The lookout?'

'As in Lovers' Lookout. There's a real pretty view of the mountain and the bridge, though I doubt that was the main attraction. Kids used to park there to make out, until one night when a couple set their car a-rocking and rocked right over the side.'

'You're kidding, right?'

Chuck shrugged. 'Mountain lore, though I'm told that's why the road was closed.'

It didn't bear thinking about. 'So, about the

gunshot that Josh heard – it must have been the same one Daisy and I did.'

'And yet, *I'm* only hearing about it now.'

'You're absolutely right. Though in my own defense, nobody had any idea a gun was involved until this morning.'

'Score another one for Earl's eagle eye. First he spotted the hole and then recovered the slug from inside the tire itself.'

'What kind of shape is it in?'

'You mean, is it likely matched to the weapon that fired it?'

'Yes.'

'Probably not, having hit the wheel rim. And, anyway, most reliable ballistics matches today are because of the extractor mark on the shell casing when it's extracted. We're not going to find that until we have the position of the shooter and, even then, there's the terrain to deal with. Even if the casing didn't roll down a hill or off a cliff, someone who could make that shot is likely smart enough to pick up the brass.'

Talk about looking for a needle in a mountain-sized haystack.

'But back to Joshua Eames.' Chuck slid a paper across his desk so he could read it. 'That young man has four outstanding citations for excessive speed. And, given how fast he likely had to travel to hie himself out of there before fire and rescue came upon you, he scored a fifth.'

'I saw him leave the station, so apparently you didn't haul him off to the slammer.'

'I didn't, though I gave him a stern talking to.'

'I'll bet you did. Softie.'

Chuck shrugged. 'Fact is, the kid doesn't have the money to pay the fines.'

'Can't his father help?'

'His daddy figures Josh earned those tickets himself and he should pay them the same way. I applaud the sentiment, so we're trying to work out some kind of payment plan.'

Probably why Josh and Suzanne were fighting as they drove away. He wasn't going to have money to take her out anytime soon. 'Well, I have to say I'm relieved that Josh came to you on his own.'

'You were worried he had something to do with the shooting?'

'It crossed my mind – didn't it yours?'

'Of course. Josh is dating the woman's daughter. Maybe Mom wasn't happy about it. Maybe there's an inheritance involved. Maybe a lot of different things. Love, greed, sex, revenge – the motives for murder are as old as these mountains. Fact is, though, that Josh didn't have to stop to help you and certainly wouldn't have, if he'd just shot out the tires of a car a few hundred yards up the road.'

'You have a point.' AnnaLise was thinking about it, when Chuck spoke again:

'Is now a good time for you to tell me about Ben Rosewood and a certain reporter on cold winter nights in Wisconsin?'

Eighteen

'How . . .' She cleared her throat. 'What do you mean?'

'My meaning, I believe, was pretty clear: when were you going to tell me about the affair you had with Ben Rosewood?'

'It's over.'

'So he told me.' Chuck's face . . . well, it didn't look like Chuck's anymore.

'He *told* you?' AnnaLise felt ambushed. First, according to the chief, Ben was 'a pain in the ass,' now he was an informant?

'The man did, yesterday. And you confirm it, every time I mention his name.'

'What did he say?'

'I'd like to hear it from you.'

AnnaLise swallowed. 'Grumpy' wasn't looking so cute anymore. 'Yes, we had an affair for about a year. It ended almost a month ago.'

'Who ended it?'

'I did.'

Chuck's eyes flickered. 'Rosewood says the opposite.'

AnnaLise wasn't surprised. 'Ben is a man who doesn't like to lose. At anything. I can show you the text messages, if you like.'

She started to paw through her purse for the cell.

'You ended a year-long affair by text message?'

'Of course not. What kind of person do you think I am?'

'I know the kind of person you used to be.'

AnnaLise stopped searching for the cell and looked at her friend. At the man who'd been more than a friend. 'Chuck, I—'

'The texts?' He nodded toward the bag.

AnnaLise nodded and returned to digging through the bag, trying to hold back tears. *I don't cry*, she told herself. *I never cry.*

'Chuck, you're scaring me,' she said without looking up. 'I'm me, AnnaLise Griggs. Remember?'

'I remember. But a woman is dead and you admit having an affair with her husband. I need to ask these questions.'

'I had an affair. Past tense.' AnnaLise tried to sound calm, despite the knot of fear growing in her stomach. Not to mention the self-loathing. 'And if you honestly think it's a factor, shouldn't you be looking into Ben as well?'

'Except he's the one who came to me.'

'Ben thinks I killed his wife?' The knot was more like a boulder now. 'That can't be right. I just talked to him yesterday, too, and he seemed fine. In fact, he was blaming the accident on Joy for serving wine to Tanja.'

'I assume he's a good actor, not surprising for a trial attorney. Or maybe he hadn't noticed the missed call from you on his cellphone yet.'

'Missed call? When?' AnnaLise was wracking her brain. When was the last time she'd called Ben? She couldn't even remember.

'The night of Tanja Rosewood's accident – and yours. In fact, not an hour after you left the scene.'

138

Left the scene? A uniformed officer had taken AnnaLise and Daisy to Ida Mae's and – 'Oh, wait. I know.'

'Then I'd be grateful if you'd tell me and clear this all up.' Still no clue as to how the chief of police – because this clearly was the 'chief,' not her friend Chuck – was reacting. His face gave nothing away.

'Daisy and I were at Ida Mae's and Daisy mentioned that the car Earl Lawling had spotted was yellow. I immediately thought of the Porsche.'

'And called Rosewood?'

'To see if he and his family were all right,' AnnaLise said uncomfortably. 'Early that afternoon, we'd seen them at Mama's and Tanja asked how long it would take to get up to the spa.'

'So you knew where she'd be.'

'Yes.' AnnaLise was staring at her friend in horror. 'But Daisy and I were together at her doctor's appointment. Chuck, you can't possibly think I stalked this woman and shot out her tire!'

'Like I said, Lise, I don't know what to think.' The use of the nickname was the only trace of warmth.

'Listen to me, Chuck. I dialed Ben's number that night because I was worried. Then Daisy interrupted me toward dinner, so I hung up. And was glad that I had. I'd been badly shaken up by the accident and had some wine, so I wasn't thinking clearly.'

'As it happens, you were. It *was* both the Porsche and Tanja Rosewood.'

'But it was no longer my . . . duty to call. You've got to believe me. Ben and I were over

139

– unequivocally and irretrievably – back in Wisconsin two weeks before I drove here to Sutherton because of Daisy's—'

'You can stop there. I know the rest.'

'Here.' AnnaLise was fumbling out her cell-phone. 'Let me punch up the messages. I kept them all – they'll prove I ended it with Ben and he wasn't taking no for an answer.' She was frantically pushing buttons. 'You should be looking at Ben for this, not— Oh, no.'

'What?' Chuck leaned forward.

AnnaLise looked up from her phone. 'They're . . . All my saved text messages from him are gone.'

Ben must have deleted those messages yesterday, AnnaLise thought as she escaped Chuck's office, barely raising her hand in acknowledgment of Charity's 'See ya later, AnnaLise.'

The D.A. had her purse in his hand, bag open, when she'd come down the stairs at the inn. If he'd looked under text messages and his name, the conniving asshole could have deleted the whole bunch with one push of a button.

But why? To erase all record of their relationship? Then why would he have gone to Chuck and admitted the affair?

The obvious answer scared AnnaLise more than the question. Ben was no longer trying to pin Tanja's death on Joy – he was trying to pin it on AnnaLise instead. But it didn't make any sense. No one yesterday knew that someone had fired at Tanja's Porsche, striking the tire and sending the car off the road.

No one, that is, except the killer.

140

Nineteen

You wouldn't confuse the Torch of today with the Griggs Market of even just a year ago.

Gone were the deli counter and shelves full of bread, cans and dried goods. The walls of the big square room had been painted slate gray and round tables filled the floor in front of a half-moon stage. On three walls, long, bar-height tables gave patrons a clear view of the entertainment.

It was at one of these counters that AnnaLise and Joy sat, not paying the slightest attention to either the decor or the performer, tonight a thankfully subdued pianist.

'Wow,' Joy said, tossing back a tequila shot. 'It's just like *Fatal Attraction*. You love that movie.'

'Not when I'm cast in the role of Alex Forrest.'

'Who's he?'

'She. You know, the character played by Glenn Close? Michael Douglas's one-night stand that rapidly becomes his worst nightmare?'

'Honestly, who but you would remember that whack-job's name? All I know is she boiled a bunny. You didn't do that, right?' Joy was signaling for the waitress.

AnnaLise, on the other hand, had been nursing her glass of Hefe-Weisen, a North Carolina wheat beer from Olde Hickory Brewery, located in the foothills of the Blue Ridge Mountains.

She'd also been trying to figure out why she was talking to Joy, other than the fact that she already knew about AnnaLise's affair with Ben. 'No, of course I didn't boil any bunnies. Or puppies or kittens, for that matter.'

The waitress who'd just arrived at their table turned on her heel.

'Now see what you've done?' Joy said, watching the woman disappear in the other direction.

'It wouldn't hurt you to pace yourself anyway.'

'This was my first. Besides, I'm surprised you're not hitting the stuff harder, given the circumstances.'

'"The circumstances" are exactly why I need to keep my wits about me. I could go to jail for something I didn't do. Oh my God, this state has the death penalty. I could fry.'

'Nah, execution is by lethal injection here. Sort of *The Big Sleep*, courtesy of the North Carolina Department of Correction.'

'Cold comfort,' AnnaLise muttered.

'Cold is right. But I don't see what you're worried about. From what you told me, it's your boyfriend's word against yours.'

'My *ex*-boyfriend,' AnnaLise hissed, 'is a district attorney, a prosecutor. If anyone knows how to frame someone, it's him, the slimeball.'

'And they say love is blind.' After the waitress shunned them, Joy raised her empty glass for the bartender to see and got a nod in return. 'So, let me get this straight.'

'Better hurry before that shot gets here,' AnnaLise interjected. 'Or you won't be able to get *anything* straight.'

'*As* I was saying,' Joy plunged on, unfazed: 'you think your D.A. killed his wife and is trying to pin the murder on you, right?'

'Right.'

'But why?' Joy nodded her thanks to the waitress who deposited the tequila crisply and departed immediately.

'Sure, I'll have another beer,' AnnaLise called to the waitress' back before returning to Joy. 'The why of framing me? No clue, except that I dumped him. Maybe his ego can't take it.'

'And so . . .' Joy prompted.

AnnaLise was warming to her subject. 'And so, think of it: District Attorney Benjamin Rosewood kills two birds with one stone. Gets rid of the wife and sticks it to the former lover as revenge.'

'Hmm.' Joy seemed to be taking AnnaLise's advice and nursing this second tequila. 'I like it. She's rich, I suppose. The wife, I mean.'

AnnaLise nodded. 'Loaded. Or at least her family is.'

'Well, there's your motive.'

But AnnaLise was thinking back to her conversation with Chuck. 'Apparently Ben asked permission to use the shooting range while he was in town.'

'Not very smart, if he intended to kill his wife.'

'True, but . . .' The reporter leaned forward. 'He never intended for the bullet to be found. The whole thing would have been written off as a tire blowout if it hadn't been for Earl.'

'Or drunk driving,' Joy agreed, taking a sip of her tequila. 'Sounds to me like Chuck is a fool

143

– or worse, negligent – if he ignores the possibility that Rosewood is involved. And if it were me, I'd also be looking into your omnipresent – not to mention, seemingly omniscient – Earl the Mechanic.'

AnnaLise was too upset over the conversation with the police chief to worry about Earl Lawling right now. 'Chuck is no fool, believe me. You should have seen how he set me up, Joy, complaining about what a pain Ben was. All the while my old friend – hell, old *boy*friend – was waiting to pounce, to drop the bomb about Ben and me, so he could see how I'd react.'

'He *is* a crafty one, our chief,' Joy said. 'He doesn't seem to be paying the least bit of attention when you talk with him, but then he can parrot back what was said chapter and verse. Only Chuck's known you for twenty-three of your most formative years. He can't honestly believe you killed this Tanja woman.'

'That's what I would have thought,' AnnaLise said. 'But if you'd seen his face, Joy. He was . . . disgusted with me.'

'Well, that's unfortunate. What's the use of having your gay former boyfriend become police chief if you can't count on him to overlook evidence?'

'There is no evidence!'

'So what are you worried about?'

AnnaLise couldn't get Chuck's expression out of her mind, but she had to pull herself together. 'You're right. All they have is Ben's word against mine.'

'And the text messages you sent to him, maybe?'

144

'Maybe, but I'm certain I never said anything that could be construed as wanting to get back with him. It does bother me, though, that I can't produce any of Ben's messages to me. They would have proved that I ended it, at least.'

'Because he was begging you to come back?'

AnnaLise rolled her eyes. 'It's obvious you don't know Ben. Begging is not his style. The messages were more like suggestions that I come to my senses.'

'Got you. And, of course, he wouldn't have shown those to Chuck. What about your friends in Wisconsin?'

'What about them?'

'Would any of them be able to testify,' she waved down the alarm in AnnaLise's eyes at the word, '*if* it came down to it, that you broke up with him?'

'At the time? I'm afraid not. I did tell Bobby Bradenham, but that was just last week.'

Joy looked sorry for her. 'Wait a second, you didn't confide in *anyone* while this was all going on? What kind of woman are you?'

'Ben and I agreed that we wouldn't.'

'That's how they get you, you know. They isolate you from your friends.'

'Who, they?'

'Predators. Abusers.'

'I honestly don't think Ben is either of those.'

'Oh, I'm sorry,' Joy said, holding up her hands. 'You're absolutely right. You just think he's a murderer.'

When you put it that way . . . 'OK, so maybe

145

he didn't kill Tanja,' she said, backtracking. 'Maybe it *was* just some yahoo with a gun.'

'You said it couldn't have been a hunter.'

'No, not in that area, according to Chuck. Think about that stretch – it's just road and cliffs, with no wooded area for wildlife to hide. But that doesn't mean someone couldn't have been hanging out taking potshots and accidentally hit the car.'

Even as she said it, AnnaLise could hear Ben: 'My wife is dead and *some*one has to pay.'

'. . . reckless, but have it your way,' Joy was saying. 'Only, speaking of "accidents," what about your text messages? Could you just have hit the wrong button and erased them yourself?'

'Uh-uh. I don't make mistakes like that.' But AnnaLise was thinking back to her visit to the inn the day before. 'I went there looking for you, you know.'

'Where?'

'The inn yesterday, when Ben must have messed with my phone. I'd tried you at the spa first, so I could warn you that Ben was gunning for you as the cause of his wife's accident. That's before,' she said ruefully, 'I knew he was gunning for me, of course.'

'Nobody knew the tire of the car had been shot out then.'

'Except the person who did it,' AnnaLise reminded her.

'Which is why you're suspicious of your boyfriend. Go on.'

AnnaLise ignored the present tense use of

146

'boyfriend' this time. 'Anyway, I was upstairs at the inn, leaving you the note, when Ben and Suzanne came in the front door. He could easily have seen my handbag on the hall table the moment they walked in.'

'So he knew you were there. Would he have said anything to his daughter?'

'No, I'm sure he didn't, because I could hear their conversation. Ben wanted Suze to stay and she wanted to be with Josh.'

'Josh?'

'Joshua Eames, her boyfriend. Suzanne sounded like a whiny brat, especially under the circumstances, but eventually she and her father agreed that she'd go with Josh and be back for dinner. The door opened and closed, so I thought she'd left and nearly collided with her as I started down the steps.'

'She set a trap for you.'

'No, she'd just forgotten her jacket. She brushed right past me on the stairs, grabbed it and left. From her attitude both then and earlier in the day, I figured she must know about the affair, but Ben says no.'

'So while this all was going on, Ben was busy deleting your messages?'

'I came downstairs right after Suze left and Ben was just coming in from the front hallway, with my bag in his hand. I bet he dug out my phone and cleared it when Suze ran upstairs.'

'Entirely logical, if he did kill his wife and planned to pin it on you. But have you thought about why he might "mess with your phone," as you put it, if his wife's death was an accident,

147

as you so schizophrenically suggested just moments ago?'

'I don't know,' AnnaLise admitted. 'I'm just trying to be open-minded and look at all the possibilities.'

'OK, so how about this one: maybe he thought you'd dumped him for another man and was checking your cell for messages or pictures. It's a time-honored tradition.'

AnnaLise sat up straighter in her chair. 'A new man is the last thing on my mind right now. It never occurred to me that Ben might suspect I'd already found one.'

Joy shrugged. 'It *is* the classic reason to give someone the old heave-ho.'

'I suppose he could have seen me chatting with James Duende at Mama's Monday morning and read something into it,' AnnaLise admitted. 'Though given Ben's ego, I doubt he could fathom any male being preferable to him. And if *I* thought so, it would just be proof I wasn't worthy of *him*. Ben, I mean.'

'Damn,' Joy said, studying her face, 'this guy really got into your head.'

Or AnnaLise had gotten into Ben's head. An even more terrifying thought. 'No,' she said, then qualified with, 'Or, at least, not anymore.'

'Good.' Joy didn't look like she believed her friend. 'So let's assume, just for the time being, that your D.A. is a normal human being, with very real insecurities and fears of his own.'

AnnaLise's shrug said, *If we must.*

'You kissed him off and then – in his mind – fled here. Mightn't he ask himself why? Why

148

now, and why Sutherton? It's not much of a stretch to think you might be running *to* someone, not away from him.'

'I'll grant you that,' AnnaLise said. 'But the real reason, my mom, was more logical. Besides, even if Ben knew nothing about Daisy's problems, Sutherton is my childhood home. I could certainly come here without it having anything to do with him and our breakup.'

'According to you, he's an egotist at best and a sociopath or even psychopath at worse,' Joy said, shifting in her chair. 'Having had experience with two out of those three in the person of Dickens Hart, let me just say that type of man, that type of person, believes *every*thing revolves around them.'

AnnaLise had a mental picture of Ben as the sun, with Tanja and her rotating around him, sometimes one closer, sometimes the other.

'I mean, look what he did to his own daughter,' Joy continued. 'Who sends his kid to college just so he can cheat when he visits her?'

'No, no, no,' AnnaLise said, shaking her head. 'I wasn't living here when Suze enrolled and Ben had no way of knowing that I would be.' Then she hesitated, adding: 'Or staying here temporarily, I should say. Besides, whatever he intended, I'm pretty sure it was a chance meeting with Joshua Eames that decided Suzanne on U-Mo.'

'Must have been a happy coincidence for your Ben. And as for your not living here at the time, so what? You'd both have built-in excuses for visiting. Beats the hell out of having to come up with reasons to take off for somewhere anonymous to do the dirty.'

Joy's tone bespoke more personal experience than accusation, but AnnaLise still felt herself flush. 'I'm done with "the dirty" as you put it. And, as we both know, Sutherton is just the opposite of anonymous.'

'What can I say?' Joy shrugged. 'Lover-boy's not from a small town. He didn't realize there was no way you could come here and *not* stay with your mom.'

AnnaLise could just imagine Daisy's reaction to her daughter's 'shacking up' with her married lover. And in her childhood room, no less. 'She'd get out one of my father's guns and run us both out of town. But you're wrong about Ben. He was born in northern Wisconsin. I can't remember where, exactly, but I remember him saying how much he loved hunting and fishing with his dad.'

Her face changed. 'It was in the context of how much he'd wanted a son. Both Suze and Tanja found the idea of the north woods off-putting.'

'Bet that's not all he told you his wife found "off-putting."' When AnnaLise reacted, Joy spread out her hands. 'Hey, believe me, you're not the first one to be fed a line and, if you'll excuse the expression, swallow it – hook, line and . . . dinker.'

As Joy started to snicker, AnnaLise leveled her with a stare. 'Enough. We were talking about my text messages.'

'I told you, he thought you were fooling around on him, so he did what any right-minded person would: he checked your phone.'

'God knows I'm no expert on right-minded people, but whatever Ben did, he certainly couldn't have found anything besides the occasional message from you or Sheree.'

'You don't get texts from Chuck or Bobby? Rosewood wouldn't have any way of knowing one is your brother and the other's gay.'

'Bobby is *not* my brother.' AnnaLise was reaching the end of her patience. 'And Chuck . . . well, OK, so Chuck is gay. But no matter what Ben found or what he thought, why would he delete his own texts and leave everything else?'

Joy shrugged. 'OK, let's look at it from another angle. You said Rosewood didn't want you to confide in anyone about the affair. Maybe he was shocked you still had his texts and deleted them to make sure you could never come back and use them against him. Maybe he's planning to run for president or something.'

AnnaLise thought about that. 'I'm trying to find a hole in your logic, but that actually makes some sense, knowing Ben.'

'Why, thank you.' Joy downed the rest of her tequila. 'It's amazing how stupid people can be about cellphones. I dated a guy once who sent me weenie pictures.' She glanced at AnnaLise. 'Don't worry, it wasn't your biological father.'

'I'm relieved.'

'Honestly,' Joy continued, 'I never understood photographing body parts. I mean, what's the point if you don't see them in . . .' She seemed to be searching for a word.

'Context?' AnnaLise supplied.

151

'More like scale. You know, include a ruler or something.'

AnnaLise didn't know what to say, so she settled for, 'Sure. Though, ultimately, parts is parts.'

But Joy was looking past her. 'Speaking of parts – and I'm betting good ones, at that – Sheree and James Duende just came in.' She waved.

AnnaLise plastered a smile on her face and turned. Much as she loved Sheree and liked James, the last thing she wanted to do right now was make small talk and watch Sheree defend her turf in the person of James. 'Not a word about what we've been discussing, you hear?'

'My lips are sealed.'

'Hey, girls – isn't it a little early in the week to be doing shots?' Sheree nodded toward the glasses on the table.

'It may be Wednesday,' Joy said, 'but it sure feels like Friday. Join us?'

'Happily,' Duende said, pulling out the chair next to AnnaLise and sitting down. 'Thanks.'

'Drink?' AnnaLise asked, signaling for the waitress.

The woman turned and rushed off.

Twenty

'What in the world did you two do to her?' Sheree Pepper asked as she took the stool on the other side of Duende.

'Not me,' Joy said. 'AnnaLise alienated her by talking about boiling bunnies.'

'Ahh, *Fatal Attraction*,' Duende said approvingly. 'One of my favorite movies.'

'Mine, too. Until now.' AnnaLise threw Joy a warning look and changed the subject. 'I'm glad you're both here – Joy and Sheree, I mean. No offense, James.'

He patted her hand. 'None taken. Want me to leave?'

'No!' the three of them chorused. The James Duende fan club.

'I understand you're working on a website for the town,' AnnaLise started.

'That we are,' Sheree said. 'Fact, James has been kind enough to write some copy for us, so he knows all about it, too.'

Famous biographer, writing website copy. Maybe the relationship between James and Sheree was more serious than AnnaLise had thought.

'That's awfully kind of you,' she said to Duende now. 'Are you looking for content?'

'Why? Are you offering your services?' Sheree jumped in.

'Careful, partner,' Joy said. 'For all you know,

AnnaLise wants to serialize Dickens Hart's memoirs.'

'First I'd have to write them,' AnnaLise said. 'But seriously, what I'm thinking about would be much more informal. I wouldn't write it, the town would.'

'The town?' Sheree repeated. 'And what do you have in mind? Home maintenance tips from Fred Eames? Wiring no-no's from Scotty the Electrician?' She leaned forward to peer at Joy past both Duende and AnnaLise. 'Now that AnnaLise poses it, I believe this idea could raise us some revenue, don't you?'

'No, no,' AnnaLise said, 'I'm talking about a simple blog where people could post about their lives or maybe their memories.'

'Like your suggested historical profile of the inn, Sheree,' Joy said. 'But I'm fairly certain you don't plan to pay for the privilege.'

'No more than you do for your 'Fitness Facts,' Sheree snapped.

AnnaLise looked at Duende and he shrugged. 'It's been a bit of a rocky start-up.'

'I can see why.' Back to Joy and Sheree, with an emphasis on the latter, since AnnaLise had already broached the idea with Joy. 'No, no fix-er-upper ideas. I'm thinking of a weekly blog by the locals here. People like you, Sheree, or maybe Ida Mae, Mama or Daisy. Anyone with a Sutherton story to tell.'

Duende had been studying her face. Now he spoke up. 'I think that's a great idea.'

'You do?' Sheree asked. 'Seems a little . . . well . . .'

'Podunk?' Joy supplied. 'Cheesy? Down home?'

AnnaLise elbowed her. She'd expected Joy to support the idea.

'Exactly,' Sheree was saying. 'And meaning no offense to Daisy and Mama, AnnaLise, they're not writers.'

'But that's the beauty of it,' Duende said. 'Genuine people who have lived here all their lives. You could title it "Voices of Main Street."'

'Voices.' Sheree seemed to be warming, though whether it was to the idea, or the man 'voicing' it, wasn't clear. 'You know, I think I like it. After all, a town *is* its people.'

'Or what's left of them,' Joy said, in full argument mode. 'Forgive me since I'm fairly new as a full-time resident, but last year you had a skier choke on gum and die on her way down the ski slope and two fishermen squished by a Land Cruiser in front of the bait vending machine. And just last week, a woman nearly bled out at the blood drive,' an apologetic glance toward AnnaLise, 'and two bodies snagged up or washed up from the lake, one bludgeoned and the other shot. Do we *really* want to let potential summer folk and skiers know the wackiness that is Sutherton's Main Street?'

Sheree looked at Duende. 'She has a point, you know. We're trying to attract tourists to Sutherton, not scare them off.'

'Oh, please. No one will blog about those things,' AnnaLise protested.

'Because our citizens are so reliable?' Joy said. 'Hell, AnnaLise, your mother actually *committed* one of "those things."'

155

'That whole incident was blown way out of proportion,' AnnaLise protested. 'Mrs Bradenham didn't lose more than a pint.' In addition to the one she'd already donated officially.

'You're missing Joy's point,' Sheree said. 'How would you have us stop them from posting whatever they wanted? I certainly don't have the time to monitor a blog and neither does Joy.'

'We're trying to keep the basic website as timeless as possible,' Duende explained, 'so updating will be limited to things like the calendar of events.'

'We certainly could put a blog on the home page,' Sheree said. 'And I do think it would be effective to have something interactive on a page that's otherwise relatively static, especially if we don't have to write it.'

Joy shook her head. 'But I say again: there's no way that we could let people post just anything they wanted. We'd need a gatekeeper and, as Sheree said, neither of us has that kind of time.'

AnnaLise could feel them looking at her. She sighed. 'Fine. I'll do it with Daisy's help. But remember.' She raised a finger. 'I'll be heading back to Wisconsin at the end of the month.'

'We're talking the Internet – do it from China for all I care,' Joy said. 'Now let's drink on it.'

'That would be a whole lot easier,' AnnaLise said, 'if we had drinks.'

'I'll go to the bar,' Duende said, getting to his feet. 'Red wine, Sheree, and tequila for Joy. AnnaLise, are you sticking with beer?' He pointed at her empty pilsner glass.

'Please. Hefe-Weisen.'

'As good a taste in beers as you have in movies.' Bowing with a flourish, he left them for the bar.

'Good taste,' Sheree said crankily. 'I hate movies like *Fatal Attraction*. They give me nightmares.'

'It's just a movie,' AnnaLise said. 'Make-believe. If anything should give you nightmares, it's the litany of real-life happenings Joy just recited.'

Sheree shivered. 'And she didn't even include the very latest.'

'You mean the Rosewood woman's car going over the cliff?' Joy asked, earning a glare from AnnaLise.

'That poor man,' Sheree said, now tick-tocking her own head, but sadly. 'Losing the two of them in less than that many days.'

AnnaLise's head jerked around. 'Two of them?'

'Why, I'm sorry,' Sheree said. 'I thought you must know.'

Joy glanced at AnnaLise and then back to Sheree. 'Know what?'

'You neither? Why, however long have you two been in here?' Sheree asked. 'It's all over town. There was a shooting.'

'Where?' AnnaLise's lips could hardly form the word.

'On the mountain.' Duende had come back with the tequila and the wine.

AnnaLise felt herself relax. Maybe she'd misunderstood.

'The tire on the Porsche?' Joy said. 'Sure, we knew about that. Ouch!' This last as AnnaLise kicked her.

'The tire was shot out?' Duende asked, not making a move to go back for the rest of the bar order. 'By whom?'

AnnaLise and Joy shrugged in unison.

'Interesting,' Sheree said. 'It does make one wonder if the two incidents might be connected.'

'So there *was* a second?' AnnaLise asked. 'Shooting, I mean?'

'Worse, a double shooting,' Duende said. 'Presumably attempted murder/suicide.'

Oh God, oh God, oh God. AnnaLise's brain repeated it over and over again until the words blurred into the dull roar of water rushing over rocks, the feeling of going under and never—

'AnnaLise, are you all right?' Duende's voice.

The journalist tried to get hold of herself. Ben. Suzanne. Had Suzanne suspected her father of killing her mother and exacted her revenge, then taken her own life? 'You ... Did you say "attempted murder/suicide?"'

'Technically,' Sheree said, 'I believe it would be murder/attempted suicide.'

'He's dead?' AnnaLise said in a strangled whisper.

'No, no.' Duende was shaking his head. '*He's* the one still alive, more's the pity. Shot the girl in the head and then turned the gun on himself, but either lost his nerve or wasn't much of a shot.'

Lost his nerve, AnnaLise thought. Ben was a good shot. Or so he claimed. But then Ben believed he was a success at everything. And now he'd succeeded at killing his daughter.

But why?

'. . . in a critical condition,' Duende was saying.

'Has anyone asked him?' AnnaLise said.

'Asked him what?'

'Why he did it? Why he killed his daughter?' God help her, she'd almost added, *And his wife.*

Trying to get control of her breathing, AnnaLise closed her eyes again. When she opened them, everyone was looking at her.

'Whatever are you talking about?' Sheree asked.

'Ben Rosewood. Have the police asked him why he killed Suzanne?'

James Duende put his hand gently on her shoulder. 'I'm sorry, AnnaLise. I'd forgotten that you know these people.'

'You do?' This from Sheree.

AnnaLise remembered that while James had been in Mama's when she'd first seen Ben and his family, Sheree had no way of knowing even as much as Duende did.

'From work.' Joy was trying to help. 'Rosewood is – or probably was, given what's happened – the County District Attorney and AnnaLise being a police reporter and all . . .' She let it trail off.

Sheree shook her head. 'I'm not sure where you two got the idea that it was Ben Rosewood who killed his daughter, but you have it all wrong.'

AnnaLise sat bolt upright. 'Ben didn't shoot Suzanne?'

'Of course not. Whyever would he?'

'I don't know, but . . .' She shook her head. 'Then who did?'

'Who? Why, Joshua Eames, of course.'

159

Twenty-one

Joy Tamarack pushed the tequila shot over to AnnaLise. 'Drink.'

AnnaLise Griggs had nearly chugged her second beer so she obeyed her friend, but just took a sip. 'Ugh.'

'Don't make faces. James sprung for the good stuff.' Joy pulled back the glass and downed the rest of its contents, then paused to wipe her mouth before continuing. 'Sure are glad they left, though. Hard to talk when they're around.'

Right now, the only thing AnnaLise wanted to do less than talk was think.

'First the wife, now the daughter,' Joy prattled on. 'Maybe you're right about your friend the D.A.'

AnnaLise gave another shudder. 'Don't say that. Don't even think it.'

'Why not?' Joy asked. 'You are.'

'Actually, I'm trying very hard not to, and you're not helping.' She waved to get the waitress' attention, but at least this time the woman was busy at another table. 'Can you get our check?'

Joy ignored her. 'You honestly don't buy this new murder/suicide scenario, do you?'

AnnaLise shrugged. 'Apparently the police do.'

'You don't know that. James and Sheree were just telling us what they'd heard on the TV news

160

tonight.' Joy held up one finger and used it to do an air-signature on her other palm. Now the waitress actually rushed over to drop the slip of paper on the table before marching away again. 'Are you going to tell Chuck?'

'I assume he already knows,' AnnaLise said, slipping cash out of her wallet for the bill.

'You know damn well I'm not talking about the shootings.'

'I do.' AnnaLise stood up and picked up her jacket from the back of the chair. 'What would you have me say?'

'Exactly what you told me,' Joy said as she hopped off her chair. 'That you suspect your boyfriend killed his wife for her money and is trying to pin it on you.'

'Like we said earlier, Chuck is smart. He'll put it together on his own. Right now I'm too tired to think, much less build a case for him.'

'So you get me all wound up and now you're just going to wash your hands? What happened to the woman who was going to fry?'

'She found out about lethal injection.' AnnaLise wound her way between the tables to the door and stopped. 'I'm sorry to have dumped on you. I know I'm shutting down, but . . . I'm confused. I don't know what to think.'

'That's why you have me,' Joy said, pushing the door open. 'I'll tell you what to think.'

'OK,' AnnaLise said, stepping out onto the sidewalk. 'What do I think about Josh supposedly killing Suzanne?'

'The word "supposedly" is a dead giveaway.'

'Don't use dead, at least not tonight, OK?' And

161

maybe never. 'But . . . I have to admit, I have trouble seeing Josh killing Suzanne. Yes, he has a bit of a checkered past and yes, I understand that people saw them fighting. In fact, the last time I saw them together they didn't look happy.' She was remembering the two in Suzanne's Camry, leaving the police department as she'd arrived.

'Only why in the world would he kill her?' AnnaLise thought aloud, but at least she was thinking again.

'A good question. An even better one: why would Josh then shoot himself?'

AnnaLise shook her head. 'I don't know. Lovers' quarrel is what people will say. You know, Suze ended it and Josh wouldn't take no for an answer.'

'Who does that sound like?'

'You mean, Ben?' AnnaLise had an idea. 'Assuming it ran in the family, maybe Josh ended it and Suzanne couldn't take it.'

'So she killed herself at his house. And then what?'

'Josh found her and was so devastated he shot himself?'

'Have you – at any point, during your worst moments – considered killing yourself over Rosewood?'

'No, of course not. But then Ben hasn't killed himself.'

'More's the pity, as James would say.'

'That's a terrible thing to even mull over silently,' AnnaLise said. 'Shame on you, Joy Tamarack.'

162

'This from the woman who was seduced by this much older man, who then followed her here and she now suspects of God-knows-what.'

'He's not much older.'

'You're twenty-eight and he's what – forty?'

'Forty-six.'

'I rest my case.' Joy stepped aside to let a couple exit Torch. 'We're blocking the door. Let's go around the corner to your place.'

Why not? AnnaLise wasn't going to get any sleep that night anyway. She preceded Joy down the sidewalk toward the front door. 'So you've been asking me what I think. What's your theory?'

'Collateral damage.'

'Collateral damage?' AnnaLise stuck the key in the big wooden front door. 'What's the collateral damage? Tanja's Porsche?'

'Not what, who. I think Josh was collateral damage. You know, like poor Ronald Goldman in the O.J. Simpson case.'

'The targeted victim was Nicole Brown Simpson. Doesn't she at least deserve it to be her "case," not O.J.'s?'

'Perhaps, but "should be" and "is" are two different things. And you're avoiding the subject.'

AnnaLise unlocked the Griggs' front door and shoved it open, sending it swinging nearly 180 degrees and into the sill of the window on the wall next to it. 'If you mean by the "subject" Joshua Eames being collateral damage when "my boyfriend" – as you insist on calling him – supposedly killed his own daughter? Yes, I guess I am avoiding it.'

163

'There's that "supposedly" again, but I'm not sure I'm buying it this time.'

'You don't have to "buy" anything,' AnnaLise mumbled, tossing her purse on a small bench next to the telephone.

'Listen, I understand completely,' Joy said, stepping through the door and closing it behind her. 'After all, it's so much harder to believe that your . . . that Rosewood killed his daughter *and* her boyfriend than that he killed his *wife*.' The sarcasm virtually drooled from Joy's mouth. 'You were perfectly happy to speculate about *that* possibility just an hour ago.'

'That's all it was, speculation.' AnnaLise flicked on the light over the kitchen table. 'Daisy must have already turned in, which is good. At least we won't have to relay the latest in Sutherton's checkered recent past just yet.'

'Very recent past. The body probably isn't even cold.' Joy pulled out a chair and turned it around to straddle it.

'Come on, Joy.' AnnaLise was feeling a little sick. 'An innocent girl is dead and a young man I've known all his life is seriously wounded. How about you cut the crap for awhile?'

'Wow, sorry. I always thought you appreciated my rapier wit and unrelenting bluntness.'

AnnaLise almost smiled as she sat down across the table from her friend. After all, this wasn't Joy's fault and she had been nothing but supportive. 'I admit your candor is . . . refreshing. But best in small doses.'

'Point taken.' Joy stretched and started to lean back, only catching herself at the last minute so she didn't tumble off her reversed – and thereby backless – chair. 'Well, I suppose I should go. It's getting late.'

'No!' AnnaLise caught herself in an entirely different way than Joy just had. 'I mean, we just got here. Maybe I should make coffee.'

'So I can sober up before walking the four whole blocks to the inn?'

'Sure.' AnnaLise went to fill the coffee pot.

'You're scared.' It wasn't a question.

'I . . . Yes, I guess I am.'

'Of the man you dated and, knowing you, probably thought you loved for . . . how long?'

'Nearly a year.' Was AnnaLise truly afraid of Ben targeting her, too?

In some ways, maybe. His air of authority could be intimidating, especially for someone who had been raised in a fairly loosey-goosey all-female household. And his ability to convince, to use words to change opinions. It was a power she admired to a point, but as a journalist she believed in providing unbiased information and letting people make up their own minds. To bend information – or to lift even accurate facts out of context, then stringing them together in an effort to mislead. Yes, it was definitely something she feared. At least if it was turned against her.

But, was she afraid of Ben physically? She'd have said no, until . . .

AnnaLise remembered a day, not very long ago, when someone took a shot at Dickens Hart and Chuck suggested they might have been aiming for her. The chief had been kidding, but just for a moment, AnnaLise had wondered whether –

165

'. . . a good thing, at least,' Joy was saying.

'Good?' AnnaLise repeated. 'I'm sorry?'

'Hey, if I'm going to refrain from spewing "crap," as you so genteelly put it, the least you could do is pay attention to my righteous words of wisdom.'

'You're right and I apologize,' AnnaLise said sincerely. 'You were saying?'

'I was saying that, amidst all this, you may be missing the most important facet of the latest development. At least for you.'

'For me?'

'Of course. Don't you see, AnnaLise? Your three theories are, number one,' she held up a thumb, 'your district attorney shot his daughter and Josh. Two,' the index finger joined the first, 'the police are right and Josh killed Suzanne and then shot himself, or three,' middle digit joined in, 'Romeo and Juliet – Suzanne killed herself and then Josh attempted suicide. Right?'

'You forgot one. Suzanne could have tried to kill Josh and then committed suicide.'

'Fine, four,' Joy admitted, raising her ring finger. 'But do you know what these multiple theories have in common?'

'They're all crazy supposition?'

'Yes, but more than that.' Joy leaned over across the table to waggle her four digits in front of AnnaLise's nose.

'They all let *you*, my friend, off the hook.' Joy leaned back. 'At least on the Suzanne/Josh incident, if not the wife/sports car one.'

Twenty-two

Despite Joy's reassurance, AnnaLise didn't sleep that night. In fact, she'd very nearly unlocked her father's gun case to stash a loaded handgun under her bed.

The only reason she hadn't, in fact, was that the whirl in her mind made her afraid she'd be more dangerous to herself or Daisy than she would be to a bad guy.

Whoever that bad guy was.

Ben? She and Joy had certainly constructed a case for that. But in the light of day and after a cup of coffee, it seemed over the top.

'They're saying Joshua Eames killed that girl,' Daisy said, putting down the *Charlotte Observer* as she got up to get the coffee pot.

Charlotte was two hours southeast of Sutherton and the very fact the daily paper of North Carolina's largest city was carrying the story was an indication of widespread interest. And it was only going to get worse. If the deaths of Ben's wife and daughter hadn't gone national by tonight, AnnaLise would shred her reporter's pad.

'Such a shame,' Daisy continued, filling AnnaLise's cup and then her own. 'This will kill his father.'

'You think Josh did it?' AnnaLise asked, surprised. 'I thought you liked him.'

'I do. Or at least I did until *he* did what he did.'

167

AnnaLise took a sip of coffee, despite the fact her stomach was already churning. 'Innocent until proven guilty, Daisy. They have to convince a jury.'

'According to this,' she slid the paper over to AnnaLise's side of the table before sitting back down, 'it won't be all that hard. They're even looking into the possibility that he had something to do with the death of the girl's mother.'

AnnaLise should have felt 'off the hook,' as Joy put it, but having Josh take her place there wasn't much of a relief. 'Have they gotten a statement from him?'

Daisy shook her head. 'Article says he's still unconscious.'

'That would have been from last night, when they went to press,' AnnaLise said. 'We could get more up-to-the-minute information online.'

'You go right ahead and do that,' Daisy said, finishing her coffee. 'But I prefer the more direct route.'

'Calling the hospital?'

'Heavens no.' She rinsed out her cup and put it in the sink. 'Mama's. If it's not being gossiped about, it's not worth knowing.'

'Wait,' AnnaLise said, 'I'm coming with you.'

The place was packed.

'Move those menu boards there, AnnieLeez,' Mama said, 'and you can sit in my booth.'

AnnaLise did as she was told, stacking the dry erase boards on the bench next to her.

Daisy slid in across from her. 'Told you everyone would be here.'

No exaggeration. Every seat was taken. 'Shouldn't we help pour coffee or something? I've never seen Mama's like this.'

'Believe me, you don't want to get in Phyllis's way,' Daisy said, reaching across to pick up one of the menu boards. 'Oh, dear, she mis-spelled "casserole" again. I don't know why she doesn't just wait for me to do these boards. And besides, my handwriting's better than hers, too.'

It was an old argument between the two friends, one that AnnaLise knew to ignore. 'You know, maybe Mama,' she paused to let the woman in question pass by in response to the jangling of the electric door chime. 'Maybe she should "lighten" the menu after what her doctor said about her blood pressure.'

'Cholesterol, not blood pressure, and you're smart to not let her hear you. She *is* trying.'

'Really? The menu looks the same to me.'

'Right here, see?'

'Between the "Tuna Noodle Casserole" and "Scalloped Cream Corn Topped with Buttered Ritz Crackers"? I can't quite make it out.'

'Steamed br . . .' Daisy peered at it, then sighed. 'She's gone and spelled "broccoli" wrong as well.'

'Looks like "brassiere,"' AnnaLise said, squinting.

'I'd appreciate your changing that, before I get another complaint.' Chuck was standing next to their table.

AnnaLise slid sideways to make room for him, relieved that her friend seemed to have warmed some since they spoke in his office yesterday.

'Another? You're kidding right? Who would complain to the police chief about a restaurant's menu?'

'It was "Peking Duck,"' Daisy said ruefully. 'And both words were mangled. Not our finest hour.'

'Peking . . . Ohh.'

'"Ohh," is right,' Chuck said. 'How much did you spend to send this girl away to college, Daisy?'

AnnaLise laughed – it felt like the first time in days, and maybe it had been. 'A veritable pittance compared to what U-Mo would have been.' The reference to the University of the Mountain reminded her of Suzanne Rosewood and the smile faded. 'Speaking of the university, we heard about Suzanne and Josh.'

'It's horrible,' Daisy said, turning over Chuck's coffee mug for him, toward Mama's next round of coffee pouring.

'I'll tell you straight, Daisy,' Chuck said. 'I've never seen anything like what's been happening here the last couple of weeks.'

'And all since AnnaLise arrived,' Daisy said.

'Thanks, mother-of-mine.' AnnaLise slid the creamer to Chuck, slopping a bit of it.

'I don't have my coffee yet.' He didn't look at her.

'If you put the cream in now, before the coffee is poured you won't have to stir it.'

'Your daughter's an odd bird.' This again, directed to Daisy. 'Does she give this much thought to everything?'

'Regrettably, no,' AnnaLise answered before

170

Daisy could. 'Only the things that don't matter.'

Chuck glanced at her. 'Self-awareness is the first step, they say.'

'I'm sorry.' AnnaLise didn't know if she was apologizing for not telling Chuck about her relationship with Ben, or the relationship in general. Chuck seemed angry about both, though AnnaLise would have thought that he, who had feared people's reaction to his own secret, would under—

'Sorry for what?' Daisy had looked up from the menu board.

'Spilt milk,' Chuck injected quickly, holding AnnaLise's eyes as he took the pitcher and poured about half of it in his cup.

'Have a little coffee with your cream,' AnnaLise said. Chuck's doctoring of his caffeine was a long-standing joke. She slid the tall glass sugar dispenser to him as well.

Chuck shook his head, and reached for a small plastic bin. 'I've switched to Splenda.'

'Ah, health kick, huh?'

'I do what I can.' Chuck tore open three sweeteners and dumped them in, cocking his head toward Daisy, who had gone back to the menu.

AnnaLise shook her head in answer to Chuck's unspoken question. No, her mother did *not* know about her affair with Ben. Then the journalist clasped her hands, as if in prayer, aiming the knuckles toward him. *And please don't tell her.*

Chuck nodded as Mama buzzed up to the table. She peered into his cup. 'Hand to God, you're going to run me right out of business with all that cream.' She filled the rest of the cup with coffee and was gone.

He looked down at the brown-tinged combination. 'Now you've gone and done it.'

'What?'

'Got me in trouble with Mama.'

'For using all that cream? You've done that for years.'

'But *she* didn't know it. I'd just ask for half a cup of coffee and then add the cream. She thought I was *saving* her money.'

'The police chief is afraid of Phyllis "Mama" Balisteri?'

'Hell, AnnaLise, everybody is afraid of Mama, you included. Now are you going to ask me about the shooting?'

'If she doesn't, I will,' Daisy said under her breath, still seemingly entranced by the menu board.

'The news is reporting that Josh killed Suzanne and then turned the gun on himself.'

'That's the way it looks,' Chuck said, drinking his coffee.

AnnaLise was used to asking questions, so she decided to conduct the discussion as she would an interview. 'Who' and 'what' accounted for, she turned to 'where' and 'when.' 'The shooting was at the Eames' house, right? Was Fred there?'

'This was late afternoon, just before five. He wasn't home yet.'

'Likely working,' Daisy said, looking up. 'Which is where Josh should have been. That reminds me, AnnaLise. Didn't you say Scotty was supposed to wire the garage today?'

'That's what Fred said yesterday,' AnnaLise

172

said. 'But I didn't see him when we left, and I'm certainly not going to bother Fred about it now.'

'Well, don't try to deal with Scotty directly,' Chuck said, setting down his cup. 'The man is a nasty piece of work and his employees even worse. I'd love to close him down.'

'Should we even be using them?' AnnaLise asked, thinking back to Scotty's truck that had tailgated them on the mountain the day the Spyder had been totaled. In fact, if it hadn't been for the shiny black panel truck, she and Daisy would have stayed on Ridge Road instead of turning onto the supposed dead end and there mightn't have even *been* an accident.

Chuck was shrugging. 'Unfortunately, if you want anything electrical done, you don't have much choice. The company has a veritable monopoly.'

'I hear Scotty threatened the last electrician who dared set up shop here in Sutherton,' Daisy said. 'And don't even think about having him work on wiring he didn't install in the first place.'

'That's ridiculous. How can— You leaving, Chuck?'

The chief was digging bills out of his pocket, tossing some of them on the table, as he stood up. ''Fraid so.'

'Wait!' There was so much AnnaLise wanted to know, but wasn't sure how to find out. She also wasn't sure what to say, if anything, to Chuck about Ben's possible role. 'I assume you've talked to Ben Rosewood? Is he . . . umm, how is he doing?' she settled on.

While AnnaLise's motive for talking to Ben

173

was clear to her, it obviously wasn't to Chuck. His face changed. 'He's at the inn. I suggest you ask him yourself.'

As Chuck left, AnnaLise shot her mother a look. 'Way to go, Daisy. If you hadn't brought up the electrician, I might have actually gotten some more information from Chuck.'

'I don't think it's me you're irritated with,' Daisy said lightly. 'Besides, don't flatter yourself, dear. The chief only gives out as much information as he wants people to know, even you. Are you going to go see your friend?'

'He's not my . . . Yes, I thought I'd go by and offer our sympathy. Do you want to come?' She made the offer, hoping for a negative answer.

'No, I'll stay here with Phyllis. The place is an absolute zoo today, and she'll need help with more than just her spelling.'

AnnaLise got up. 'I thought you said we should stay out of the way.'

'No, dear. I said *you* should stay out of the way. You do tend to complicate matters.'

AnnaLise couldn't argue with that. 'I may also stop by the hospital. Maybe I can see Josh.'

'The hospital is thirty miles away, on the far side of Boone,' Daisy said. 'What if you "stop by" and they don't allow you to see him?'

'Well, then, I'll talk to his father. This can't be easy for Mr Eames.'

'When you see Fred, would you ask about Scotty? I know it's bad timing, as you say, but winter is coming, and I'd like to get the car back into the garage.'

Daisy had a point. It was already the middle

174

of September and snow could arrive in the High Country at any time.

'Sure,' AnnaLise said. 'Might as well kill two birds with one . . .'

She let it drift away, remembering she'd said the very thing about Ben last night – if he'd killed Tanja and successfully pinned it on AnnaLise, the woman who'd spurned him.

Given recent events, though, AnnaLise couldn't even begin to figure out body counts and who was wielding the stone.

Twenty-three

While Joy Tamarack had guessed Benjamin Rosewood's age at forty, today he looked every bit his forty-six years. Plus another decade.

AnnaLise was again sitting in the Sutherton Inn's parlor on the red chair. Ben Rosewood was across from her on the couch, his head in his hands, tousled hair covering his eyes.

'That bastard killed my daughter. And for what?'

'Maybe we'll find out when he wakes up.'

'A bullet went through his head. If he lives, it will likely be as a vegetable.'

'He was . . . He shot himself in the head?'

'First he killed my daughter, then the coward ate his gun.' When Ben raised his head, his eyes were blazing.

'But why?' AnnaLise asked, feeling sick. 'What could be his possible motive?'

'Like I told your chief, I believe Suze tumbled to what he'd done.'

'Meaning your wife's accident.'

'It wasn't an accident!' He slammed his fist down on the end table next to him, making the lamp and cellphone on it jump.

AnnaLise, who had jumped, too, sat up straighter in her chair. 'Your latest theory – after blaming Joy and the spa, of course – was that I had something to do with it. Nice of you to share that with Chief Greystone.'

'I'm sorry, but *someone* shot out the Porsche's tire, resulting in the car going over the cliff and killing my wife. I didn't imagine that fact. *Or* that you called me shortly thereafter and hung up.'

'I started to call to see if you were OK. I thought better of it.'

'Why?'

'Because you and I were no longer a couple, below-board or not. I didn't have the right.'

'Or the responsibility.' He looked up, his eyes regretful. 'I did love you, you know. Of all the women I've known, you were –'

She wasn't buying the puppy dog act, '– the only one you reported to the police?'

Ben put his head in his hands again. 'I . . . I had to tell the chief about the affair. I knew he'd find out eventually, so it was best to be proactive.'

'By throwing me under the truck?' AnnaLise had another thought. 'You knew that if the affair was discovered, you'd be the prime suspect. The husband always is – I can't remember how many times I've heard even you say that.'

The face rose a little. 'I didn't kill my wife.' Perfectly bland. Controlled. 'And I didn't throw anyone "under the truck," as you so charmingly put it. I just reported the facts.'

'You couldn't possibly have believed that I harmed your wife. Why? I ended the affair, Ben, did you forget? Or do you now believe your own lies?'

'That's not the way I remember it.' The way he said it would have made AnnaLise believe him. If she hadn't lived it, too.

'You deleted your text messages on my phone.'

He spread his hands wide. 'I honestly don't know what you're talking about.'

'Fine. You can continue to deny it and I, of course, have no way of proving otherwise.'

'Lise.' He shook his head sadly. 'Do we really have to have this discussion now?'

The use of Chuck's nickname for her raised hackles, but she fought to remain calm. This man fed on confrontation.

AnnaLise took a deep breath. 'You're right. What happened between us is over, so we should let bygones be bygones.'

'Thank you.'

'Please let me know if there's anything I can do for you while you're here.' She stood up as a phone rang in another room. 'I assume you'll be—'

Sheree stuck her head around the corner. 'Excuse me. The chief is on the phone. He says he's been calling, but your cell goes right to voicemail.'

AnnaLise glanced down at her handbag. 'I don't—'

Ben overrode her, nodding to the BlackBerry on the table. 'I turned mine off. Too many crank calls. Is the chief still on the line?'

'Yes,' Sheree said. 'You can take it in the kitchen if you'd like some privacy.'

'Thank you.' He turned to AnnaLise and extended a hand. 'And thank you so much for coming. Now, if you'll excuse me?'

AnnaLise shook hands wordlessly. As Ben left the room, Sheree followed, sending a questioning look in AnnaLise's direction before she rounded the corner.

Left alone in the room, the reporter eyed the BlackBerry. It was the same as hers, so she'd have no trouble turning it on and punching up the text messages. Couldn't hurt to have a look, she thought, moving toward the table. After all . . .

'Excuse me.' Ben's voice was behind her, and his hand jabbed for the BlackBerry. 'I'll be needing that.'

AnnaLise whirled to face him.

'Contact numbers.' Rosewood held the phone up for her to see.

But he had a smile on his face.

Twenty-four

The man was a pathological liar, AnnaLise thought as she began the drive to the hospital. So why had it taken her so long to see it?

'Because he's so damn *good* at it,' AnnaLise said out loud. She pounded the steering wheel with one fist, sending the Chrysler swerving slightly and earning her a surprised look from the driver of the pick-up truck next to her.

But this was the High Country, so there was no horn being blared or finger being thrown. When you were stupid in the mountains, you were expected to realize it and do better next time.

And boy did AnnaLise realize it. Now how could she do better?

For whatever reason, Chuck was currently on the fence about her. Angry, disappointed, even disgusted – AnnaLise wasn't sure, but she did know that something had shifted between them.

Even if AnnaLise went to him at this point and poured out her fears about Ben Rosewood, she wasn't sure the police chief would listen. The undisclosed affair had complicated everything including, presumably, AnnaLise's perceived reasons for trying to reciprocally throw Ben under the same bus previously rolling over her.

No matter what Chuck said about the Wisconsin

180

D.A. not being on the same 'team' as the Sutherton police, the justice system was entirely capable of closing ranks, especially given that Ben was utterly convincing and AnnaLise utterly devoid of proof he'd done anything wrong. In fact, despite her theories, even she herself couldn't be sure he had.

'Just because he's a lying bastard doesn't make him a murderer.'

'The patient is still unconscious and can*not* receive visitors at this time, 'the gray-haired woman at the nurse's station told AnnaLise.

It wasn't a surprise, nor was the police officer she could see sitting on a chair outside a room about two-thirds of the way down the hall.

'I understand,' AnnaLise said to the woman. 'Do you know if his father is with him? I'd like to offer my . . .' What did you offer a man whose son was likely to be charged with murder, assuming he survived. Condolences? Best wishes?

'I'm sure Mr Eames would be very glad for your company,' the nurse said. 'I believe he's in the cafeteria right now, having lunch.'

'Thank you,' AnnaLise said gratefully. 'Can you tell me how to get there?'

'Just follow that green line you can see on the floor by the wall opposite there? Oh, and be certain you don't switch over to the turquoise accidentally. That'll end you up in Radiology.'

The woman's tone and manner reminded her of the nurses who had taken care of her father

– her real father, as far as she was concerned – before his death.

AnnaLise may have been just five, but she recalled the sounds and bustle of the hospital vividly. And, more than anything, she remembered the calm kindness of the nurses who brought coloring books and crayons to the little girl in the waiting room.

The nurses did for her, and her mother and her father, what they would do again and again and again for other families. It was a gift – one that AnnaLise wasn't sure she was capable of giving.

But she was very grateful others were.

'Thanks again,' AnnaLise said, following directions. About halfway there, she no longer needed the line – her nose could have led her to the big room, filled with round tables and chairs. They say that scents trigger memories, even more so than the sights and sounds evoked by our other senses.

'Trays are to your right,' the woman at the cash register said.

AnnaLise nodded her thanks. Passing by the long aluminum buffet counter, she looked around. It was nearly noon, so many of the round tables were already filled with people, a sea of white lab coats and blue or salmon scrubs. Amongst them, AnnaLise caught sight of a familiar blue plaid shirt bent over a soup bowl.

'Mr Eames,' AnnaLise said when she'd reached his table. 'I don't mean to disturb you.'

'AnnaLise,' Fred Eames said, hefting himself to his feet. 'Are you visiting someone here?'

'Actually, I was hoping to see Josh, but I'm

182

told he's still unconscious.' She gave the man a hug.

'I'm afraid so, but that's kind of you.' He was staring at her and she saw tears brimming in his eyes. 'So very, very kind.'

'Please,' she said, waving him back into his chair. 'Don't let your lunch get cold.'

'Won't you join me?' Mr Eames said, more a plea than invitation. 'They have the most wonderful soup. Make it right here. I can't tell you how long it's been since I had homemade beef barley soup. Not that this is quite homemade, of course. More "hospital-made."' An awkward laugh.

'I remember their soup,' AnnaLise said. 'I spent a lot of time here when my dad was sick.'

'You were very little,' he said. 'I'm surprised you can recall that.'

AnnaLise sat down. 'Chicken noodle was my favorite. They made it with those thick noodles you couldn't keep on a spoon. I'd pretend they were trying to escape back into the bowl before I could eat them.'

'Bet your mama loved that. Them big egg noodles splash some.'

'They surely do,' AnnaLise agreed with a smile. Then, 'How is Joshua, Mr Eames?'

'Holding his own, is all they'll say.' He shook his head. 'I tell you, it's been a long night. I . . . I didn't think anyone would . . . Well, it's very, very kind of you to come.'

Poor man. In such pain and here he sat here all alone, except for the guard at his son's door. 'Do you have family coming in?'

'No, no. It's just Joshua and me. We're doing fine, though, just fine.' He was staring at his soup.

'Mr Eames?' AnnaLise put her hand on his. 'I truly don't believe Josh did this.'

And the big, burly man started to cry.

Twenty-five

An hour later they were still sitting at the table. Fred Eames had had a second bowl of soup – this time chicken noodle at AnnaLise's recommendation – and AnnaLise had joined him. Between them on the table was an asymmetrical haystack of cellophane wrappers from the saltines they'd broken into their bowls after the noodles had been slurped out.

Finally sated, AnnaLise sat back. 'Delicious. How can something I associate with such an awful period in my life still taste so good?'

'Maybe because it was the only thing that helped at the time?'

AnnaLise considered. 'And the nurses. I remember them fondly.'

'They have been saints,' Eames said, raising his water bottle in salute. 'Not one of them has looked at me like . . . well, like some other people have.'

'You mean like the father of a murderer?'

'You are a plain-spoken woman, AnnaLise.'

'I learned it from Joy Tamarack,' she said. 'Not to mention being a police reporter.'

'There's been some of them around here, too,' Mr Eames said. 'Though I'm not certain our local papers have police reporters in particular.'

'Not the weeklies, I'm sure, but the *Observer* most likely does. If you are interviewed by

185

reporters, and I'd suggest you consent to that at least briefly, you should think through in advance the things you want to say. Then, everyone you talk to, keep repeating those same things.'

'Is that what you wanted your own – what would you call them, interviewees – to do?'

'Heavens, no,' AnnaLise said. 'I wanted just the opposite, for them to be off the cuff so I could get a striking quote.'

'Well, I don't rightly know what I should say.'

'You might ask your lawyer.'

'Don't have one yet.'

'Well, you need one. Or, more precisely, Josh does.'

'The chief told me the same and I'm looking into it.'

AnnaLise wished she had somebody to suggest, but all the attorneys she knew were in Wisconsin – except for Ben Rosewood, of course.

'They're saying that maybe Josh killed the mother, too,' Fred Eames said. 'What with him being on the mountain around the same time.'

Presumably Monday night, when Tanja Rosewood was killed and AnnaLise and her own mother had nearly followed the poor woman over the edge.

'Which is just plain stupid,' Eames continued, 'seeing as we live right there.'

'Daisy and I were near the bridge, too.'

'Josh told me so. Said he called nine-one-one for you.'

'He did,' AnnaLise said, bobbing her head.

'Given that, would you maybe know something that might help my son?'

186

'I'm afraid not,' AnnaLise said regretfully. 'Daisy and I heard what we thought was a shot as we drove up the gravel trail between Ridge Road and the bridge. I just don't know where Josh was at the time.'

'Could've been on that trail, himself. He tramps through there for a shortcut to our place.'

AnnaLise had been so turned around, literally and figuratively that night, that she had no idea where Josh's truck had come from. 'If so, that means he couldn't have been on the other end of the bridge, shooting the Porsche's tire out.'

'That would be mighty good news,' Mr Eames said. 'Though I don't know how we'd know for sure, what with Joshua still unconscious.'

'Even if he weren't,' AnnaLise said, 'we'd have to prove it.'

'I watch the lawyer movies and TV and all,' Mr Eames said, focusing on her, 'but I have no idea how to go about "proving" anything. You being a reporter and all, I'm thinking maybe you do.'

'I'm not an investigator really,' AnnaLise said. 'Reporting is mostly about answering the questions your readers have. You know, the "who, when, what, where, why and how"?'

'Well, that seems a pretty solid start.'

'It is, if we could get all the answers. You said the police think Josh shot out Tanja Rosewood's tire. Did they say why?'

'Just that she didn't approve of him and her daughter dating, but I think that's hooey. The father didn't seem to have a problem with it. And if Josh killed every parent who didn't want him to see their little girl . . .' Eames flushed.

187

'Josh does have a reputation as a bad boy,' AnnaLise said with a grin to soften it. 'Which girls love, of course.'

'And the boy earned it, I'll have to say. But Joshua has straightened up, though some won't believe it.'

'Well, we'll prove them wrong,' AnnaLise said. 'Now tell me the rest of the police's theory. I understand they think Josh shot Suzanne and then himself. Again, why?'

Eames rubbed his beer belly. 'That's harder to flush out. You can understand they're not giving me a whole lot of information, though I have heard talking out in the hall.'

'Outside Josh's room?'

'Sure. On shift changes, the officer taking over might have some update. Best I can tell, the shooting took place in my own living room.'

'So you haven't been home since it happened?'

'No, ma'am. Or at least no closer than where I park my car. The police stopped me and when they wheeled Josh out, I just went right along with everybody to the hospital.'

'Did they say anything about the crime . . . about the scene? Where the gun was and all?'

'Not where, but one of them did say Josh's fingerprints were on the gun.'

'Not a good sign.'

'Unless it was one of ours, which supposedly it was.'

'The gun?' AnnaLise asked. 'You'll understand that's not exactly encouraging either.'

'I do. But maybe someone broke in and Josh tried to stop them.'

'And the assailant got the gun away from Josh and shot both of them?'

'Had to be a mighty big man,' Eames admitted. 'Joshua's no shrimp. And he's not exactly a slouch with a gun, neither, though he does have trouble with killing things. You saw yourself the other day, AnnaLise. The boy couldn't even do in that spider properly. How can they believe my son could, could . . .' Eames voice broke.

AnnaLise reached across the pile of cracker wrappers. 'Mr Eames, have you thought at all that maybe it was Suzanne who had the gun?'

'You mean she shot Joshua?' Eames thought about that, rallying a bit despite the horror of it. 'Well, I do suppose that's possible. I hear they were arguing.'

'I heard that, too, but do you know what about?'

'Not first hand, but what they're saying is she thought Joshua killed her mother. Not that he did, of course.' He glanced around to see if anyone had overheard.

'Of course not,' AnnaLise confirmed loudly. 'Just a theory.' The last thing the Eames needed was for someone to say they'd overheard Mr Eames say Josh had killed Tanja Rosewood. It might not hold up in court, but it sure could turn the tide of public opinion.

Not that public opinion was on the Eames' side in the first place, given the lack of support AnnaLise had seen so far.

'It's Suzanne's father I can't understand,' Eames said now. 'Joshua said he seemed OK, even if Mrs Rosewood wasn't hot on Josh dating the daughter. I can't imagine why this Rosewood would turn like that and accuse Josh.'

AnnaLise had her theories, but instead asked: 'You said the firearm involved was one of yours?'

'Again, that's what I'm told, though I don't know which one.'

'How many guns do you have?'

'Not many. Maybe five or six rifles and seven or eight handguns.'

Despite being born and bred in the High Country, AnnaLise thought twelve to fourteen firearms in one house was 'many.'

Eames shook his head. 'Though we may still be down one. Josh told me he loaned a piece out just this past weekend and I'm not sure it got brought back.'

AnnaLise's ears perked up. 'He lent a firearm to somebody?'

'Yup, and he's not easy—'

'Who?' AnnaLise interrupted. 'Mr Eames, who did Josh give one of your guns to?' AnnaLise had a feeling she already knew the answer.

'Why, Benjamin Rosewood himself. Seemed he wanted to do some target shooting.'

Twenty-six

AnnaLise just bet D.A. Rosewood had some shooting in mind for the gun Joshua Eames lent him.

'Do you know which firearm he borrowed, Mr Eames?' AnnaLise asked as they followed the green line back toward Josh's room.

''Fraid not. Nor even whether it was a rifle or a handgun. And I wouldn't trust my own count of those still in my house.' A sigh. 'Assuming the police will let me back *in* it. Otherwise, when Joshua wakes up, he can tell us.' Eames raised his chin.

'And I'm sure he will.' She glanced past the uniformed officer to get a glimpse of Josh tangled amongst tubes and IV drips.

'Are you . . .' Eames broke off and waved AnnaLise to move away from the hospital room door and the man who guarded it.

When she did, Mr Eames' eyes had grown wide. 'Are you thinking this Rosewood killed his own daughter?'

AnnaLise shook her head. 'I'm not thinking anything, Mr Eames. Just gathering information, which is what a reporter does.'

'I understand.' Fred Eames wasn't buying it, but he also seemed eager not to upset the wisp of an applecart – in this case, AnnaLise's offer to help – by asking too many questions.

191

'It would be helpful to know what gun was lent and whether it's back in your gun cabinet or wherever you keep them.'

'They're all over. The rifles in a closet. The handguns wherever we think they might come in handy.'

Lovely – just terrific. Good thing there weren't any small children toddling around the Eames' house. 'When you have a chance, maybe you could look around. Is there any chance Rosewood already returned the gun?'

'I suppose. He's had it since Sunday – or maybe even Saturday – though the boy didn't tell me until after the fact. He knows I don't hold with lending firearms.'

AnnaLise had seen Ben and his family for the first time on Monday, but it made sense that they'd been there earlier, since move-in for U-Mo had been Thursday and Friday of the prior week, as witnessed by the rental trailers and vans that had clogged the local roads. 'And when was it he told you?'

Eames cocked his head, thinking. 'Yesterday, maybe, or the day before? So much has happened, I . . .'

'Of course,' AnnaLise said. 'But so far as you know, Ben Rosewood still has it.'

'Unless it found its way back after Josh and I talked.'

They looked at each other, thinking the same thing: *Or the killer brought it back to the house, used it on Suzanne and Josh and left it at the scene.*

'Even if Josh could testify it was the same gun,

we'd be hard-pressed to prove it,' AnnaLise said, thinking out loud.

'They wouldn't believe him?'

'It would be his word against Ben Rosewood.' And if AnnaLise hadn't liked her chances again the D.A., she didn't think Josh stood a chance.

'Maybe someone saw it,' Mr Eames said. 'Josh said Mr Rosewood was going to use the new police range. Could be someone there—'

'Uh-uh.' AnnaLise was shaking her head. 'The chief didn't give him permission, so that's no good. Of course, Suzanne might have seen the gun, but—'

'Not much of a help now, is she?' He glanced back toward Josh's room. 'I'd like to go sit with my son for a while.'

'Of course,' AnnaLise said, walking him to the door.

The police officer stood. 'I'm afraid no visitors other than Mr Eames, ma'am.'

'I understand.' She gave Fred Eames another hug, feeling bad about leaving him alone. 'I'll let you know if I find out anything.'

The uniform stepped aside so Eames could enter, but Josh's father turned at the door. 'Say, that Scotty *did* show up this morning, didn't he?'

AnnaLise smiled. 'Mr Eames, the last thing I want you to do is worry about that right now.'

'I knew it. He didn't, did he? The bastard thinks he owns this town. Well, I'm going to show him different.'

'Truly—'

'Nope, nope.' He was getting out his cellphone. 'I've about got another electrician lined up and this one has balls—' Eames blushed. 'Excuse me, AnnaLise. No reason to offend your ears with what I have to tell Scotty. You run along and I'll take care of this properly.'

The man was punching numbers as AnnaLise left. Reaming out Scotty would likely be the high point of his day.

Not that it would have taken much, given this particular day.

As AnnaLise walked to her mother's car in the parking lot, she saw three women she recognized from town clamber out of a van at the hospital's entrance. They were carrying covered dishes, a fruit basket and, if AnnaLise wasn't mistaken, an entire coffee cake.

Apparently the Main Street cavalry hadn't deserted Fred Eames. They'd merely needed time to arm themselves.

Twenty-seven

'Still no Scotty?' AnnaLise asked.

It was late afternoon and AnnaLise had arrived home to find her mother in the kitchen. Not unusual, in and of itself, but this particular time Daisy was actually cooking.

'Not a sign of him.' Daisy lifted the lid off a big pot of what looked like brown gravy. 'Though someone named Miles called, telling me he'd be taking over the electric side of our job and was it all right if he arrived at eight a.m. tomorrow? I said if he was going to get me my garage wired, I'd have coffee hot and ready by six.'

'I left Mr Eames on the phone at the hospital, saying he was going to fire Scotty. I think it was a nice distraction.' AnnaLise stuck her nose over her mother's shoulder. 'What you making?'

'Beef birds.' She picked up a spoon and stirred, then reseated the cover.

Called *rouladen* in Germany and *braciole* in Italy, Daisy had always referred to the stuffed rolls of thinly pounded steak her mother – and her mother's mother – had made as 'beef birds.'

The Griggs women filled theirs with onion, a sliver of bacon and a pickle spear, then tied them up with cotton sewing thread before browning each roll. Any caramelized bits left in the pan were then made into a gravy to which the birds were returned and cooked for hours. By the time

195

they were finally deemed ready, the meat would be fork tender and the gravy to die for.

You just had to make sure you didn't eat the thread in your enthusiasm.

'Mashed potatoes, too?' AnnaLise asked, reaching over to raise the lid to get a sniff.

'Of course. They're always part of the meal,' Daisy said, taking the cover away from her and replacing it. 'Now leave things alone so they can cook for another hour or two.'

'Rare' meat didn't stand a chance in a Griggs kitchen. 'You haven't made beef birds for ages,' AnnaLise said. 'What's the occasion?'

'No occasion,' Daisy said, turning to the kitchen counter. Turning back, she had a three-by-five-inch notecard in her hand. 'But here, I wrote down the recipe for you.'

AnnaLise took the card, feeling uneasy. 'Did something happen?'

Daisy picked up the frying pan and took it to the sink. 'Happen? What do you mean?'

'I mean this.' She waved the card, though Daisy now had her back to her. 'Did you have another memory blip, which made you want to write down a recipe you know by heart?'

The back of Daisy's head shook. 'Not really. It's just that this afternoon, I set up those tests the doctor wants me to get. And that started me thinking.'

'Well, don't.' AnnaLise said, coming up behind her mother to wrap her arms around her waist.

'Think, you mean?' Daisy asked, twisting to give her a little smile. Unfortunately, a *very* little smile.

'Worry, I mean. Whatever the tests show, we'll deal with it.'

'I know. Now are you going to let me finish up these dishes? I need to start peeling potatoes.' Daisy nodded at the five-pound bag on the kitchen counter. Making three times the amount needed was another proud Griggs tradition.

'I'll help,' AnnaLise volunteered.

'By the way,' she continued as she hunted through the drawer for a potato peeler. 'I talked to Joy and Sheree and they'd love to put a blog right on the front page of the new Sutherton website.'

'"Love to" or are they just doing it because you asked?'

'They were genuinely enthusiastic about the idea.' AnnaLise came up with the peeler. 'It's going to be called "Voices of Main Street" and I'm going to oversee it.'

'That's wonderful.' This time Daisy actually swiveled to face her and the smile was full-sized.

Life-sized.

'I know – should be fun,' AnnaLise said, realizing she meant it. 'You're going to have to do the recruiting, though. We need people with good stories, including you.'

'Good stories are no problem,' Daisy said, handing AnnaLise a newspaper. 'Good writing may be the challenge.'

'Just write the way you talk and you'll be fine.' AnnaLise opened the paper – the previous week's *Mountain Times* – and spread it on the counter to catch the peelings.

197

'You don't want me to do the first one, do you?'

'Blog entry? Why not?' AnnaLise honestly hadn't given it much thought, what with everything else going on. 'It'll be easy.'

'For you.' Daisy got a big kettle out of the cabinet next to the stove and put it in the sink to fill. 'For me, not so much. What would I write about?'

'Sutherton lore. God knows we have enough. The only problem will be choosing something that won't scare off visitors.'

'True.' Daisy put the half-full pot of water on top of the newspaper.

'Since we're moving toward ski season, maybe something about the mountain rather than the lake.' AnnaLise dumped her first peeled potato into the water.

'I don't know as much about the mountain,' Daisy said. Employing a large slotted spoon, she dredged up the potato. 'You didn't dig out the eyes.'

'OK, give it back.' AnnaLise held out her hand. 'Maybe we should have Ida Mae do the first blog then. She's lived on the mountain for years.'

Daisy kept the potato. 'I want to do it.'

'The potato?'

'No, the blog.' She handed over the spud. 'It's easier to get out the eyes with your peeler than it will be with a knife. I'll cut up the potatoes when you're done.'

AnnaLise stabbed the tip of the peeler into the spud and dug out the offending eye. 'Better?'

'You missed one.' Daisy pointed.

'Fine.' AnnaLise applied herself to the potato

198

and then held it up. 'Does it meet your specifications now, Inspector?'

'Just barely.' Daisy took the potato.

AnnaLise moved onto the next. 'So you'll do a few paragraphs about the mountain. Some story from the past, but linked to current time in the lead paragraph. You know, "I was driving up Sutherton Mountain today, remembering—"'

'You sure have a lot of rules,' Daisy grumbled, guillotining the potato with a small cleaver. 'Why don't you write it?'

'That, my dear mother, would defeat the purpose. Tell you what?'

'What?' Another vicious chop.

'I'll set you up on the computer after dinner and do the introduction. You know: new blog celebrating an area steeped in history, blah, blah, bla— What?'

Her mother had stopped slicing and was looking at her. 'You just pulled that out of thin air?'

'I *am* a college graduate and professional writer, you know?' She dumped another potato in the kettle.

Daisy sighed and skimmed out the potato. 'Good thing. If I'd sent you to cooking school, you'd have starved to death by now.'

Dinner, as predicted, was wonderful. AnnaLise filled Daisy in on Josh and her conversation with Fred Eames as they ate.

'You just can't stay out of these things, can you?' Daisy said. 'If you're right, this friend of yours has killed his wife and daughter. Why would you think that's possible? Does he have a history of violence?'

AnnaLise, of course, still hadn't told her mother about the affair and had no intention of doing so if she didn't have to. 'Not that I'm aware of, but he is fairly ruthless in his dealings. Granted, his job allows him to do it under the guise of justice, but . . .'

'All the more reason to stay away from this man, AnnaLise.' Her mother leveled blue eyes at her. 'This isn't in any way your responsibility.'

Oh, but it was, AnnaLise thought. Much as she wanted to spill her guts to Daisy in hopes of having her say otherwise, AnnaLise kept her thoughts bottled up, except for, 'I guess I just feel like if I hadn't talked up the area to Katie, Rosewood's paralegal . . .'

Daisy held her eye for two, three beats, seeming to will her daughter to say more. When AnnaLise didn't, the older woman sighed and stood up. 'We'd best put this food away.'

Many beef birds had been consumed but, despite the two women's best efforts, three-quarters of them and about a gallon of mashed potatoes remained toward leftovers.

'The beef birds I can freeze or maybe take them over to Fred Eames,' Daisy said, sliding the leftovers into the refrigerator. 'What should we do with the potatoes?'

'You'll be eating patties and croquettes until next spring,' AnnaLise said. 'Why do we always make too much?'

'It's the Kuchenbacher way,' Daisy said, adding soap to the dishwasher and closing the door. 'As it was, as it is, as it will always be.'

The Rule of Three – even her mother used it.

'Speaking of things as they were, I'm going to get you set up on a page and write a quick opening, then you can start the blog.'

'Well, if you really want me to write what people want to read, plunging off the mountain roads has a long history in Sutherton. I can pin it to recent events, like you said.'

'Please don't mention the Rosewood woman's death,' AnnaLise begged. Then she had an idea. 'You know, Chuck was scolding me about our taking that dead-end shortcut.'

'I'm not surprised,' Daisy said. 'The police have been trying to keep people from using it since even I was young.'

'He says it's dangerous.'

'That's what was claimed when they put up the signs after the bridge opened, but I think the major danger was to the preservation of the local kids' virginity.'

'So why don't you write about that and the lore that surrounds it?' AnnaLise suggested. 'We were just up there, so the lead-in can talk about how that was a reminder of your own misspent youth.'

'I didn't say my crowd hung out there,' Daisy said. Her tone was indignant, but a smile played around the edges of her mouth. 'At least, not that much.'

'See?' AnnaLise said. 'It's already bringing back nostalgic moments. Just don't give driving directions or Chuck will have our heads.'

Sitting down at the computer, the daughter worked up a quick intro to the new blog in general and her mother, the first blogger. When AnnaLise was ready to show it to the older woman, however, she was nowhere to be found.

'Daisy?'

'Upstairs. I'm getting dressed to go over to Torch. You want to come?'

It was sad to be a twenty-something whose mom had a better social life than you did. 'No, but I thought you wanted to work on the blog?'

'I need to let the ideas percolate,' Daisy said, coming down the steps. She was wearing straight-leg jeans and a sparkly shirt that AnnaLise wouldn't mind borrowing. Her mother, truth to tell, also had sexier underwear than she did.

'You look nice,' AnnaLise said. 'Meeting someone?'

'Who knows,' Daisy said. 'The night is young and so I am. Sure you don't want to come?'

'To be my mother's wing man? I think not.'

'Don't worry, dear,' Daisy said, parting a curtain at the front window to look out. 'I'm not prowling for a new daddy for you. Just socializing.'

'Good thing,' AnnaLise said. 'I already have one more than I want.'

Now, though, she glanced out the window as Daisy moved to the door. 'What were you looking at?'

'I just thought I saw a car.' Daisy put her hand on the knob, then said over her shoulder, 'Have I mentioned I'm sorry about that?'

'About what? Dickens Hart being my biological father? You have, but I'm sorry – it just doesn't ring true.'

'Water over the bridge, dear.' Daisy picked up

her purse with her free hand. 'You can't change yesterday by regretting it today. You just have to move—'

A combination of sounds and sensations: shattering, splintering, spraying.

When AnnaLise opened her eyes, a window pane was gone.

The first police officer was there within minutes, probably because AnnaLise told Coy Pitchford, who was manning the desk, about the bullet hole in the wall.

That officer was soon followed by Chuck and a crime scene technician.

'Daisy was just looking out that window, Chuck,' AnnaLise said, keeping her voice down, partly because she was afraid it, too, would crack if she raised it.

'I think she knows that, AnnaLise,' Chuck said. 'Why are you whispering?'

'I don't want to upset her.'

'Heavens, I'm not upset.' Daisy had come up behind them. 'In fact, it's rather . . . exhilarating?'

'Think how "exhilarating" it would have been if you'd been hit,' AnnaLise scolded.

'You're all right, Daisy?' Chuck asked. 'You don't think we should transport you to the hospital?'

'No, no – I'm fine. Is there anything else I can do for you?' Daisy was picking up her handbag from the floor where she'd dropped it when the window exploded.

'Where are you going?' AnnaLise demanded.

'Torch, as I told you. Honestly, AnnaLise,' she said, swinging open the door. 'You really should have your own memory checked.'

The door closed behind her.

AnnaLise looked at Chuck. 'So what do you think?'

'Me? I think your memory's passable, but you *do* tend to nag.'

AnnaLise rolled her eyes. 'I meant about our window being shot out.'

'Could have been a drive-by.'

'In Sutherton?'

'Not exactly big-city kind of drive-by. More like good ol' boys on Main Street shooting into the air. You never know where the bullets are going to come down.'

'But usually not by making a ninety-degree horizontal turn through a vertical pane of glass.'

'Maybe not, but it could have been a ricochet. Or some other odd, unpredictable thing. We're just going to have to wait on the crime scene guys telling us more.' Chuck turned away.

AnnaLise swallowed, feeling sad and alone.

She followed him to where he was conversing with his first-responder. 'Chuck . . . um, Chief, when you're done, could I talk to you? Alone?'

He looked surprised. 'Sure.' Then to his officer. 'When you're done here, get somebody to cover this window, then Waddell and you can head back to headquarters.'

The officer nodded and Chuck and AnnaLise moved away to the small parlor.

They didn't sit.

'Chuck, are you angry with me?'

'Why?'

'I don't know. It's just,' she looked over her shoulder, 'ever since I told you about my relationship with Ben Rosewood . . . or didn't first tell you, I've sensed a . . . difference in you.'

Chuck's face in the light coming from the kitchen didn't change. 'Toward you?'

'Yes. I'm really sorry I didn't tell you everything right away, but it's not something I was – or am – proud of.'

Still no response.

'Will you at least say *some*thing?'

Chuck cocked his head and then slowly shook it. 'I'm not mad, Lise, so much as surprised. I mean, you? With a married man?'

She closed her eyes and took a deep breath. 'I know. And I'm ashamed, but . . . like Daisy said, we can't change yesterday, we just have to go forward. Ben Rosewood is not a good man.'

'Please, don't take that tack.' The chief's eyes didn't leave hers, didn't blink. 'Don't make this all Rosewood's fault, because he was married and you weren't.'

'I'm not. It's just, just that he . . .' She took a deep breath and tried to compose herself. 'I'm sorry, Chuck. I thought that you of all people would –'

'– understand? Why?' Now he did look angry. 'Because I'm gay? Monogamy isn't valued only in the straight community. Nor is honesty.'

Chuck went to move past her toward the front door, but stopped. 'Sometimes, Lise, not being bound by the rules makes it even more important to play by them.'

'You're right,' she whispered hoarsely, closing her eyes against the tears that were welling in them. Then AnnaLise felt a squeeze of a hand on her arm and, when she opened her eyes, Chuck was gone.

The window was boarded, but AnnaLise didn't feel safe. She felt . . . hollow. Empty.

It was only nine p.m., so sleep was not an option. She considered joining her mother next door at Torch, but despite the desire for some normality, she didn't want to have to make small talk.

That seemed to leave just the Internet. AnnaLise's computer was still on, with the start of Daisy's blog glowing on the screen. AnnaLise saved the document into a new folder, at first hesitating, then naming it 'Blog.'

'Pithy, huh?' she said to her computer. 'Afraid that's about all the creativity you're likely to get from me at the moment.'

Just above 'Blog' alphabetically was a folder labeled 'Ben.' 'Equally pithy, no? Although if I named the file "Bastard," it would not only be closer to the top, but more descriptive.'

AnnaLise considered deleting 'Ben' in a grand gesture without opening it. With the exception of the last few texts Ben had purged from her phone, she'd heeded his advice and kept very little on either her computer or phone that could be incriminating.

Incriminating. The word reminded AnnaLise of the legal system and, therefore, Chuck. Had she actually thought that because he was gay, he'd think cheating was OK?

Or, if not OK, at least . . . less bad?

Irritated with herself, AnnaLise double-clicked on the 'Ben' folder. As she'd expected, there wasn't much. Indeed, there was just one substantive document and it was entitled 'end.' She hadn't even bothered to capitalize the word.

She clicked.

'*Why can't we be together?*' the copied and pasted incoming message read.

Then AnnaLise's trilogy reply, carefully composed on the computer: '*Three reasons: you have a wife, you have a daughter, and I have a mother who needs me.*'

Complete with creation date, if not when ultimately sent by text, thereby at least supporting AnnaLise's claim that she'd been the one to break off the adulterous relationship. Not that it mattered much anymore.

AnnaLise reread her reply.

'Oh, dear God.'

Twenty-eight

'So, what are you thinking? Two down and one to go?'

AnnaLise had called Joy Tamarack and asked her to come over. Her reward was her friend's company.

Her punishment was her friend's mouth.

They were sitting at the kitchen table again, and AnnaLise rubbed her sore head. 'I honestly don't know anymore.'

'You want me to tell you? Your message to him said you two couldn't be together because of his wife, who is dead; daughter, who is also dead—'

'And my mother,' AnnaLise reminded her.

'Yes, the one who was just shot at. Any idea whether it was the same gun?'

'That shot out our window? It couldn't be the Eames weapon,' AnnaLise said. 'That was left at the scene and the police have it.'

'Does it match the bullet from the Rosewoods' tire?'

'I don't know,' AnnaLise said, sitting up straight and reaching for her cell. She stopped.

'What?' Joy asked.

'I was going to call Chuck.'

'Then call him.' She looked at the kitchen clock. 'It's only ten.'

'Our chief isn't very happy with me,' AnnaLise

said. 'My affair with Ben Rosewood, remember?'

'Oh, right. Do you want *me* to call him?' Joy asked, picking up AnnaLise's phone and thumbing through contacts. 'I can tell him about your suggested hit list, too.'

'Are you kidding? It's as much an indictment of me as it is Ben. In fact, I'm surprised he hasn't already shown it to the police.'

'Maybe he has and that's the reason Chuck's not speaking to you. With it, you've become his prime suspect.'

AnnaLise shook her head. 'The prime suspect now is Josh, I'm afraid.' She filled Joy in on that side of the situation.

'So there's a police officer stationed at his door?'

'I assume when Josh wakes up, they'll read him his rights and place him under arrest. *If* he wakes up,' she amended.

'Hope they're being as careful about who they let in to see him as who they let out,' Joy said.

'They are. In fact, when I was there . . .' She stopped. 'You're saying that Josh could be in danger?'

'From what you've told me, he's the only one who knows what really happened at the Eames' house. If you're right about Rosewood, Josh's the only one who can wreck his plan.'

'Josh *is* the real threat to Ben,' AnnaLise said, impressed again with Joy's reasoning. 'Unless Ben knows somehow that the poor kid won't regain consciousness. Maybe, as a prosecutor, he's seen enough similar cases to know which headshots are fatal and which aren't.'

'And which scramble the brain and which don't.'

'True, but even so, even if he actually believes Josh's not a danger, why target Daisy? She certainly doesn't pose a threat to him.'

'Yeah, but her daughter does. And don't forget: you're the one who put Daisy – and Tanja, and Suzanne – on your list.'

For which AnnaLise Griggs didn't think she could ever forgive herself.

That night, AnnaLise did get a revolver from her father's gun cabinet, loaded the cylinder, and slept with the weapon under her pillow.

Sleep proved tough to come by, and when she did fall off she dreamt about their front window. In the dream, it was a simple lighted frame, first with Daisy's head silhouetted in it, then AnnaLise's, as she looked out to see what had caught Daisy's attention. And then . . . everything went black.

The next morning, AnnaLise sat down at the kitchen table with a cup of coffee and called the police station. Not sure that she wanted to talk to Chuck – or that he would be willing to talk to her – AnnaLise was relieved when Charity Pitchford answered the phone.

'I heard what happened at your mother's place last night. Is she all right?'

'Yes,' AnnaLise said, glancing toward Daisy sitting at the desk and in front of the computer. 'Up pre-dawn and composing a blog.'

'A blog? Bless her heart, that woman is a marvel. And so resilient.'

'She certainly is,' AnnaLise said. 'Whereas I'm the worrywart in the family. Did you get any *other* reports of gunfire last night?'

'In fact, we did. Let me see.' AnnaLise could hear the clacking of keys and the rustling of papers. Then Charity was back on the line. 'The other report was from Church Street, just a block and a half away from you.'

'Did anybody see the shooter or shooters?'

'No, although this other homeowner had damage as well. Three brand-new front windows blown out.'

AnnaLise whistled, all the while feeling relief that perhaps the Griggs weren't solely the intended targets of the shooter. 'Lucky we have just the one window facing the street.'

'If everyone and their brother didn't have a gun, we wouldn't have all these shootings,' Charity said.

'Very true,' said AnnaLise, remembering the police officer was not native to the High Country where people like Fred Eames considered four-teen weapons a modest cache. Speaking of . . . 'Any word on Joshua Eames' prognosis?'

'Much better than the girl he shot,' Charity said dryly. 'Looks like he's going to be just fine.'

'Really?' AnnaLise was astonished, but relieved. 'I stopped by the hospital to see his dad yesterday and Josh was still unconscious.'

'"Was" is right. He came to last night. In fact, the chief went right from your house over to the hospital, for all the good it did him.'

'Josh wouldn't talk to Chuck?' Maybe Fred Eames had taken AnnaLise's advice and hired a lawyer.

'Oh, he'd talk, but what he told the chief isn't worth the paper it's written on.'

AnnaLise smiled at the expression. 'What do you mean?'

'I mean, Joshua Eames says he doesn't remember a thing. Convenient.'

And, perhaps, true. After all, the young man had been shot in the head. 'Is Josh under arrest?'

'He is, and we'll most likely be transporting him to jail as early as this afternoon if all the tests come out clean.'

'So soon?'

'The gun must have slipped as he pulled the trigger and missed doing any real damage. Like I said, though, we'll know more later in the day. Well . . .'

Charity's voice signaled she was getting ready to say goodbye.

'Wait, before we hang up,' AnnaLise said hastily. 'I meant to ask Chuck yesterday if he'd been right about the slug in Mrs Rosewood's tire. Did it match the weapon used at the Eames' place, like he thought it would?'

A silence. 'Well, I could transfer you over so you could ask the chief himself –'

'No, really. Don't bother him, I—'

'– but since I just sent the information over to the press, I don't think there's any harm in telling you what little we know. As was expected, the slug was so damaged the only thing the lab can be certain of is that it's twenty-two caliber.'

'Is that the same caliber as the gun that killed her daughter?' AnnaLise left out Joshua Eames, since Charity obviously wasn't a fan.

'And most deer rifles you'll find around here.'

'Deer rifle?' AnnaLise looked at her cellphone like it was lying to her. 'How in the world does someone shoot himself with something as long as a deer rifle?'

'Simple. You take your sock off, put the rifle between your legs – butt end down, of course, barrel in your mouth – and use your toe to fire the weapon.'

'You're kidding.' AnnaLise was trying to picture how that might be done. *Without* picturing the result.

'AnnaLise, we're of fairly short acquaintance,' Charity said, 'but of one thing you can be sure: I don't joke about something like this.'

'Sorry, of course you don't. I'm just . . . and you're sure it was a hunting rifle because it was left at the scene?'

'Correct. Right there on the floor next to its owner's son. And his discarded sock.'

AnnaLise slid the phone onto the table. Then she picked up the morning's *Charlotte Observer* and stared at it, before setting that back down, too.

Could she have been wrong? Had Joshua Eames killed Suzanne and then shot himself? The evidence seemed damning.

But . . . it *was* evidence, something a seasoned prosecutor like Ben Rosewood might know about. AnnaLise was trying to imagine the man she knew removing Josh's sock and shoe while the boy lay there—

'"Dead end" – one word or two?' Daisy swiveled from the desk.

213

'Two,' AnnaLise said.

'Makes sense,' Daisy said. 'Otherwise it could be confused with "deadened."'

'That has an extra "e."'

'What does?' Daisy was clicking away at AnnaLise's keyboard.

'The word "deadened," as in "the pillow deadened the sound of the gunshot."'

'Well, aren't *we* a ray of sunshine? And speaking of sunshine, maybe you should get outside and absorb some. You're pale as can be.'

'What is today – Saturday?'

'AnnaLise, you're too young to lose track of the weekly calendar. Today is Friday.'

'It's from not working. Not being on a schedule.'

A phone rang and AnnaLise looked around.

'Isn't that your cell?' Daisy asked.

'It is, but where's my purse?'

'There.' Her mother pointed at the bag on the chair next to the desk. 'But it's the newspaper next to your coffee cup that's ringing.'

AnnaLise dug her cellphone out from under the *Observer*. The caller ID read: Sutherton Auto.

'Hello?'

'Ms Griggs. This is Earl, over at Sutherton Auto? I just got in a used car you might like to see.'

'I'm sorry Earl, but I don't think I—'

'It's Japanese, like your Mitsubishi, but the current model year. The owner is anxious to sell and will take any reasonable offer. I told him I'd broker the deal.'

'Well, I—'

'It's clean as a whistle or will be if you can

214

give me an hour or two. We're usually closed on Fridays, but I'd be happy to stay until you get here.'

Closed on Fridays? Welcome to the High Country. Our slogan? 'I'll do what I damned well please.'

AnnaLise looked toward her mother's back, hunched over the keyboard. She was busy working on the blog and AnnaLise did need a car.

'Sounds good, Earl. I'll come take a look.' She checked her watch. 'It's ten thirty and you said you need an hour to get the car ready to show?'

'Better give me two,' he said. 'It's a beauty but was owned by a student and you know the kind of mess they can make. CDs, clothes, food – you'd swear the girl practically lived in the vehicle.'

The 'girl'? And a student. It couldn't be. It just plain . . . 'Earl, what kind of car did you say it was?'

'I don't believe I did, but we're talking a Toyota.'

'A Toyota Camry?'

'Yes, ma'am. A new XLE with all the bells and whistles.'

'It's red.' AnnaLise's reply wasn't a question.

'Barcelona Red Metallic, the manufacturer calls it,' Lawling said. 'But how did you know?'

Because Suzanne Rosewood drove a red Toyota Camry.

'Earl, I'll be right over. Meanwhile, don't start cleaning up – or out – that car.'

'Don't—' But AnnaLise had already broken the

215

connection, grabbed the keys to her mother's Chrysler, and yanked open the front door to their apartment.

'Love you, too,' Daisy said, sounding more absent-minded than sarcastic to her daughter as she hit the sidewalk.

Twenty-nine

AnnaLise drove to Sutherton Auto, not knowing what she was going to do when she got there. She was sure what she'd find, though, and she was right. She also should have known Earl Lawlings wouldn't be able to resist tidying it up.

'This is Suzanne Rosewood's car.'

Earl Lawling whistled. 'Good eye, though it's true that anything that's not a truck, an SUV or another four-wheel drive vehicle does stand out around here. You can be sure, though, that I did have every intention of telling you the previous owner met a violent death.'

'Of course.' AnnaLise didn't really believe that, but she didn't much care right now. 'Her father is selling it?'

Lawling nodded. 'What with all that's happened, he needs to tie up the loose ends here, then fly back north to make arrangements.'

'So sad,' AnnaLise said, with what she hoped was the right note of sympathy for the scumbag. 'But with the Porsche totaled, how will he get to Charlotte/Douglas for his flight if he does sell this?'

The High Country was not Boston or New York, where you could flag a cab to the airport. Which, by the way, was between two and two-and-a-half hours away, depending on traffic. And weather.

217

'He's taking one of my SUVs as a rental and leaving it at the airport tomorrow.'

'Tomorrow?' AnnaLise repeated. 'That's quick.'

'Like I said, the man's got multiple arrangements to make for both his wife and daughter's resting places.'

'But what about the investigation – or investigations, also multiple? I'm surprised Mr Rosewood doesn't feel like he needs to stay until those are concluded.'

'Well, hard for me to answer for the man, but I don't see things can get too much more "concluded" than they already are.' Lawling opened the driver's-side door. 'Leather-trimmed seats. Nice, huh?'

'Beautiful.' replied AnnaLise. 'But what do you mean about the investigation?'

'Well, they already have the killer.' Lawling shook his head sadly. 'I've known Fred Eames for thirty years. He surely doesn't deserve the kind of sorrow he's seen.'

'You're convinced Joshua Eames killed Suzanne?'

'Not just me, but pretty much everyone from what I hear. And not just the girl. I stopped down at the police station to see how they were coming on that slug I pulled out of Mrs Rosewood's tire and the chief told me it could've come from the very same gun that killed the daughter.'

Earl Lawling swept his hand toward the car. 'Why don't you just slide on in? See how she fits you.'

AnnaLise complied. 'Mr Eames told me that Josh'd lent that gun to someone.'

218

About to swing the door closed, Lawling froze. 'How could that be? It was found right there next to the boy from what the chief told me.'

AnnaLise noticed there was no mention of the sock. 'Maybe someone brought it back. Like the killer.'

Lawling gave a strangled laugh. 'Sounds like someone's been watching too much television, though I'm not sure if it's you or Josh coming up with these wild theories.'

'Josh's been unconscious, or he was until last night.'

'The boy's woke up?' Lawling apparently hadn't heard that news, at least. 'Well, then, if you're right, he should be able to tell the police what happened.'

'Joshua Eames doesn't have any memory of that night, at least not yet. And even if he eventually does remember . . .' AnnaLise decided to leave it there. Naming Ben Rosewood would not only be stupid, but might land her in a courtroom defending herself against slander charges on top of everything else. 'Well, even if Josh says he does recall, who knows?' she ended lamely.

'Well, I certainly don't,' Lawling said, dangling the key. 'And sounds like you don't neither, so how about you take this little beauty out for a test drive?'

AnnaLise hesitated.

'Multi-stage, heated front seats.' Lawling reached down to push a button on the door side of her seat. 'Plus eight-way power-adjustable driver's seat with lumbar support.'

AnnaLise's seat was undulating. 'Ooh, nice.'

The car really did have everything, including a blue, glowing gauge cluster, navigation system and . . . 'Oh, my Lord, is that a USB port?'

'It surely is. I'm telling you, no expense was spared. That Mr Rosewood truly seems to have loved his daughter.'

AnnaLise wasn't so sure Ben loved anything or anyone, except himself. Still . . . she looked around. 'I do need a car.'

'And I'm telling you, the price is right. Mr Rosewood said that if you wanted it, he may be willing to negotiate. Might let it go for as little as sixteen.'

'Thousand?'

Lawling looked offended. 'This is the V-6, with only eight thousand miles on it. Fully loaded like it is, the vehicle would have fetched over thirty, thirty-five new.'

'I'm sure it did, but I was really looking for something closer to . . . Did you say if *I* wanted it? Did Mr Rosewood ask you to offer it to me, specifically?'

'Why, sure.' Lawling hiked up his pants. 'He remarked on your accident and I told him you were likely in the market for a car. He said this was a way of something good coming out of the tragedy.'

'So Ben Rosewood had you call me?' AnnaLise asked. 'Why not do it himself?'

'Well, now, this is only my opinion, but I think he was feeling badly about selling the car in the first place, though what with him having to leave and all . . .'

And all, being the operative part. Still . . .

AnnaLise ran her hand over the leather covered steering wheel. Her Spyder's had been grubby tan plastic and sticky in places.

'I suppose it couldn't hurt to take it for a spin.' She held out her hand for the key. 'Are you coming?'

'I believe I can trust you.' Lawling dropped the key-fob in her hand. 'In fact,' he pulled out his cellphone and checked the time. 'I see it's nearly noon, and I promised my girlfriend I'd take her over to the outlet mall. If you don't mind, I'll ask you to park the car right here where you found it and drop the key in there.'

AnnaLise followed his index finger to a box on the wall next to the door of the sales office.

'You're going to just let me take it?' AnnaLise was looking for the ignition on the steering column. 'Don't you want me to leave my ID or charge card or something?'

'Well, I'm fairly sure I know where to find you if you don't bring her back. Besides, this way you can take a nice long test drive and see what you really think without worrying about me back here waiting on you.'

'All right, if you're sure,' AnnaLise conceded. 'Where's the ignition?'

'Right there.' Lawling pointed to a button on the dash.

AnnaLise looked at the fob in her hand which, now that she noticed, didn't have an actual key attached. 'Ohh, this is one of those keyless ignitions.'

'Not just that, but it's also a remote starter.'

Wait. 'You mean in the winter I could stand

inside at a window and start my car like on the commercials?'

'Yup, as long as that window's not more than, say eighty feet away from your car.' Earl seemed to sense he had a live one. 'See, you just push unlock on this remote twice quick and then hold it down for three seconds.'

Voila. Like magic, the Camry started.

Ben had purchased this scientific marvel for an eighteen-year-old? AnnaLise bought the Spyder – already rode hard and put away wet – when she moved from Sutherton. It hadn't even had remote *locks*, much less a remote starter.

'To turn the car off, you just push unlock. Not only that,' Earl continued, 'but if you set the temperature you want the car to maintain, it'll have it all toasty for you by the time you climb in.'

AnnaLise was thinking about those long, cold Wisconsin winters. Longer and colder, seemingly, than what she remembered from growing up in the High Country.

She tried not to seem too eager. 'Well, then, what's to be done with this?' she asked, holding up the fob.

'Anything you want. Your handbag or pocket, or right here in the cupholder, and you're good to go.'

'Gotcha.' AnnaLise dropped it into her jeans pocket. Asking another question – this one about what would happen if she left the fob in the cupholder and got out and locked the car – would only serve to damage her bargaining position even more. 'Thanks, Earl. I'm sure I won't have it out long.'

'Take your time. Like I said, no hurry.' Lawling had already started away toward what she presumed was his black SUV, dialing his cell as he walked, probably calling his girlfriend toward the trip to the mall. Shopping in the High Country – like getting to the airport – was often a major expedition.

Inching down the gravel driveway so as not to ding the Toyota's finish, AnnaLise wondered where she should go on *her* expedition. So far the car drove like a dream, but she knew that if she were to splurge for the Camry she needed to put the unfamiliar vehicle through more demanding paces than a few miles of state highway before driving it through the mountains and back to Wisconsin alone.

Girding herself, AnnaLise turned right toward the Blue Ridge Parkway. Heading north on the highway took her past the upper entrance of Sutherton Mountain and then, as the road veered west, the gated access to Grandfather Mountain. Here, visitors could pay an entry fee and explore the pristine landmark including, if one were so inclined, crossing a mile-high swinging bridge on foot.

AnnaLise had never been so inclined. In fact, she'd have to be prone and comatose to even consider it.

Which reminded her of Josh. Now conscious but apparently clueless in the hospital. If Ben was leaving tomorrow, he must not consider Josh a threat. And, therefore, Ben wasn't a threat to Josh, at least in a physical sense.

Deep in her thoughts, AnnaLise missed the

entrance to the Parkway, only realizing when the road she was on dipped under the Blue Ridge. Five years away from the High Country hadn't helped her sense of direction, which had never been particularly good anyway. In fact, after she'd gotten her driver's license, she'd become very adept at avoiding any routes that would take her on roads she viewed to be 'scary.'

Like a nonagenarian who preferred to make only right turns, AnnaLise would get there eventually, but it might take her awhile. In the mountains it took a *long* while and the paralyzing fear really had shadowed her teen years. She'd be a fool to let it continue through to her thirties.

AnnaLise finally found a place where she could turn around safely and head back to the Parkway entrance. Taking a right at the small Blue Ridge sign this time, she followed the road as it snaked around and stopped at a stop sign. This part of the Parkway circled Grandfather Mountain. Counterclockwise took you north around the mountain to the Linn Cove Viaduct. Clockwise, or south, was less challenging and had the advantage of putting you on the side of the two-lane road closest to the mountain instead of to the abyss.

AnnaLise planned to go safely south for this first foray, so she turned left onto the Parkway, which should have taken her in that direction. It was only when she caught a glimpse of a 'North' sign that she realized she'd gotten turned around and was heading the wrong way.

No worry, she told herself. Although the Linn

Cove Viaduct was much higher than the bridge on her own Sutherton Mountain, it had an absolutely gorgeous view. In AnnaLise's experience, though, it was tough to appreciate that when you're sobbing hysterically from fear.

Still, there had to be at least one or two scenic overlooks before she'd reach the viaduct itself. She could pull through the gravel apron of the overlook and back onto the Parkway heading the other way – blissfully and safely southward.

AnnaLise checked her rear-view mirror and saw to her dismay that a dark SUV was closing in on her. The maximum speed on the Parkway was forty-five miles per hour, even lower in some sections. But no matter the posted limit, it always seemed about ten miles an hour too fast for AnnaLise. Other motorists disagreed – especially locals who actually needed to get somewhere and were sick and tired of timid tourists puttering along.

With no way to pull over and let the other vehicle pass, AnnaLise pressed lightly on the Camry's gas. The car jumped forward, startling her. The Spyder hadn't been nearly as responsive.

More nervous by the moment, she nevertheless chanced another look in the rear-view and, though reassured the other vehicle was still well back, she did manage to miss a turn-off for one of the Parkway's scenic overlooks.

Damn. Ahead she could see the Linn Cove Viaduct snaking alongside Grandfather Mountain, supported by nothing more than giant, concrete toothpicks. Whether AnnaLise liked it or not, she would be on the bridge in mere moments, with nothing to be done but remember she was a big girl and push through her fear. Preferably without wetting any undergarments.

One more curve, and the sound of the road under the Camry's tires changed from the rumble of asphalt to the whoosh of concrete. An engineering wonder: an S-curve four football-fields long and cast in 153 fifty-ton segments so it could be lowered into place without damaging even the surface of one of the oldest mountains in the world. The only work done on the ground was the drilling for the footings of the seven abutments – AnnaLise's concrete toothpicks – that supported the viaduct.

AnnaLise knew all these facts and figures as she crept along, white-knuckled hands strangling the steering wheel while she tried to concentrate only on the road in front of her and ignore the nothingness to her right and the SUV nosing ever closer behind. She even appreciated the vision and tenacity of the engineers determined to complete the most complicated concrete bridge ever built and do it at a height of over four thousand feet.

But she dared not focus on any of that. All AnnaLise should think about was getting to the end of their viaduct. Turning the steering wheel at just the right angle to hold the curve, feeding the Camry just the right amount of gas as it came out of the turn. Every small movement was exaggerated in importance, every millisecond like an eon.

And through it all, AnnaLise wanted nothing

more than to let go and close her eyes. To let the big kid in the schoolyard finally tag her in a game she knew she was destined to lose anyway.

Just to get it over with.

'Chicken-shit.' AnnaLise had said it aloud, and now she said it even louder. 'Chicken-shit!'

Her mother drove this road. 'Hell, ninety-year-old Mrs Peebly drives this road,' AnnaLise yelled into thin air. 'I am no . . . chicken-shit!'

Her hands were relaxing on the wheel and she tried to become one with the last of the curves, riding inside it instead of fighting its centrifugal allure. Skimming along the beautiful stretch of road, instead of fearing it. Delighting in the changing colors of the trees below while hugging that last bend like a downhill skier.

And AnnaLise was, finally, on solid earth.

She didn't dare look back, but she wanted to. Maybe let out a hoot and a holler. 'I did it,' AnnaLise said, also aloud. 'Not only that, but I genuinely enjoyed it.' A hesitation. 'At least the last part.'

She heard a light tap-tap of a horn behind her and glanced in the mirror. Could that be Earl in the SUV? The Blue Ridge was one possible way to the mall he said he and his girlfriend wanted to visit and, in fact, the most direct route. Since the windows of the bigger vehicle were tinted, AnnaLise couldn't make out who was driving or even how many people were inside.

She raised her hand in greeting, in case it was Earl, or in apology if it wasn't. AnnaLise was feeling a little light-headed as the adrenaline faded away.

'Chicken-shit,' she said again, and this time laughed.

The driver tapped his or her horn again and AnnaLise realized she should pull off at the next overlook, not only as a courtesy, but to get out and walk around. Relax a little before heading back, this time south across the viaduct.

More circle-driveway than actual lot, the next turnout she came to had just enough room for perhaps two or three vehicles to park nose-in on either side of a small stand of trees. AnnaLise turned off anyway, raising her hand again in a 'thank you for your patience' gesture to the driver behind her, only to realize the SUV was turning in behind her.

Wonderful. Probably going to tell her what a bad driver she was. Or, even worse, ask if AnnaLise was all right. *Or maybe it's Earl and he wants to introduce you to his girlfriend*, she told herself. *Or take the Camry back for risking it on the Parkway*, she replied.

But when AnnaLise pulled into the first, angle-parking space, the SUV continued past to park on the other side of the trees. Not Earl, because this SUV – an Explorer – was dark blue, not black.

Likely some long-suffering family praying their vehicle wouldn't get stuck again behind 'the tourist' who'd already led them on a painfully slow trek across the viaduct.

Not to worry, AnnaLise thought as she turned off the ignition and swung open the Camry's door. She'd wait to let them leave first. Maybe get out and stretch. Take in the view. Even the thought of standing at the railing didn't seem as daunting as it once had.

Slipping out of the test-drive Toyota, AnnaLise checked her pocket for the fob. With cellphone service sometimes chancy, she didn't want to lock herself out and find she had to walk back across the viaduct, if that were even possible. She sure hadn't seen anything that suggested a pedestrian path. But then, she hadn't seen much of anything except for those last few feet of terra firma.

Leaving her purse in the car, AnnaLise swung the door closed and locked up with the fob, sliding it into her pocket as she approached the lookout.

Still not quite brave enough to walk all the way up to the railing, she nevertheless managed to get within two feet of it. 'Not bad,' she said.

'Talking to yourself again?'

AnnaLise turned to see Ben Rosewood, feet planted at shoulder-width, and looking all the more menacing for seeming to be relaxed.

Thirty

The man of AnnaLise's dreams. Or nightmares, to be more recently accurate.

'I'm very proud of you for making that drive over the viaduct,' Ben said, edging closer without seeming to move at all. 'I know how frightened you must have been.'

AnnaLise crossed her arms. 'Actually, I was fine.'

Ben smiled – a genuine smile, not the self-effacing one he used in public, practiced in the mirror. The one that made him seem a little embarrassed by his own accomplishments. 'So fine you barely broke ten miles an hour? I thought you were going to oversteer that Camry right off the edge.' He hooked a thumb over his shoulder. 'How do you like it, by the way?'

'It's a very nice car.'

'Good. I've never driven it, but the thing should be, for what it cost me.'

'Suzanne must have been thrilled.'

'Barely said thank you, actually. But then that's kids these days.' This smile was wistful, with a little 'whatcha-going-to-do' thrown in.

'Well, I'm sure Suzanne appreciated it.' Polite conversation, to mask the fact that AnnaLise was trying to figure out what Ben was doing there. On the other side of the trees, she could just make out the sound of his Explorer's engine still running.

Set for some version of a fast getaway? AnnaLise stepped back from the low railing and the carpet of flame-colored trees below and toward her test-drive Camry.

Ben followed gracefully, then settled his butt on the pristine car's hood. 'Well, I'd like you to have it.'

'Have what?'

The district attorney looked down and actually blushed. 'The Camry.'

AnnaLise shook her head. 'I can't take that car from you. Why would you even suggest it?'

'Because I care about you.' He held her eyes for a beat or two and, when she didn't respond, he continued anyway. 'I'm flying back to Wisconsin tomorrow to make the necessary arrangements. I don't need another car and, even if I did, I don't think I could bring myself to drive this one.'

AnnaLise could feel herself softening, doubting. What if she'd been wrong? What if her former lover had nothing to do with the death of his wife and daughter? He'd lost so much in the space of four days.

'Ben, I'm sorry.'

'Me, too.' He reached over and squeezed her hand. 'That's why I followed you here.'

AnnaLise's heart skipped a beat, and not in the good way. 'You followed me from Earl's garage?'

Ben shrugged. 'As I said, I'm leaving tomorrow. I wanted to see you, but dropping by your mother's place wasn't an attractive – or viable – option.'

'Good thinking,' AnnaLise said. 'But I don't

think we have anything left to say.' Even as she spoke those words, she began reconsidering them, not because she had any intention of continuing on with Ben, but because she wanted to see what his next move would be. 'Unless . . .' She practically batted her eyes at him.

Ben looked startled. 'Unless what?'

'Unless we can drop the pretense and become an above-board couple. After a suitable period of mourning, naturally.'

'I don't think that's a good idea.'

'But why not?' AnnaLise persisted. 'Tanja is dead and you're free. It's what you told me you've always wanted.'

'I never said I wanted my wife dead.'

'Of course you did,' AnnaLise said, channeling Glenn Close, just inches away from boiling a bunny. 'You said Tanja was a bitch. Once you even said that if she were to go down on a plane, we—'

'For God's sake, AnnaLise, grow up.' Ben moved her back with the palm of his hand. 'If I had a dollar for every time I told a woman I loved her or used that—'

'Every time?' AnnaLise knew she shouldn't have been surprised, but . . . she was. Bad enough to be singularly, volitionally, stupid, but to be nothing more than one generic fool in a herd of stupid women?

Ben was shaking his head regretfully, as if facing a witness incapable of finding her way to the witness stand, much less answering a question competently. 'Yes, of course. Before I met you, while we were together and subsequent to our break-up. I never said there weren't other,' finger quotes in the air, "other women.'"

AnnaLise felt like part of a tag team – Ben Rosewood's Gullible Ladies of Mattress-Wrestling. 'You never said there "were."' Responding finger quotes.

A shrug. 'You didn't ask.'

AnnaLise's eyes narrowed. 'Oh, but I did. Our first time together, in fact. I recall your exact words: "No. No one but you." Then you kissed me.'

Ben shrugged again. 'There happened *not* to be anyone but you, at that particular moment.'

'And in that particular room.' AnnaLise was shaking her head. 'What did I need to do? Specify a time period and GPS coordinates?'

'Honestly? Yes. And if you had, I'd have told you the numerical truth. Though no names, of course.'

'Of course. Because you're such a gentleman.'

'Ahh, the sarcasm doth drip. But who are you angry with, AnnaLise? Me, or yourself, for being so naive? I have to admit, I was surprised you didn't probe further, given how smart you seemed to be. But then, when I saw where you came from,' he spread his hands out wide, palms up, 'I appreciated the naivety.'

Speechless with rage – and not just a little wonder at his ability to pull off such fraud – AnnaLise just stared at him. What had life with this man been like? No wonder Tanja stressed she wasn't a good 'sharer' upon their meeting that morning at Mama's. It hadn't even been personal. Ben's wife was just playing the percentage bet.

AnnaLise took a deep breath, trying to remember that the real issue here was not that the man was a cheater – she'd always known that, God help her – but that he was a murderer.

And she was standing alone on a cliff with him.

'You're absolutely right. I was naive,' AnnaLise said. 'But that's the unchangeable past. Let's return to the Camry. If we're negotiating, what do you want for it?'

Ben looked surprised at the abrupt shift of subject, but went along with it. 'As I said, I thought about giving it to you outright, but that might look odd under the circumstances.'

And God forbid we should look odd.

'. . . enlist Lawling as the middleman,' Ben was saying. 'I've told him he's to accept any offer you made.'

Now AnnaLise was genuinely surprised. 'Really? Earl said you might take sixteen thousand.'

'I bet he did,' Ben said. 'Lawling's getting a percentage of the sale. Tell him you can't go over seven and then let me know what you agreed on, so he doesn't pocket more than his share of the deal.'

The district attorney was not a 'truster.' Probably because he knew *he* couldn't be trusted himself. 'I don't think Earl would do that.'

'Of course you don't, Pollyanna. Only good and honest folk here in the High Country.' Ben, who'd been leaning on the hood of the car, drew himself up and met her eyes. 'Let me remind you that one of your upright citizens killed my wife and daughter.'

'That hasn't been proven,' AnnaLise snapped, realizing the bastard planned to do figuratively to Josh what he'd done quite literally to AnnaLise. And she was damned if she was going to let that happen.

But Ben just shook his head. 'Still the champion of the young. And the stupid.'

AnnaLise knew the district attorney was talking about their disagreement over the charge he'd leveled against the teen in Wisconsin. 'All kids do stupid things. Everyone does. I know for a fact you routinely speed. Why should that girl back home go to jail for doing the same thing?'

'Because she killed someone, and I didn't.'

'So it's just simple chance.' AnnaLise wanted to smack the smug expression off his face. 'An accident.'

'If you take someone's life, there's a penalty that must be paid.' He seemed almost bored.

'And what about you, Ben? What's your penalty for what you've done?'

'Fine. I've told you I was sorry. You were much too young, too immature for me to—'

'I'm not talking about the affair, you pompous, egotistical asshole,' AnnaLise exploded. 'I'm talking about your wife and daughter.'

'AnnaLise.' The district attorney shook his head sadly. 'I know you've been through a lot with your mom and all, but have you thought that maybe her problems are less random and more . . . genetic? Perhaps you—'

AnnaLise slapped his right cheek. Hard.

The district attorney staggered back as he

235

grabbed her wrist, his face white with rage. 'Try that again and you're dead,' he hissed. 'Do you hear? *No one* hits Benjamin Rosewood.'

Given their height and weight differential, AnnaLise was being lifted off the ground and onto her toes, the grip on her forearm so painful it was all she could do not to cry out. 'Let . . . me . . . go!' she said between clenched teeth.

Ben twisted her arm the wrong way against her elbow, and this time she did scream.

'Say it.' He thrust her away from him. 'Say you think I killed my wife and daughter.'

AnnaLise tried to catch herself, but fell backwards, landing hard on her rear end. 'Sure I'll say it. And I'm betting so has Joshua Eames, now that he's regained consciousness.'

'No. He has not!' Ben exploded.

'But he has,' AnnaLise said, rubbing her aching wrist. 'The bullet missed his brain. You made a mistake. A bad one.'

Ben, nearly shaking with rage, took steps forward, bringing his face directly over her. AnnaLise skittered away like a crab, until the upright of the rail fence bit into her back. In the heat of the moment, she hadn't realized how close she'd come to leaving the overlook.

And life, permanently.

'Stay away from me!' AnnaLise screamed as loudly as she could manage with her heart in her throat.

Ben backed off and looked around as a lone car passed by on the Parkway. 'I'm sorry, I'm sorry,' he said, holding up his hands, palms forward.

'I could have gone over,' AnnaLise said, glancing behind her. 'Is that what you wanted?'

'Of course not. Are you hurt?' Ben put his hand down as if to help her up, but she slid sideways from him.

'I'm OK, but no thanks to you.' Still too near the edge for her comfort, AnnaLise crawled on hands and knees until she felt confident that she could stand up without tipping over backward.

Ben said, 'Please, AnnaLise, this has gotten out of hand,' coming closer again.

'Back off!' AnnaLise rose unsteadily, feeling in her jeans pocket.

No cellphone. She'd left it and her purse in the Camry.

Even if AnnaLise didn't have a chance to dial, at least if her phone was nearby and something happened, they'd locate her via its GPS. Daisy wouldn't wait . . .

'Wait,' Ben echoed. 'Can we start this whole conversation over?' He appeared to follow her directions, but in reality was just circling – or semi-circling, given the cliff. 'You have to know what kind of damage this will do to my career if you—'

'If I what? Tell the truth?'

Ben was moving clockwise toward her. Doing the same in order to keep her distance would take AnnaLise over the cliff. He said, 'And what do you think is the truth?'

'What do I *think*?' AnnaLise stood her ground, hand still in her pocket. 'I think the good voters of Urban County hit the trifecta when they elected you. Liar/Cheater/Murderer, all on one

237

easy-to-pull lever. How's that fit your "Rule of Three"?'

'You have to stop this –' He was just past the left front fender of the Camry now.

AnnaLise pressed. Two quick and then one . . . two . . . three.

The Toyota started.

Startled, Ben whirled around toward the car. 'What the hell—'

But AnnaLise was on the move and by the time the district attorney turned back, she'd already hopped into his rented, still-running Explorer and locked the doors.

Thirty-one

AnnaLise had never driven that fast down the Blue Ridge Parkway. The fact she was recrossing the viaduct and piloting a large and unfamiliar vehicle – the Explorer Ben Rosewood had rented from Earl Lawling – made it even more remarkable.

Passing within range of the Toyota on the way out of the overlook, she'd employed the Camry's fob once more, this time pressing 'unlock' on the remote once. The engine shut off just as Earl had promised.

'"The Key is in Your Hands,"' AnnaLise yelled back. 'Too bad you didn't practice what you preach for once.'

She wasn't sure Ben would appreciate the irony, even if he'd heard her. 'The Key is in Your Hands' was a campaign he'd spearheaded to reduce car theft by enforcing a law already on the books – fines for car owners who left their keys in their vehicles.

And now he *would* pay. Having left his own keys and cellphone in the SUV that AnnaLise was now driving – and unable to start the Camry without the fob that she also held – Benjamin Rosewood would be going nowhere fast. Walking or hitching a ride were his only options and whichever he chose, AnnaLise would be safely to Sutherton before Ben was even off the Parkway.

As her fear started to subside, it left behind anger. Since she didn't have her phone, her plan was to drive directly to the police station.

She didn't get the chance.

At the sound of the siren, AnnaLise pulled over, having gotten as far as the state highway. The squad parked behind her and, as it did, another squad pulled past and stopped at an angle across the front end of the Explorer.

The officers exited the cars with their guns drawn.

I'm driving a stolen car, AnnaLise thought. And, *Ben reported me somehow.* She carefully kept her hands where they could see them.

'Step out of the car, ma'am,' said the shorter of the two officers, handgun drawn.

'Coy,' AnnaLise said, complying. 'Coy Pitchford. It's me, AnnaLise Griggs.'

'AnnaLise?' He was still keeping the muzzle on her, unwavering. 'Whatever are you doing stealing a motor vehicle?'

When Coy said the word 'vehicle,' the letter 'h' was not silent.

Nor was AnnaLise. 'I didn't steal it, Coy. I borrowed it to get away from a killer. He has my car.' *Or more precisely he has his own car. Fat chance he'd be selling it to AnnaLise now.*

'And your cellphone, apparently.'

AnnaLise turned to see Chuck Greystone, who was the second officer on the scene. She'd been so rattled, she hadn't even realized. 'Chuck, thank God you're here.'

'Boyfriend trouble?' Chuck waved for Coy to holster his weapon.

AnnaLise started to deny it, but then thought what the hell. '*Killer* boyfriend trouble. Ben Rosewood is a murderous ass, pure and simple.'

Chuck leaned down to peer into her face. 'Whatever are you talking about, AnnaLise?'

'The term "killer."' AnnaLise was dithering and she didn't seem to be able to stop herself. The words just kept tumbling out. 'It can also mean "great," like that was a "killer" chicken recipe, and—'

'And this all has what to do with Ben Rosewood calling me on your cellphone to report you'd stolen his Explorer and left him stranded at an overlook?'

'It's not his Explorer,' AnnaLise said. 'It's Earl Lawling's. The Toyota I left with him is Ben's. Or Suzanne's, though I can't imagine he would have put it in her name, what with insurance premiums and all.'

Chuck turned to Coy. 'Cuff her and bring her in for questioning.'

The chief of police was sitting forward in his chair, left elbow on the desk, his left hand tented against his forehead like he was battling a headache.

Coy hadn't actually handcuffed AnnaLise, but she was now seated in one of Chuck's two guest chairs.

The chief said, 'OK, tell me.'

And so she did. But after she'd laid it out – all of it – there was silence.

'Chuck?'

'I'm thinking.'

'Please don't let your opinion of me cloud your judgment. This is about Josh. I'm not accusing Ben Rosewood because of an affair which I ended.' And boy-oh-boy, wasn't she glad now that she had.

Chuck let loose of his head. 'Lise, I love you – you're one of my best friends. I may not like what you did with Rosewood back in Wisconsin, but I certainly don't believe you'd accuse a man of killing his wife and daughter and wounding a third person just because you were pissed at him.'

'Thank you.' When Chuck said he loved you, you could take it to the bank.

'I do need to think about this and see how your theory – and so far it is only that, a theory – fits into what we know of the facts.'

'But what about Ben?' AnnaLise asked. 'You can't leave him roaming the streets.'

'I know where to find Rosewood, thanks to you, and I'll bring him in for questioning. I can't say that there'll be anything to hold him on, though.'

'I'll press charges,' AnnaLise said. 'For assault.'

'From what you said, he didn't assault you.'

'He grabbed my wrist.' She held up said appendage and was sorry to see there was no bruising.

Chuck cocked his head. 'I believe you, but with no proof, it's just not enough.'

'So because I religiously take my vitamins and don't bruise easily, I'm out of luck?'

'We'll see.' Chuck leaned across the desk and patted her hand. 'Listen, I'll have someone watch your place. I promise you and Daisy will be safe, OK?'

242

Instead of feeling relief, AnnaLise felt a chill run up her spine. 'You think he could come after us?'

'Honestly, Lise, I don't know. And I won't know until I interview him, and even then, maybe not.'

'What about Josh?'

'We plan to take him into custody when the doctors release him.'

'Can you maybe hold off on that?' AnnaLise asked. 'At least until after you talk to Ben?'

'We'll see.'

AnnaLise smiled ruefully. 'Damn that inscrutable Cherokee blood line of yours.'

'It would behoove you, I think, to get your tasteless ethnic stereotypes right. It was Charlie Chan who was inscrutable and not only was the character Chinese and *not* Cherokee, but Warner Oland who played him wasn't even Asian.'

'He was Swedish,' AnnaLise said. 'I love that you know this stuff.'

'If it was about cops or detectives, as I was growing up, I watched it. Or read it. My dad and I were really close.'

'That's right, your mother and father were divorced,' AnnaLise said. 'Maybe that's why you have a soft spot for Josh. He grew up without a mother, too.'

Chuck escorted her to the door. 'It was probably tougher on Josh. He was ten when his mom took off. I never even knew mine.'

AnnaLise kissed the chief on the cheek as the phone on his desk began to ring. 'Poor woman. She doesn't know what she missed.'

243

Finally outside the Sutherton police headquarters, AnnaLise realized she didn't have transportation.

Daisy's Chrysler was at Earl Lawling's yard, the Toyota was presumably still on the Blue Ridge, and the police had impounded Ben's rented Explorer.

'Huh.' AnnaLise stood in the parking lot outside the station and looked around.

Where was a cab when you needed one? 'New York City,' she said aloud.

'Talking to yourself?' Charity Pitchford was just coming out of headquarters.

'More and more, these days,' AnnaLise admitted. 'I don't know where my head is. Or my car.'

'You've lost your car?'

'Not technically. I just . . . well, I got a ride here, and . . .'

'By one of our squads, I understand,' Charity said, producing her car keys. 'Coy told me. Need a lift?'

'I do, but I'm afraid it's to Sutherton Auto. That's where Daisy's car should be.'

'Hey, no problem,' Charity said, waving her to a Ford Escape which had to be her civilian car. 'I thought you might want me to take you all the way up to the overlook past the viaduct.'

'No, that wasn't exactly my car. And I left it with the owner, anyway.'

'When you stole his.' Charity started her mid-sized SUV. 'Busy day.'

'You don't know the half of it.'

'Do you mind if we head south first and stop at the hospital? Coy's there standing guard over

244

the Eames kid and I told him I'd bring lunch.' She reached back and picked up a brown paper sack. 'He's trying to take off some weight and doesn't trust himself in that cafeteria.'

'They have great soup,' AnnaLise said as they backed out of the parking space. 'And that's not bad for you.'

'It surely is, if you pair it with a loaf of bread, a pound of butter and cheesecake for dessert. The man has absolutely *no* will-power.' Charity pulled up to the stop sign at the top of the cop lot. 'So, hospital first?'

'You bet,' AnnaLise said. 'In fact, I was hoping I could talk to Josh. Do you think that's possible?'

'I don't see why not,' Charity said. 'As long as you don't mind either Coy or me being right there, too.'

'Not at all.' AnnaLise glanced sideways at her driver. 'I understand the plan is still to arrest him?'

'Now, AnnaLise, you're not trying to pump me for information again, are you?'

'Yes, but don't take it personally. I do it with everyone.'

'Must be the journalist in you. Makes you nosy.'

'Or being nosy, which makes you want to be a journalist,' AnnaLise admitted. 'I've never quite been sure which is the cart and which is the horse.'

When they got to the hospital, Coy was in Josh's room and Fred Eames was nowhere in sight.

'Fred's with the lawyers,' Coy said as he emerged. 'Hope he doesn't spend everything he's worked so hard for trying to push off the

245

inevitable. Though I have to say you introduced a nice new wrinkle to the plot.' This last was directed at AnnaLise.

'What do you mean?' Charity asked, handing the lunch bag to her husband.

'Well, the chief just called and had me ask Josh about whether he lent this Ben Rosewood a gun. The boy's brain is fuzzy – no surprise, what with a bullet having whizzed right past it – but he says he does recall doing that, just not which gun or exactly when.'

'Probably just grasping at straws,' Charity said. 'You put the idea in the kid's head.'

'I don't think so,' AnnaLise piped up. 'Fred told me about the borrowed gun yesterday, so this isn't something Josh just came up with – or went along with, as you say – to dodge the charges against him.'

'Well, it's going to take a whole lot more than that, I'm afraid,' Charity said.

AnnaLise was afraid, too. 'Can I see Josh?'

'Don't see any harm,' Coy said. 'I'll have to sit with you, but I'll mind my business and eat my lunch. Want half, Charity?'

'Heck, no,' Charity said. 'If AnnaLise is going to be here for twenty minutes or so, I'll run over to the cafeteria.'

Coy looked pained, but he kissed his wife. 'Have fun, darlin'. Eat something I'd like.'

'Oh, I will,' Charity said, turning to walk the green line. 'Cheesecake or tapioca?'

'So help me, if that woman comes home with cheesecake on her breath,' Coy said, leading AnnaLise into the room, 'I'll divorce her.'

'I've never been much for that particular treat,' AnnaLise admitted.

'Then you haven't had this here hospital's cheesecake,' Coy said. He waved AnnaLise toward Josh and seated himself in a reclining chair in the corner, sack lunch in his lap, Coke on the floor next to him.

'Don't know why everybody is enthusiastic about this hospital's food,' Josh said by way of welcome as he pushed away the rolling table that was across his bed. His left cheek was covered with a gauze patch and the rest of his head bandaged in a kind of figure of eight, like somebody with a bad headache in an old-time movie. 'Stuff turns my stomach.'

'Then I'll get rid of this,' AnnaLise said, guiding the table to the door side of the room and returning to sit down next to him. 'How are you doing?'

'Not good,' Josh said. Whatever painkillers they'd probably given him couldn't take the edge off the fear in his eyes. 'They're saying I somehow killed Suze.'

'Do you remember anything?'

'Not a thing. After we got to my house and sat down there on the couch, that is. We'd been fighting.' He glanced over at Coy, but the officer seemed engrossed in what looked – and smelled – like a hard-boiled egg sandwich. 'And since my dad wasn't home we . . . um, thought it'd be a good time to . . . well, make up.'

AnnaLise couldn't suppress a smile. Oh, to be this young – and that naive – again. Seemed like

247

just yesterday. 'And you don't remember anything after you sat down?'

'Nothing that had any guns or shooting in it, and I'd swear to that.'

Now AnnaLise laughed outright. 'I may have some good news for you.' She leaned closer. 'The chief is bringing in Ben Rosewood for questioning.'

'Really? The chief thinks he's the one who shot us?' The hope in Josh's voice made Coy glance over, but then he kindly went back to eating.

'It's possible, and using the . . . firearm you lent him.' Tempted as she might be, AnnaLise knew she shouldn't give anything away – including that the murder weapon was a deer rifle. 'Are you sure you don't remember anything about it? Like which one of your dad's it was?'

Josh had begun shaking his head before AnnaLise finished her question. 'I wish I could, believe me. Heck.' A sideways look toward Coy. When he turned back, Josh had tears in his eyes. 'I'd have made something up if I thought it would help.' His voice was barely a whisper.

'Don't do that, whatever you think of,' AnnaLise warned softly, as Coy's cellphone started to ring. 'If there's anything I know, it's that the chief recognizes a liar when he sees one.'

For Josh's sake, AnnaLise hoped her words were true.

Coy said, 'Pitchford' into the phone and listened.

'I should probably go,' AnnaLise said to Josh. 'I just wanted you to know what was going on.'

'I appreciate that, AnnaLise,' Josh said, sticking out his hand.

When AnnaLise took it, the palm was understandably sweaty, but still firm. 'It's going to turn out OK, Josh.'

He nodded and looked down at the floor, and AnnaLise had the sinking feeling that he was experiencing the same surge of fear that she had, when Chuck had tried to reassure her. That if someone felt they had to tell you everything was going to be OK, that maybe it wasn't. Couldn't be, even.

She stood up. 'Daisy said to say hi.'

Now Josh smiled. 'She's a real trip, your mama is. Mrs Peebly, too, though I have to say she scares me sometimes.'

'Don't feel bad,' AnnaLise said, patting his shoulder. 'She scares me, too, and I lived next door to her most of my life.'

That got a laugh out of him. 'Still, you were lucky to grow up with Daisy and Mrs Peebly around. Mama Philomena, too. I—'

'Excuse me?' Coy was standing, the phone still in his hand.

'I'm sorry, Coy, I was just leaving. I didn't mean to overstay my—'

'No, that's not the problem, AnnaLise. I just need to talk to Josh and, well, maybe it's best if you're still here for that.'

AnnaLise sat back down and took Josh's hand.

Thirty-two

'I couldn't believe what I was hearing.'

AnnaLise was again in the passenger seat of Charity's Escape, the two women heading toward Sutherton Auto so AnnaLise could pick up Daisy's Chrysler.

'I know,' Charity said, turning onto the highway. 'How did Josh take it?'

'He was ten years old when his mother "left."' AnnaLise's air quotes went unseen, the officer wisely keeping her eyes on the road in front of them. 'Now her remains are found in the second car recovered from the gorge this week. I don't think he knows *how* to feel.'

'I'm not sure I would either.' Charity looked sideways at AnnaLise. 'Did Coy tell him about the man with her?'

'No.' AnnaLise felt her eyes go wide. 'A man? Do we know his identity?'

A shake of the head. 'Not yet. The license plate on the car was still intact, so it was easy enough to figure that the female remains were Robyn Eames' and get dental records confirming it. We don't have as much to start with on the male, though I'm certain the chief is talking to Fred right now, see who he thinks it could be.'

'Presumably, the guy she was having the affair with,' AnnaLise said. 'And there are probably lots of people willing to dredge up that little tidbit.'

'Was the man from Sutherton?'

'I think so, though most of what I know is second-hand – through either Daisy or Mama.'

'You weren't here?'

'That was my first year of college at Wisconsin. From what I heard, there'd been talk about the two of them, no surprise, and when they both disappeared it was assumed they'd run off together.' AnnaLise shook her head. 'Who knew it was the road they'd run off?'

'Well, not exactly "run" and not precisely "road,"' Charity said. 'From where the car landed, it's more likely to have slipped off that Lovers' Lookout near where Daisy and you had your own accident.'

Some ends are deader than others, AnnaLise could hear her mother saying. 'Talk about your unsafe sex,' she muttered.

Charity laughed. 'I've heard tell of such things. And to make things worse, neither had a seat belt on.'

'Or the parking brake, apparently.' AnnaLise relayed what Chuck had told her about a particularly amorous couple rocking their car off the cliff, even as they were rocking each other's worlds. 'I put it down to urban legend.'

'Sutherton doesn't strike me as urban, but I get your point. Well, here we are.' Charity turned the Escape into Sutherton Auto's drive.

'The Chrysler is right up there next to the office,' AnnaLise said, pointing. 'But you can drop me any—'

'Excuse me.' Charity's cell was ringing, so she conscientiously pulled over and put the car in park, 'Charity Pitchford.'

251

AnnaLise opened her door and signaled that she'd just walk the rest of the way, but Charity held up one finger.

'My God, Coy, why did you . . .' She listened. 'Don't blame it on . . . Is he . . . Well, that's good, at least. Do we have a description . . . OK. I'll be right there. Hang on, babe.' She clicked off, shaking her head almost violently.

'What?' AnnaLise asked.

'Coy. Apparently the hard-boiled egg sandwich didn't agree with him and he had to make a bathroom run. Josh was sleeping and Coy figured things would be fine, but—'

Oh, God – what did the kid do? 'Don't tell me. Josh bolted?'

'Worse. He was attacked.'

'Oh, my God.' AnnaLise said, her hand going to her mouth.

'Don't worry, Josh's not much worse off. He woke up and started yelling, scaring the guy off apparently.'

'Ben Rosewood.'

'As good a guess as any,' Charity said. 'The chief questioned him, but decided he couldn't hold him with what we had. Especially since the judge had already issued an arrest warrant for Josh on the same crime.' She shifted her car into drive. 'Listen, I need to get back to the hospital, but let me get you up to your car first. I'd hate to have you stranded in this deserted lot if it doesn't start.'

'No.' AnnaLise plucked at the officer's sleeve. 'I really mean, it *was* Ben Rosewood. I told him that Josh had regained consciousness.'

252

'But that's no secret,' Charity said. 'The whole town likely knew hours ago that Josh was awake. Hell, they're also probably chewing on his mother's body being found, given how fast news travels around here, courtesy of Mama Philomena's and the rest of the Sutherton grapevine.'

The journalist waved that aside. 'You don't understand. I . . . umm, I may have told Ben that Josh identified him as his and Suzanne's attacker.' AnnaLise ducked her head. 'Don't you see, Charity? This could all be my fault.'

Thirty-three

AnnaLise watched as Charity Pitchford's SUV bounced back down the drive, a rooster tail of gravel splaying out behind it. The officer had called Chief Greystone and reported what AnnaLise had just told her about the conversation with Ben.

AnnaLise had been able to hear the 'You're telling me she did what?!' but, mercifully, Chuck had lowered his voice enough for Charity to be able to return the phone to her ear for the rest of the brief conversation.

When they finished up, AnnaLise hopped out of the Escape and insisted that she'd walk the rest of the way to her mother's car, while Charity headed off toward the hospital. Clearly upset both by what had happened to Josh and by Coy's role, Charity agreed, but only after handing AnnaLise her card and making her promise to call if the Chrysler didn't start or some other problem intervened.

AnnaLise had promised, despite the fact that she'd left her cell in the Escape, which was why Ben had been able to call Chuck and report it stol— 'Shit!'

AnnaLise searched her jean pockets, but came up with only the fob for the Toyota Camry. 'Fat lot of good you'll do me,' she said to it.

Because, of course, the keys to the Chrysler

were in her purse, also in the custody of either Ben Rosewood or the Sutherton police.

Unless . . .

AnnaLise trudged up the dusty drive to the Chrysler and felt under the right front fender. 'Eureka! The hidey place.' When she snaked her hand back out from under, it held a magnetic key case.

Only problem was, when she slid it open, the thing was empty.

'Looking for this?'

AnnaLise jumped and turned to see Earl Lawling holding the valet key from the Chrysler in his hand. She hadn't noticed the front bumper of his SUV just visible behind the building, nor the light inside.

'My God, Earl. You scared the life out of me.' She put her hand over her heart.

'I'm mighty sorry, AnnaLise.' He looked around. 'Where's the Camry?'

'I left it with Ben Rosewood,' she said truthfully. 'It's a bit of a long story, but I think it's best you contact him and see what the situation is.'

Lawling cocked his head. 'I sure can do that, AnnaLise, but—'

'Oh, wait,' she interrupted, digging through her pockets. 'Here's the fob.'

He took it. 'Now, how in the world did Mr Rosewood—'

She shrugged. 'Must have another fob he didn't give you. Like I said, best you ask him. For now, though, where did you find that?' She gestured toward the Chrysler key.

Standing here alone in the deserted lot with

255

Lawling, she was remembering Joy's comments about him appearing at every pertinent juncture. Why in the world would he remove the key from Daisy's hidey place?

'When you weren't back yet, I thought maybe you'd decided to keep the Camry.' Lawling was looking a little crestfallen, presumably because that clearly wasn't the case. 'I was thinking I should drive Daisy's car down – you know, make it easier for you. Before I called and made the offer, though, I wanted to make sure I had the means to follow up on it.'

'That's very nice, Earl,' AnnaLise said. 'But how did you know where the key was?'

Lawling snorted. 'Everybody older than forty in this county has one of those.' He pointed at the magnetic key-coffin in her hand. 'And every single one of 'em thinks nobody knows where they put 'em.'

He knocked on the Chrysler's bumper like it was a door. 'There's only so much metal on cars these days, so it doesn't take a wizard to know where they'll stick.'

AnnaLise laughed, but held out her hand. 'I'm starting to think you may be the smartest person in Sutherton.'

'You're just *starting* to think that, AnnaLise?' He regarded her for a moment and then dropped the key in her palm.

'Thank you, sir,' she said and closed her hand on the key. Climbing into the car, she started the engine – the old-fashioned way, with a real key – and rolled down her window. 'I'll be in touch about the Camry.'

Lawling didn't look like he believed that. He raised his hand in farewell. 'You take care now.'

'And you.' AnnaLise shifted in drive and started to pull out. When she was far enough away for comfort, she called to him.

He'd started for the office and turned. 'Yes?'

'If you were going to drive this down to Daisy's for us, how on earth were you going to get back?'

AnnaLise Griggs didn't give Earl Lawling time to answer.

Thirty-four

'Honest to God, AnnaLise, have you descended to the point that you trust no one?' Daisy was where AnnaLise had left her, in front of the printer working on her first blog entry. 'And that poor Earl Lawling, him and his girlfriend, probably, just trying to do us a favor by ferrying the car down.'

'I'm not sure there's any such thing as a "poor man,"' AnnaLise said. 'They're all playing the angles, I just don't know which particular ones are Earl's. Beyond wanting to sell me that Camry, of course.'

'Well, that's a terribly jaded way of looking at life,' Daisy said, getting up to put paper in the printer. 'And love, I might add. Whatever happened to you today?'

Oh, Daisy, you don't want to know, AnnaLise thought.

And then she told her.

When the whole sordid story was out, both of them were sitting down at the table, Daisy leaning forward on her elbows.

'So . . .' the mother began. 'This Rosewood, your married lover, used a gun Joshua Eames lent him to shoot out his wife's tire and send her off the road toward certain death.'

'He knew she didn't wear a seat belt.' This last was said with a flourish, since AnnaLise herself hadn't thought about it for awhile. 'And drank too much. The mountain roads were the ideal setting and seemingly everyone – first Joy, then me, and ultimately Josh – the perfect scapegoats. Ben, always the lawyer, was setting up "reasonable doubt."'

Daisy looked like she had some doubt of her own. 'And his daughter?'

'The way I see it, Ben was fed up with Tanja and killed her to get out of the marriage without having to forfeit her money. Then, somehow, Suze – Suzanne – became another stumbling block. Maybe there was a trust fund, containing more money than Ben wanted to sacrifice, or maybe she just tipped to what her father had done.'

'But what about Joshua? He had to die, too?'

'With Josh dead, Ben would be free to pin the whole thing on him.' Make that killing *three* birds with one stone.

Daisy was wagging her head from side to side. 'Oh, AnnaLise. How in the world could you get involved with a man like this?'

'Take this to *any* bank, Daisy: you don't need to tell me how stupid I was.'

'Beyond stupid, daughter-of-mine,' Daisy said, reaching across the table. 'And I know from personal experience. Maybe if you'd asked me—'

AnnaLise put her hand up to her ear like it was a telephone receiver. 'Hello, Daisy? I'm thinking of having an affair with a powerful, married man. What do you think?'

'See?' Daisy said, with a smile. 'This all could have been avoided. If you can't tell your mother

259

about something you're considering, then just don't do it.'

'Words to live by.' AnnaLise squeezed her mother's hand and then let go. 'Time to pack?'

'Pack?' Daisy asked. 'Where are we going?'

'Anywhere but here,' AnnaLise said. 'Ben Rosewood attacked Josh and – at least as of a half an hour ago when I called Chuck – the police still hadn't found the bastard. Chuck says we should go somewhere safe and I agree.'

She didn't tell her mother where Chuck, kiddingly, had suggested AnnaLise go. At least she hoped he was kidding.

'But where?' Daisy asked. 'Phyllis'?'

Phyllis 'Mama' Philomena lived behind her restaurant. 'I'd prefer farther away.'

'Ooh, I've got it,' Daisy said, getting up and going to the phone. 'We'll go to Ida Mae's. She'll love all this!'

AnnaLise just bet she would.

Daisy insisted on driving her car and, given AnnaLise's adventures of the day, her daughter had agreed.

As they slung their overnight bags onto the back seat, the kitchen phone began ringing. AnnaLise, who had been in the process of locking the apartment's front door, ran back inside to answer it.

When she returned to the car, she was smiling. 'Good news. We don't have to go anywhere. Ben has been arrested.'

'That's wonderful news, dear,' Daisy said, giving her daughter a hug. 'Only, we're still going.'

'But why? We're not in fear of our lives anymore.'

'Oh, yes we are. I told Ida Mae what was going on and she's already changed the sheets in the guest room, decanted the wine and started dinner. You want *real* death threats, see what happens if you disappoint her. Get in the car.'

AnnaLise sighed, but grumbled an 'All right,' as she opened the passenger side door. She picked up a sheath of papers on the seat. 'What's this?'

'My blog. I thought you could read it as we drove.'

Ahh, the real reason AnnaLise had been relegated to the shotgun position. 'But I get carsick.'

'Only on winding roads. Read fast before we get to them.'

AnnaLise doubted the tome in her hands could be finished before they got to the mountain and started up, but she also figured she owed Daisy at least that. When AnnaLise had finally decided to confide in her mother, she had been a rock.

'This is very good,' the daughter said, squinting against the slanting sun. 'But you realize it's supposed to be a blog entry, not the Encyclopedia Suthertonia.'

'What I wrote isn't that long,' Daisy protested.

'It is, too,' AnnaLise said, paging through. 'But we can put this up on the website in installments. I had no idea this Lovers' Lookout was so popular. I love the part about you and your friends being chased out by Chuck's dad.'

'Cop or not, he was just a few years older than we were, so knew first-hand all the places to park. Here.' She slid a small rectangular sleeve to AnnaLise.

'What's this?' AnnaLise unzipped it. 'A digital camera?'

'Yup. We need to take pictures.'

'Of what?'

'Lovers' Lookout, of course. I noticed that a lot of blogs have photos with them. If we time it right, the sun should be setting.' The car made an abrupt turn off pavement and onto gravel.

'Please, Daisy,' AnnaLise heard a less-than-flattering whine in her voice. 'Pretty please, can't we go on to Ida Mae's and have a nice quiet dinner? I've had enough excitement today without off-roading at sunset. Especially somewhere the cars seem to have plummeted from fairly regularly.'

'Oh, pshaw,' Daisy said, as they bounced over the gravel road. 'It's perfectly safe up here.'

'Pshaw?' AnnaLise repeated as a bump separated her from her seat – at least as far as the seat belt would allow. 'You're too young to say "pshaw."'

'Says you.' Daisy darted the Chrysler to the right and stopped, switching off the ignition.

'We're here?' AnnaLise pulled on the door handle, swinging it wide. She was already feeling a little sick from reading in the car and needed air.

'We are, but be careful on that side. The first step can be a doozy.'

AnnaLise slammed the door shut. 'Daisy, I swear—'

Her mother cackled. 'Don't be such a weenie, dear. This is like angle parking. I nosed in so our best view is out the front windshield.'

'Great, then I can stay right here.'

'Is this the young woman who conquered the Blue Ridge Parkway?' Daisy asked, getting out on her side. 'Exit this car and claim your heritage. You, my dear, are a child of the High Country.' She swung an arm in a wide arc. 'Look.'

AnnaLise looked. The sun was bathing the mountain, the far end of the Sutherton Bridge on the opposite side of the gorge cutting a glowing white swath through the autumn colors.

It was . . . breathtaking. In a good way.

AnnaLise sighed and swung open her door again. Looking first, she stepped out. 'This isn't too scary. In fact,' she glanced around, 'it's not scary at all.'

'Of course not,' Daisy said, reaching back into the car to retrieve the camera from the console where AnnaLise had left it. 'When we used to come up here, we weren't looking to die. We were just looking to . . . well, look.'

'And touch,' AnnaLise murmured under her breath, but thinking too much about exactly what her mother had done up here wasn't any better an idea than her mother doing likewise about AnnaLise and Ben.

As Daisy clicked away, AnnaLise cautiously walked forward to the Chrysler's front fender. 'You heard they found Josh's mother, right?'

'Robyn?' Daisy kept clicking. 'Yes, and though I was surprised she was dead, I'm not surprised there was a man with her. Robyn spent so much time parked here that I'm surprised they didn't name this lookout after her. Not that you could tell Fred that, of course.'

'They say her car must have gone off here, but I don't see how it could just roll. I mean, cars had emergency brakes even back then and this area is pretty level.'

'"Even back then"?' Daisy repeated, peeking out from behind the camera. 'We're not talking about the nineteenth century, AnnaLise. Or even the twentieth, for that matter.'

'I know.' She shivered. 'Are you done? It's starting to get cold.'

'You don't fool me. You're more worried about the dark than the cold.'

'More like you *driving* in the dark.'

'Well, you needn't and, besides, I'm done.' Daisy pulled out her handbag and traded the camera for her cell. 'Let's not keep Ida Mae waiting again.'

Like the night of their accident and the discovery of the Porsche. Just four days since what Charity had called the busiest – no, wait, the *craziest* night ever. '*One call sends our guys plus fire and rescue out there, only to stumble on something altogether unexpected . . .*'

'Daisy?' AnnaLise said, putting her hand on her mother's shoulder before she could climb back into the car. 'Do you remember Ida Mae saying her neighbor had called nine-one-one, but they hadn't come straight away?'

'Of course. Barbara Jean down the way was having stomach pains and her daughter insisted she call the paramedics, but they didn't arrive for an hour. Can you imagine? Glad we don't live on the mountain. If I have pains, I just walk on over to the station.'

'Right,' AnnaLise murmured, still thinking. 'Can I use your cellphone?'

She pulled out the card that Charity had given her and dialed the number. When Charity answered, AnnaLise asked her one question.

When she hung up, her mother was looking at her. 'What was all that about?'

'Charity Pitchford was on duty at the station the night we had our accident and Tanja Rosewood went off the road.'

'And her husband Coy was right here on the scene, remember? What—'

This time AnnaLise stopped her. 'You heard the question I just asked Charity.'

'You mean how many nine-one-one calls they got? I did. But I couldn't hear her answer.'

'It was exactly what she told me in Chuck's office earlier this week. One.'

'So?' Mother was peering at daughter.

'Don't you see? That one call was Barbara Jean with her pains. The responding units stumbled on us en route.'

Daisy was looking confused. 'But that would . . .'

AnnaLise was nodding. 'Exactly right. Joshua never called nine-one-one.'

Thirty-five

'But why would Joshua Eames have said he called the emergency number if he didn't?' Daisy was looking even more confused.

'Maybe to keep us from calling ourselves?'

This time Daisy shivered and wrapped her arms around her torso. 'Can we talk about this in the car?'

But AnnaLise was looking off across the gorge. 'What if Josh was there on the road leading to the bridge heading home, not from work, but from shooting out Tanja Rosewood's tire.' She pointed toward the white glint of the bridge and the road leading to it on the opposite side of the 'c' from where they stood. 'It would be a clear shot from here, if not necessarily an easy one.'

'Now you think *Josh* is the guilty one?' Daisy asked, apparently forgetting her earlier chill. 'What about your friend, the district attorney?'

'Ben is a pathological liar and cheat, but maybe he's not a murderer.'

'But Josh, someone you've known practically all your life, is?'

AnnaLise shook her head. 'I'm wondering . . . I mean, we have only Josh's word that he lent Ben the gun. And even that he was attacked in the hospital just hours ago. If he lied about calling

266

nine-one-one, maybe he's been lying about everything.'

'What if . . .' Daisy was staring off toward the gorge, arms still wrapped around her.

'Go ahead?'

Daisy turned to her. 'What if the sirens wouldn't have scared him off that night? He told us to stay in the car, remember?'

'You're thinking he might have sent us over?' AnnaLise followed her mother's gaze off the edge.

'It wouldn't have taken much,' Daisy said. 'And if you're right that we caught him in the act . . .'

But AnnaLise was shaking her head. 'But we hadn't. In fact, we didn't even know it was Josh until he called out to us.'

'But *he* couldn't have known that,' Daisy said. 'Still . . . I know that the black truck was coming down the mountain.'

'You're sure of that? Because if so, it blows my theory to smithereens. Josh couldn't have been both here shooting off the lookout and in the truck coming down the mountain.'

'Maybe he wasn't in the truck,' Daisy said. 'You know how many dark-colored SUVs and pick-ups there are up here, and I told you I thought the truck just kept on going.'

'Didn't you say the Eames' house was very near here?' AnnaLise recalled something else. Fred Eames saying that Josh liked to 'tramp' through the dead-end as a shortcut.

'Just through there.' Daisy pointed away from the cliff. 'Fifteen minutes on the road, but probably ten by foot.'

'More like five,' a voice said from the nearby brush.

Joshua Eames stepped into the fading, slanting sunlight.

Thirty-six

'They released you from the hospital,' AnnaLise said, not knowing what else to say to the young man who stood wraithlike in front of them, his head still swathed in gauze.

'And police custody, thanks to you. Your friend Ben Rosewood is in a heap of trouble, especially now that I remembered what happened that night.'

Josh was standing with his back to the gravel road. While AnnaLise and Daisy could see his face, they were likely only silhouettes to him against the setting sun.

Good thing, because AnnaLise didn't think she could keep the horror off her face.

'Well, that's good,' she said, glancing at her mother. 'Daisy, we need to run. Ida Mae's waiting.'

'I don't think so,' Josh said, moving closer. 'We need to talk first.'

Both women were standing on the driver's side of the Chrysler and AnnaLise pulled Daisy toward the front of the car, so the open door was between them and Josh.

She'd forgotten, seeing him in a hospital bed most recently, how tall he was, and how broad. His father, but with the six-pack. 'Always big for his age,' Daisy had said. Probably even at ten.

'I'm sorry about your mother,' she said now,

as she had in the hospital when Coy Pitchford had broken the news to both of them. Though now she realized that it hadn't seemed as much of a surprise to Josh as it was to her.

'You know . . .' He stopped, his face expressionless.

'Know what?' Daisy said, looking back and forth between them. 'Whatever you heard, Josh, it was just us gossiping. You know how much we all love to gossip in Sutherton.'

'I do, Daisy. Especially you women.'

'You don't like women?' AnnaLise asked.

Josh shook his head, just once. 'I sure try to, but . . . well, don't take offense, but I've found you just can't trust 'em.'

Funny, but AnnaLise had been thinking the same about men recently. Not that she planned to mention it to Josh just now. 'We can be flighty creatures.'

'Truer words were never spoken,' Josh said. 'My mother, even Suze. Say one thing, then do another.'

'They said they loved you?' Daisy asked gently.

AnnaLise, who wasn't so sure this was a good tack to take, kept quiet.

Josh dipped his head. 'They did, Daisy. That they did. And then they left.'

A 'huh!' sounded in the woods. AnnaLise was appalled that it apparently had come from her.

'You question that, AnnaLise?' Josh said, taking another step toward them.

'I'm sure AnnaLise wasn't so much questioning,' Daisy said, sending a warning glance in her daughter's direction, 'as expressing disgust.

At Suzanne's behavior, and especially your mother's.'

'Right,' AnnaLise said, and that didn't come out quite the way she meant it, either. Sarcasm might be called for, but she'd be the first one to say it shouldn't be expressed right at the moment.

'Now you see, Daisy?' This from Josh. 'Your daughter is doing exactly what I said. Saying one thing, but meaning another.'

'My –' AnnaLise's voice cracked. There was something about having Daisy there with her that made the reporter more frightened, even, than when she'd been alone on the Parkway facing Ben. Whether it was because AnnaLise felt like a little girl, wanting her mommy to save her, or because she feared for Daisy's life as well as her own, would need further study.

Later.

AnnaLise cleared her throat. 'My . . . *skepticism*,' perhaps not the best word choice, but she'd have to live with it, 'was not that your mother and Suze betrayed you, but that they'd left you. From what I've learned – and maybe you can tell me better, Josh – but from what I know now, neither of them left you of their own volition.'

'Oh, but they did.' Another step closer and they could see his eyes clearer. Not that it mattered, because the blue eyes were dead, as expressionless as the face they were set in. 'I just . . . hastened them along their way.'

The game of tag, surrendered. 'Just to get it over with.'

'Exactly.' A smile on Josh's face, but not really. 'You understand.'

271

'Well, I surely don't,' Daisy said, and AnnaLise saw that she still had the cell in her hand, blocked from Josh's view by the car door. 'Can somebody explain?'

Josh shook his head.

'I can, Daisy,' AnnaLise said, hoping to distract the young man – the crazy young man – long enough for her mother to dial. 'I think I can explain everything.'

'Do you now, AnnaLise?' Interest was sparking in Josh's face for the first time, like a hunter whose winged prey had just taken erratic – and futile – flight. 'Then, please, go on.'

'Thank you, I will,' AnnaLise said politely. 'But where would you like me to start? At the beginning, with your mother?'

'That would be fine,' Josh said, tipping his head. 'No need to go into how lonely I was, with my father going about his business, and my mother . . . hers. Though I did do my best to please my father early on, going hunting and fishing and the like.'

Now a laugh, harsh in the peaceful twilight. 'Ol' Fred would get so irritated that I didn't seem capable of a clean kill, he eventually stopped bringing me hunting with him. Which was fine by me. That way I was free to wing quarry on my own. Takes a damn good shot to do that, you know – maim, I mean, without killing outright. And with no Fred to interfere and finish them off, I could sit and watch for hours as the light in their eyes slowly . . . flickered . . . out.'

AnnaLise felt sick to her stomach. From behind her, Daisy said, 'But about your mother?'

'I didn't get to see the light go out of her eyes.'

AnnaLise swallowed. 'Did you catch them here, Josh? Did you see your mother with her lover?'

'I did, but it wasn't just the one, AnnaLise. There were quite a few, actually.'

'Told you,' came loudly from behind AnnaLise.

'Shh, Daisy.' AnnaLise was shuddering. 'So your mother was promiscuous, Josh?'

'"My mother" was a whore. I saw her take money from those men and then get out of their cars to walk home.'

'Convenient, I suppose, Lovers' Lookout being so close to your house.' Again from Daisy, and this time AnnaLise tipped to the fact that her mother had successfully connected with someone – hopefully the police – on the cell. 'So you killed her, Josh?'

Daisy's attempt to get the young man to confess seemed way too obvious and, besides, AnnaLise wanted to live until the police got there. 'You were very young,' she said sympathetically.

Joshua Eames was looking off into the distance. 'At first, she'd buy me presents. Things I knew we couldn't afford. I figured out where the money was coming from, even if my dad didn't.'

'He found out somehow?'

'Nope.' He turned his attention back to AnnaLise.

'Then what changed? Why—'

'Why? Because she was going to leave, don't you understand? The gifts . . . *everything* was going to stop. She *owed* me for her being with *them*,' he spat out the indictment, 'when *I* was the one who needed her.'

273

'So you kept her from leaving.'

'No. I sent her away, before she could leave me.'

'How?' Daisy's voice.

'Easy.' A smirk from Josh. 'She took her car that day. I'm not sure why. Maybe the guy had a pick-up or something. Awkward for what they had in mind, you know? Her driver's door was open, just like yours is right now. And with a manual transmission, all I had to do was reach in and –'

'– put it in neutral,' AnnaLise said.

'Shh,' came from Daisy. 'Let Joshua tell us. It *is* his story, after all.'

'Sorry,' AnnaLise said. 'Go on, Josh.' And slowly, she prayed.

'No, you're right, AnnaLise, I just slid the stick from park to neutral, then all it took was a little push.'

Big for his age, AnnaLise heard in her head again. 'But your mother and . . . they were in the car, right? Didn't they notice? Maybe feel the car move and pull on the brake?'

Now Josh laughed outright. 'You're kidding, right?'

'No. Why?'

He snorted. 'Because they were in the back seat, of course.'

Thirty-seven

Daisy said, 'Fore-on-the-floor, I imagine.'

AnnaLise preferred not to imagine the scenario at all. She turned to Josh. 'And Suze?'

'She was going to leave me, too.'

'I suppose Suzanne found out you killed her mother?' Daisy asked loudly from directly behind AnnaLise.

Her daughter rubbed her right ear. 'Assuming you *did* kill Tanja.'

Josh nodded toward the gorge, as if the Porsche and its driver were still down there. 'That woman was trouble – real uppity, and she surely didn't like me being with her daughter. Suze thought if we bided our time, maybe didn't move in together right away, her mama might come around. And even if she didn't, once Suze was twenty-one, she'd have money of her own from her granddad.'

A trust fund or inheritance – Annalise had been right. 'But you . . . didn't want to wait?'

'I have to admit, I didn't quite see the point.'

'So you killed her.' Daisy, again.

'I did, Daisy, though I have to say I got lucky there. I figured shooting from here would give me a clear shot across the gorge and, what with the car being yellow, I got a good bead on it coming down around that last bend to the bridge. Even so, the shot was a lot more challenging than wounding an animal or shoving a car off a cliff.'

275

'Hey, you were only ten then,' Daisy said. 'Give yourself credit.'

'Nix the sarcasm, please?' AnnaLise hissed over her shoulder, then turned back to Josh. 'What would you have done if the Porsche had just crashed instead of going over the cliff?'

Josh shrugged. 'I'd have figured out something. In fact, I was walking over there to confirm the kill when I came across you.'

'Walking?' AnnaLise asked. 'So you *weren't* driving your truck.'

'Why? So somebody could ID it? Cutting through the woods on foot is a lot faster, anyway.'

'But then who was driving the truck that nearly hit us?' AnnaLise asked.

'Got me,' Josh said. 'It just kept on going.'

'Told you.' Daisy, again.

'You didn't call nine-one-one,' AnnaLise said to Josh.

'Nope, just like you said, talking to Daisy. That siren took me by surprise, while I was figuring out what to do.'

'With us, you mean?' Again, the sick feeling in the pit of AnnaLise's stomach.

'Of course, with you. I figured you'd seen me, AnnaLise, though as it turns out you'd closed your eyes. If I'd known that I would have just gone on my way and left you there.'

'But as it was, what if the rescue squad hadn't chased you off?' Daisy asked, like she had to know.

Josh cocked his head. 'I'm not sure. Interesting question, though. I surely have experience with sending bigger vehicles over than that crushed

Spyder of yours, AnnaLise. I could have probably picked the little thing up and tossed it.'

AnnaLise thought not, but kept her mouth shut.

'But back to Suzanne,' Daisy said. 'She figured out you'd killed her mother?'

'Worse. She told me she was leaving. With everything that'd happened, she'd decided to go back to Wisconsin with her father. I didn't expect that. We had plans. She *told* me, she loved me more than anything. Anyone.' He was close enough now that AnnaLise could see a vein in his forehead throbbing.

'Sounds like you should have killed the father,' AnnaLise's mother muttered. 'Would have saved everybody a lot of trouble.'

'Daisy!' AnnaLise scolded, though she wasn't sure why.

'I was just so angry,' Josh said, and for the first time he looked shaken. 'I showed Suze the rifle, explained what I'd done for us and that with her mother's family and all their money we'd be rich. You know how she answered me?'

'No,' said Daisy and AnnaLise simultaneously.

'Suze said, "*I'm* rich." Not us, her. Just like my mother, she was going to leave me behind. I couldn't let Suze do that.' His head dropped, as did his voice. 'I had no choice . . . I shot her and . . . and, maybe my dad was right, I'm just not capable of a clean kill.'

When he looked up, there were tears in his eyes. 'I sat there and watched her die. But it wasn't the same.' This last, a strained whisper.

'You mean, as the animals?' AnnaLise asked.

277

He shook his head, the tears streaming now. 'She . . . Suze could talk a little. She kept asking me, "Why?"'

No one spoke now.

'And you know what?' Josh finally continued. 'I didn't know. I don't know why I'm like this.'

'So you shot yourself,' Daisy said gently, the way she'd started this conversation.

Josh hung his head. 'And even that, I couldn't do right. What's wrong with me?'

He started toward them and AnnaLise swung the door as if to close it, smashing into his legs.

It slowed Josh down, but it didn't stop him. Limping, juked like an injured football player, he kept coming.

Their backs to the cliff, with less than three feet of solid earth between them and the gorge, AnnaLise pushed her mother out of his path. 'Run, Daisy!'

Daisy stumbled, but managed to regain her footing. AnnaLise held her ground as Josh rushed forward. Her plan was to sidestep when he gained shoving distance, hoping his momentum and reduced agility would send him over the edge instead of her.

As Josh reached out for her, AnnaLise went to dodge, only to have him do the same, like two polite people on a sidewalk, trying to slip past each other.

Then Josh grabbed her by a shoulder, his face wild, spittle at the corners of his mouth and tears running down his cheeks.

Daisy screamed and AnnaLise let herself go limp, wanting to take him by surprise so she

278

could thrust upward with her knee, while holding on to *him*. So that even if she went over, Josh would as well.

And Daisy would be safe.

Even as AnnaLise raised her knee, though, she felt him lift her off her feet and toss.

AnnaLise Griggs' last thought was, 'Maybe he could have thrown the Spyder over the side,' before she landed hard on some piece of solid ground.

While Joshua Eames charged past her and flew off the cliff.

Thirty-eight

'Well, at least he finally got it right,' Daisy said.

AnnaLise was sitting with her in the Griggs kitchen. Ida Mae had been disappointed they wouldn't make dinner, especially given the stories they could have told, but she understood.

And scheduled a rain-check time for the next day.

Chuck, and what seemed like the entire Sutherton police force, had arrived at the Chrysler to find AnnaLise and Daisy huddled a few feet away from the edge of the gorge, shivering.

'Good thing your phone had GPS,' AnnaLise said, now pouring her mother some wine with still-shaking hands and then emptying the rest of the bottle into her glass. 'Chuck said that despite all our talking, we never clearly said where we were.'

'Oops.' Daisy took a sip of her wine. 'I don't even like wine, yet I believe this might be the best elixir I've ever tasted.'

Elixir. 'You were wonderful out there,' AnnaLise said. 'My mom, the hero.'

'I don't feel like a hero,' Daisy said. 'I feel . . . confused.'

AnnaLise's stomach dropped. 'Confused in what way?'

Daisy flapped her hand at her daughter. 'Oh, not in *that* way. My memory of what happened would be just fine, thank you. Too fine, in fact. That poor boy.'

'That poor boy was a monster.'

'But not of his own making,' Daisy said. 'His mother was wild well before Fred Eames met her and God knows what she might have taken when she was pregnant. They say crack babies don't have a sense of right and wrong, maybe . . .' She let it drift off.

'Maybe.' AnnaLise echoed. 'I wonder if we'll ever know. I guess . . . Well, I guess I understand why somebody like Ben Rosewood doesn't believe in "accidents." It's a whole lot easier to believe there's a reason something horrible happened, something that could have been prevented. Because otherwise, we're powerless. Vulnerable. We could all become Joshs.'

'I'm not sure there's anything more terrifying than knowing that something inside of you isn't right and not being able to do anything about it.'

AnnaLise wasn't sure if her mother was talking about herself or the young man who had just thrown himself off the cliff.

But nothing would be gained tonight by asking. Instead, AnnaLise reached over and put a hand over her mother's. 'It's been a long day, Daisy. Time for bed?'

'I think so. Though I doubt I'll sleep.' Daisy stood up and started toward the stairs, hesitating at the plywood-covered window next to the front door. 'Oh, did you hear the chief say that this was the work of one of Scotty's guys? The house in the next block, too.'

AnnaLise shook her head. 'Scotty is putting hits out on people who fire him?'

'Of course not,' Daisy said. 'Just their windows. And it wasn't Scotty himself, you understand. Just an employee who was angry he was let go, business being down.'

'Not going to get any better, shooting out windows,' AnnaLise said, suddenly weary. 'The way we're going, you'll never have a working door on that garage, Daisy.'

'The door will wait.' She peered at her daughter. 'What about you? Bedtime, too?'

AnnaLise smiled. 'I think I'll sit for a while, thanks.'

This time Daisy made it as far as the second step before she turned back. 'You're a good person, AnnaLise. You made a mistake with that D.A., but you figured it out. I'm proud to be your mother.'

AnnaLise felt herself tearing up. 'Thanks, Daisy. I'm . . . I'm proud to be your daughter, too.'

Daisy was at the landing when AnnaLise's voice stopped her. 'Mommy?'

'Yes, sweetie?'

'You mind if I stay awhile in Sutherton? I mean, beyond the end of the month?'

'Of course not. You just stay as long as you like.'

Daisy continued up the steps. Maybe she would sleep tonight, after all.